Waverly Place

A woman opened the door. She looked like she'd run into a train, that was Ruggieri's first thought. He stared past her into a dark void. The place stank, what the hell was going on?

"Where are the fucking lights?" yelled one of the cops. Ruggieri pulled out his pocket flash.

Four or five pinpoints of light picked out overturned chairs, piles of clothes, bags of garbage. In a corner a baby sat on the floor, tethered to a wooden cage by a three-foot rope. Its diaper was soaked with urine and feces.

From the shadows of a hallway, a burly man in black came toward them carrying the limp, naked body of a larger child. She wasn't breathing. The diagnostic part of Ruggieri's brain did a flip as his stomach kicked over.

She looked dead.

Also by Susan Brownmiller

Against Our Will: Men, Women and Rape
Femininity

Susan Brownmiller

Waverly Place

A Mandarin Paperback
WAVERLY PLACE

First published in Great Britain 1989 by Hamish Hamilton Ltd
This edition published 1990 by Mandarin Paperbacks
an imprint of Reed Consumer Books Ltd
Michelin House, 81 Fulham Road, London SW3 6RB
and Auckland, Melbourne, Singapore and Toronto

Reprinted 1994

Copyright © 1989 by Susan Brownmiller

A CIP catalogue record for this book
is available from the British Library
ISBN 0 7493 0456 1

Printed and bound in Great Britain
by Cox & Wyman Ltd, Reading, Berks.

This book is sold subject to the condition
that it shall not, by way of trade or otherwise,
be lent, resold, hired out, or otherwise circulated
without the publisher's prior consent in any form
of binding or cover other than that in which
it is published and without a similar condition
including this condition being imposed
on the subsequent purchaser.

For Holly Forsman and Joan Corrigan,
and with gratitude and affection to
Florence Rush, Barbara Milbauer,
Pearl Broder, Minda Bikman,
and Neal Johnston.

Foreword

Early one morning in November 1987 the silence was broken on a quiet residential street in Greenwich Village. In response to an emergency call, police and paramedics entered a dark apartment and found an unconscious six-year-old girl. Three days later she died.

It couldn't have happened here. But it did. The day the child died, I began to write, to imagine how the couple from my neighborhood whose image flashed repeatedly across the television screen—a lawyer and a woman with a bashed-in face who had once been a writer—could have traveled the distance from people I *might* have known to such a nightmare, and why the ample warning signs were misperceived and misinterpreted by those in a position to sound the alarm. Aberrant in the extreme—in the following weeks, there were more headlines and revelations—this story nonetheless seemed to be a paradigm for a thousand case histories and clinical studies of family violence.

I chose to write fiction because I wanted the freedom to invent dialogue, motivations, events, and characters based on my own understanding of battery and abuse, a perspective frequently at variance with the scenarios created by the prosecution or the defense in courts of law. I did, of course, read everything that appeared in print about the case, and borrowed freely from these public accounts. The journalists assigned to cover the story did yeoman work; I am in their debt. I also read, or reread, the pertinent literature on battery and child abuse.

All the characters in this novel, central and peripheral, are products of my personal vision. I gave them names, biographies, and plausible interactions that fitted my own interpretation of the publicly reported events. I invented conversations for them and put them in situations of my own choosing. I imagined what they thought, and what others thought of them. I entered the delusional world of my protagonists to understand their *folie à deux* and to choreograph their scenes of violence, impelled from start to finish by the haunting face of a spirited little girl with red hair.

As one who has devoted her professional career to research and scholarship, with its double-checked sources and citations, I know and respect the difference between fact and fiction. I hope that my readers will respect that difference as well. No reader should assume (and neither I nor my publisher suggests) that any of the characters in this novel are accurate portraits of real people, or that the events described actually occurred. To the extent that any of the events depicted here may resemble reported incidents, my treatment generally differs in substance, detail, or motivation. This is, after all, a work of fiction.

What unquestionably did happen is that a child died and a woman was battered. I have tried to imagine how it might have been.

Susan Brownmiller
July 18, 1988

Waverly
Place

A high-priority call dumps the whole system. This one, logged by the EMS receiving operator in Maspeth, Queens, at 6:33 a.m., was a hi-pri.

Monday morning on the second of November a half-hour before dawn, *Child not breathing, request emergency aid* came in over 911. Operators in two separate locations, police and medical, took the complaint and fed the data into their computers.

In Maspeth the message jumped to the top of the queue. A blip on the screen. *Cardiac arrest. Kantor. 104 Waverly Place, Apt. 3-A, in Greenwich Village.* The EMS dispatcher read the one-line message and punched up the complaint history. *Six-year-old child not breathing.*

She called Twelve X-Ray on the two-way radio.

John Ruggieri and Brian Mahoney, St. Vincent's paramedics, were nearing the end of their tour. Two cracks on the head, a drunk in the gutter, a slow, uneventful night. Their mobile unit covered a long swath of Manhattan from West Twenty-sixth to the Battery, but eleven p.m. Sunday to seven a.m. Monday doesn't get much action in the lower end of the city.

This was a job for single men, Ruggieri liked to say. He'd been at it for nineteen years, ever since dropping out of Columbia after the student riots. Emergency work was sophisticated now, and Ruggieri reveled in the new techniques, but lately he'd been feeling burned out, unfit for human company after a tour. With twenty minutes to go, he made a turn at Sixteenth Street and headed for the garage.

The ambulance was cruising down Seventh Avenue when *Twelve X-Ray, Twelve X-Ray, Child not breathing, 104 Waverly Place, west of the park* crackled over the radio.

Mahoney whistled. "That's us, the winning ticket."

Ruggieri flipped on his lights and siren. His adrenaline surged. He shot down Seventh into Waverly, ignoring the one-way sign. The narrow, tree-lined street was empty of traffic, and he reached the house in under a minute. An unfamiliar address, not a fixed point on his mental list of every-few-months-and-they're-at-it-again calls.

Four wailing police cars and the paramedic van converged in front of the old Village brownstone in the pre-dawn gloom. Someone rang all the buzzers. A cop from the Sixth slipped the downstairs door with plastic. A tight herd of cops and paramedics, six men and a woman, stampeded up the stairs.

No doors opened and no inquisitive neighbors peered out as they made their noisy ascent. Two apartments to a floor, each black metal door with an eagle-crest knocker, minuscule peephole, and nameplate. "Where the hell are the apartment numbers?" somebody shouted. In the confusion it took them a while to find 3-A.

A woman opened the door. She looked like she'd run into a train, that was Ruggieri's first thought. He stared past her into a dark void. The place stank, what the hell was going on?

"Where are the fucking lights?" yelled one of the cops. Ruggieri pulled out his pocket flash.

Four or five pinpoints of light picked out overturned chairs, piles of clothes, bags of garbage. In a corner a baby sat on the floor, tethered to a wooden cage by a three-foot rope. Its diaper was soaked with urine and feces.

4

From the shadows of a hallway, a burly man in black came toward them carrying the limp, naked body of a larger child. She wasn't breathing. The diagnostic part of Ruggieri's brain did a flip as his stomach kicked over.

She looked dead.

The cops and the paramedics in New York have a formal understanding. In a medical emergency the cops take a back seat and the paramedics run the show.

Ruggieri put the little girl on the floor and started to work her over. His fingers probed her head. No fracture. He pulled a pediatric Ambu bag from his trauma box and placed the resuscitator over her nose and mouth, pushing away the matted strands of reddish hair. He pumped the valve. The air wasn't going in freely.

"What happened?" he shouted.

"She was fine till a half-hour ago," the father said in a flat, gravelly voice. "She got into the refrigerator and ate some fried chicken for breakfast. Must have choked on a wing. When I came out of the bathroom, she was throwing up."

Mahoney ran down to the van for a suction machine.

The woman was mute, a shadow hugging the wall. Ruggieri figured she might be the grandmother. The father trailed the cops through the dark apartment, talking a blue streak. All the lightbulbs in the house were burned out or missing from their sockets.

Ruggieri worked in the dark with a flashlight in his teeth. He tore off the Ambu mask and did a Heimlich maneuver on the motionless body. A little gob of phlegm and food came up, not enough to have blocked the passage.

"I'm getting air in and out," he yelled, checking the pulse in the child's neck. It was rapid but strong. The

5

father stood over him, a detached observer. Ruggieri could see his legs.

"Your story doesn't make sense, buddy. It wasn't a chicken wing. What really happened?"

"Last night, not this morning, you misunderstood me. She told us last night her tummy was hurting. We sat up with her all night. I don't understand, she suddenly stopped breathing."

Ruggieri racked his brains. He'd been on a case where the child got into a jar of methadone mixed with Tang. "Check the refrigerator," he called to one of the cops.

An eerie glow from the refrigerator light suffused the kitchen. The officer came back with something moldy. "That's all that was in there."

By the time his partner returned with the suction machine, Ruggieri was on the phone to the ER. "Bringing in a six-year-old female. Not breathing. Has a pulse and blood pressure."

He packed his equipment while Mahoney carried the child in his arms down the three flights of stairs. The soles of her feet were black with dirt.

A small crowd of curious onlookers had gathered on the street. They stared impassively as the little body was placed in the back of the van. The father suddenly appeared and climbed in without asking. One of the cops offered to drive. He slid into the front seat and gunned the six blocks to St. Vincent's while the kneeling paramedics continued to work over the child's inert form.

The father was still talking when they wheeled the gurney into the ER. He strolled around the brightly lit room while the gowned-up trauma team went into action.

Most people get hysterical, Ruggieri pondered. This guy's acting like he turned in a broken appliance.

I have been in the presence of evil, the paramedic thought as he left the ER.

6

7:00 A.M.

Under the emergency room lights, the pediatric resident found the dried blood in her matted hair.

"When did this child get hit on the head?"

The father didn't answer.

"Order CAT scan."

"Have security get the elevator."

They rushed the comatose child to the elevator bank.

One of the police officers motioned to his buddy as the father slipped out the door.

"Hard to stay in the same room with him—with a gun in my belt," the cop said out loud before he called the precinct from a hospital phone.

7:30 A.M.

The CAT scan showed blood pressing on the brain. A subdural hematoma, the kind of seepage that usually develops over four to six hours. The little girl was hooked up to a life-support system now, but she wasn't going to make it. It was only a matter of time before they would make the official pronouncement. Brain-dead.

8:00 A.M.–6:30 P.M.

The West Tenth Street stationhouse between Bleecker and Hudson was designed with Greenwich Village in mind. A visitor approaching the modern front entrance was momentarily diverted—and, it was hoped, charmed —by two rectangular stone troughs planted with English ivy and seasonal flowers. The Sixth Precinct's community liaison faithfully watered the troughs and pinched off the spent blooms, a grudging concession to a hypersensitive neighborhood of hysterical preservationists, touchy civil libertarians, militant gay activists, and other bohemian weirdos who drove cops bananas.

Despite the brisk weather on this early November morning, the Sixth Precinct's orange marigolds and ruffled petunias were putting on a resplendent show. In the second-floor squad room, four detectives proceeded with methodical caution. The squad commander gave out assignments to the tour coming on; the night tour had been held over.

Three cars went to 104 Waverly Place to pick up Barry Kantor and a woman identified as Judith Winograd for questioning. Nice and easy. Just come with us to straighten out some inconsistencies and clear up the investigation.

Over Kantor's objections, a female officer from the sex crimes unit untied the other child, a baby boy, and took a whiff of the rancid milk in his bottle. By daylight the "wooden cage" described in the memo books of the first cops on the scene turned out to be an inverted playpen. Aside from the filth he was wallowing in, the baby appeared unharmed. She took him to Special Services for Children.

Kantor kicked up a fuss in the stationhouse when he and Winograd were put in separate rooms. It was going to be a long day—at that point the cops didn't know how long. Everything had to go by the book. Kantor was a criminal lawyer and not entirely unknown to the precinct. A month ago two officers had been called to his apartment on a neighbor's complaint. Wife beating. They spoke to Winograd, but she refused to press charges. The cops on the call wrote her off as a nut case.

Four detectives stayed at Waverly Place all morning to

8

videotape the apartment, collect and tag material evidence, and interview neighbors. Two went to P.S. 55 around the corner to see what they could get from the principal and the child's teachers. St. Vincent's was being cautious as to the nature of the injury beyond confirming that it was a blow to the head and likely to be fatal; the hospital expected to release a definitive medical statement in the afternoon.

The case grew more bizarre by the minute. Several neighbors told detectives that the suspects weren't married and the two children were adopted. Kantor and Winograd confirmed the story, but the state's computers drew a blank on the adoption papers.

Kantor sounded like a broken record. He hugged his arms and repeated, "I'm a good father, I'm a good father. Ask the school." By lunchtime the cops had given up on him in disgust.

In the other room, Winograd was a pathetic puzzle. She looked old enough to be Kantor's mother, but she gave her age as forty-five. Somebody in the last twenty-four hours had given her a good going-over. She had a bloodied scalp, blackened eyes, a smashed nose, a split lip, probably some cracked ribs she didn't know about. Most but not all of the injuries were fresh. She shook her head frantically when they asked if she was in pain. The way she stuck to her story drove them crazy: the little girl fell down a lot on her roller skates, early this morning she had choked on her breakfast. In frustration the detectives left her alone under guard.

By early afternoon there was enough for probable cause, and they got the green light for a lockup. But the problem was Winograd. The DA wanted a statement, it would tidy things up. The detectives went in and tried one last time—maybe she'd break if they told her the child was dead. She peered at them blankly through puffy eyes. One of the detectives happened to glance at her right leg and nearly puked. From the ankle up, the whole lower leg looked infected. How could she walk on the thing? The woman was wrecked, she needed medical attention.

It hadn't taken long for the brass hats to jump in. The chief of Manhattan South detectives hurried to the precinct with his deputy inspector to help with the wrap. Then someone called from downtown and said to put a hold on the booking. Public Affairs wanted time to alert the press.

At four-thirty, Kantor and Winograd were informed they were under arrest. Kantor was allowed to call a lawyer. Winograd did not request a separate attorney for herself. The subjects were removed to individual lockups on the ground floor. Things weren't any tidier than they had been four hours earlier. The child was still on life support, and Winograd hadn't budged.

After conferring with the DA, the arresting officer drew up three charges: attempted murder, assault in the first degree, endangering the welfare of a child. When St. Vincent's pulled the plug, the DA could up the complaint to murder.

6:30 P.M.

The Sixth Precinct cops blinked reprovingly in the unaccustomed glare. Public Affairs had done a thorough job. Cameras and microphones jammed the lobby, photographers elbowed reporters behind the sacrosanct front desk.

They brought in Kantor. Flanked by officers, he bounded to the desk, a tall, disheveled man with a large, trim mustache and designer glasses. Winograd was hustled in behind him: small, scared, vacant, an incongruous blue-and-white bandanna on her frizzy grey hair.

"There's not a mark on that child," Kantor shouted to the reporters. "Check the hospital records."

It was over in a minute. They were escorted out the side door to the alley. A waiting squad car would take him downtown, she'd go by van to the prison hospital for women in Elmhurst.

With a low moan, she turned her face up to his. Their eyes locked. Flashbulbs popped in the chilly night air.

A plaster bandage on her squashed-in nose gave her the look of a boxer who'd gone down for the long count.

She mouthed "I love you" through grotesque, swollen lips.

11:00 P.M.

Cynthia Owens switched on the eleven-o'clock news. It was one of her disciplined habits. Local news at eleven, all-news radio to wake her up in the morning, that way she always knew what was hopping by the time she arrived at the paper at ten a.m.

She caught the lead story as she kicked off her shoes. "A Greenwich Village lawyer and his live-in lover were arrested tonight on charges of attempted murder."

The silent footage stopped her cold.

She grabbed the remote control and clicked to another channel just as they were winding up the same piece. The footage got her again.

She took a deep breath before she went to the phone. "The Kantor story," she said to the night editor in clipped, professional tones. "I can help."

"Cindy baby!" A gratifying whistle came through the receiver. "What angle?"

11

"Hers."

He checked his sheet. "Winograd?"

"Yes, Judith. I knew her."

"Call in a sidebar in fifteen minutes. Five hundred words. It's front-page."

"Five hundred words," she repeated. "You got it. Give me a year's leave of absence and I'll write you a book."

SATURDAY, JUNE 6, 1970

Waverly Place is one of the contrary streets of Greenwich Village. Striking a westerly course at Broadway near New York University, it loses its name at Washington Square Park, reappears east of Sixth, jogs north at Christopher, and emerges upland on the far side of Seventh Avenue South, where it meanders to a dead end at Bank Street. No one intent on getting from one point to another in the Village chooses Waverly Place as a route, but the dark-haired young man in sunglasses and jeans walking his Great Dane on this Saturday morning was headed nowhere in particular. He was taking a stroll with his brindled companion, and he happened by accident upon the Bank Street block fair.

With a springy, athletic step he strode past the food stalls, the racks of secondhand books and antique clothing, then came to a halt at a knickknack table. The object of his sudden interest was examining a green majolica vase.

He took in the wiry thick hair teased into the current fashion, the wide butt, the disdainful eyes expertly circled in black, and made his calculations. Brooklyn gypsy with a ton of hair spray, perky. A type he liked.

"Don't buy it. It's cracked."

Judith jumped, almost dropping the vase.

"You've got it filled with posies already. What kind? Roses? Nah, nothing as common as roses. Nothing ordinary for you."

He laughed and moved away. Gripping the vase, she stared at his retreating back. He is good-looking and married, she thought. Why is he in the city on a weekend?

13

Judith put down the vase. She hadn't noticed the small crack on the rim, but what difference did it make? If she bought it she'd only throw it in the closet with the chipped Wedgwood plates and the bent silver demitasse spoons and the other useless items she purchased at these street fairs to make it look less obvious that she had nothing else to do on a Saturday morning.

She searched the crowd. Blue Jeans had stopped to buy a hotdog. She watched him josh the vendor, pointing to the sauerkraut, miming "more, more" while the Great Dane slobbered at his side. She liked that, his energy. Tall, over six feet—well, all men were tall compared with her, height was not one of her priorities. What was he? Italian? Jewish? With the mustache it was hard to tell. This year every man in the city who thought he was hip wore a mustache and denim.

What the hell, be adventurous. Judith moved toward the hotdog stand.

"Peonies. You were right. The vase was filled with pink peonies. Nothing as common as roses."

He eyed her through his opaque lenses and slowly broke off the end of his frankfurter. "Open up." In one confident motion he popped the piece in her mouth and wiped an imaginary trace of mustard off her chin. "Chew before you swallow."

The Great Dane whined.

I am being picked up, she thought to herself, how about that? By a tall, dark stranger walking a dog on a Saturday morning in Greenwich Village.

Judith

What are you saving yourself for, Mama would ask. For a doctor, a lawyer? Why can't you just settle?

14

Whatever I did, it was always wrong. It was wrong to want to go to college. *What are you going to do with your education? You'll only get married. For that you don't need a college diploma.* And then when I didn't get married, it was *Why can't you just settle?*

Mama, why couldn't you see me? Why couldn't you see that I was different? I was bright, Mama, really bright. I scored higher on the IQ tests than anyone else in class. My homeroom teacher in high school wrote you a letter. *Mrs. Winograd, your daughter Judith tested in the upper tenth percentile. It would be a tragic blow to her questioning young mind to switch her from the academic track to the commercial course.* I won that battle, didn't I, Mama? I lied to you and said I was taking shorthand and typing, and I didn't quit high school at sixteen like I promised. I made it all the way to Brooklyn College, riding the subway every day for four years while you and Daddy shook your heads and said, *She'll never stick it out, she'll find some man and that'll be the end of her hotsy-totsy education.*

I fooled you. I got the diploma and I didn't get a man. The Jewish boys at college who wanted to be doctors and lawyers didn't want me. They were all escape artists, Mama, just like I was, and a machinist's daughter from Avenue U wasn't on the route out. Fuck them, fuck them hard. I didn't want them either.

JUNE 6, 1970, AFTERNOON

"Pull down the shades," he said. The dog, Thor, found a place for itself in the corner and flopped down with a thud. She busied herself at the window while he took out his stash and hand-rolled a joint. He took a deep drag and passed it to her.

She giggled. "It's two in the afternoon."

"Right. Take a deep drag. Hold it in."

Pray to God, she thought. Pray to God I don't cough. He paced her one-room apartment, surveying the Van Gogh prints on the wall, checking out her bookcase. What was he thinking? Barry, Barry, Barry, she had never been with a Barry before. She had never thought about Barrys, a Barry had never crossed her mind, much less her threshold. She must be getting stoned.

He was sitting next to her on the bed, very close. That was strange. A minute ago he was walking around the apartment. When did he sit down? She must be very stoned.

"Now what?" she whispered.

JUNE 12, 1970

Judith ran the last block. "I'm sorry."

"Goddammit, remind me never to meet you on a street corner."

"I said I was sorry." Judith almost turned around and went back to the subway. If Carol was going to be grumpy all evening, she wouldn't be able to tell her the big news. The two young women made their way into the Third Avenue bar and ordered drinks, which they sipped in slow little swallows.

The singles scene had been fun at the beginning, once she and Carol had overcome their humiliation at being so obviously on the market. She'd gotten a couple of dates out of this particular place, more accurately a couple of lays, one with a dentist who lived with his mother in a row house in Queens. Red brick, semidetached. If she ever wrote her novel, the dentist would be in it for sure. Last spring she and Carol had tried the reform Democratic clubs on the Upper West Side and in Chelsea, but all they got from stuffing envelopes in a ratty clubhouse for some congressional candidate was paper cuts on their fingers.

There was more action in the bars. A fast dance of eye movements. Yep, nope, possible. As long as you didn't make a mistake and lock eyes with a loser, you could keep your self-respect intact and your options open. Carol was terrific at sending out a teletype of brazen signals. You, no, *not you*! Without Carol Marks she'd never have the courage to go into one of these places. Last summer when they took that crazy charter flight to London, it was awesome to watch her waltz into a pub and strike up a conversation. They were really such different people. After sharing hotel rooms and eating all their meals together for seventeen days, it was miraculous that they came home still talking. It was nice having a best friend. She hadn't had one since high school, a chum to gab with and dish about boys. Pardon, *men*. Huntresses on a manhunt, that's what they called themselves. But where were the men?

"You girls from Jersey?"

A loser. Why did the losers always want to cover you with their own shit? Jersey! Was that how they looked to this overweight schmuck with beads of perspiration on his forehead?

Judith gave him her freeze-and-begone special. "We're Shriners from Oklahoma in town for a convention."

Carol swirled the ice in her drink, suppressing a chortle.

BB, Before Barry, life had begun to look like a long row of dentists who lived with their mothers in semidetached red-brick houses in Queens. Follow the red-brick road. *You* follow the red-brick road.

"See any prospects?"

"Nope. You see any?"

"Nope. Let's get out of here and grab a burger." Carol

17

drained the last of her drink. Judith left a fifty-cent tip.

At the hamburger place on Lexington, Judith leaned back in the vinyl booth while Carol gave her the weekly update on the married man in her office, an account exec who closed his door and let her blow him before he caught the 7:42 to Syosset. Usually Judith liked to hear the unchanging details of Carol's story. It confirmed her opinion about the possibilities of unhooking and rehooking married men. Married men were never her thing. She believed in the sanctity of home life, always had, even if she was a nervous twenty-eight and dying on the vine, BB. Carol's situation was one she could empathize with, but not one she could see herself in. No future.

Carol reapplied her lip gloss. "So, anything new?"

Her cue. Judith savored the moment.

"I met a man." The simplicity of it astounded her. She felt no need to go further.

"Is he married?"

Judith allowed herself a small, triumphant smile. "I shouldn't be telling you any of this, I don't want to jinx it before it happens. No, he's not married. His name is Barry Kantor, he's a lawyer, and he lives by himself in the Village with a huge Great Dane."

The exultation was almost too much to bear. Barry Kantor. That was the first time she had said his name out loud to another person. She braced herself for the questions, but Carol was silent. One girl's luck is another girl's reminder of failure, and at this moment she was the luckiest girl in the world.

"The best sex I ever had in my life."

Carol looked almost relieved. "Oh, a cocksman."

"No, not a cocksman. A wonderful human being." Okay, Carol was asking for this. "A wonderful human being who gives great head."

"Judith!"

"I kid you not. Two arms, two legs, great head. And

everything else. A Jewish lawyer who grew up in the Bronx, but there's nothing Bronxy about him. Single. Did I say that? Single. He's twenty-nine, a year older than me. We found out inside of two minutes that we were both only children."

"Where did you meet him?"

The words were almost out of her mouth. *I met him last Saturday morning at the Bank Street fair. We went back to my place and got stoned out of our skulls. At two in the afternoon.* But a warning buzzer went off in her brain, and instead she fibbed quickly, "We were introduced by an aunt of mine he represented in a legal matter. Really."

Why had she told Carol that small fib? A hangup from her bourgeois days, no doubt. People got introduced, they courted, got married, had children. Love and marriage. Where did Barry Kantor fit into that picture? She flashed on her darkened studio apartment last Saturday morning, the shades down, the two of them coiled together on top of her madras spread.

"He took me to a great Italian restaurant on Bleecker Street."

Now she was really gilding the lily. In another minute she'd be blathering about the antipasto and zabaglione. Would Carol be less impressed if she told her the truth about how she met Barry Kantor? A young lady who blows a married man in the office before he catches his train to the suburbs does not stand in judgment over a young lady who smokes a joint with a stranger in her own apartment. Does she?

But Carol's tawdry affair and her own great new romance had nothing in common. That was why she preferred to tidy up the public version. When she had Barry Kantor firmly in tow, they could have a laugh about how they had met. One day they might even tell their children.

Judith

Once, maybe when I was eight years old, I got lost coming home from school. I took a different street, and then I got turned around somehow, and when I tried to find Avenue U it wasn't there. I kept turning corners expecting to see Tookie's Upholstery and the New Parkway Jewish Center, but none of the houses and stores looked familiar. It was getting dark, so I sat down on the sidewalk and started to cry. A man came by and asked me where I lived. He took me right home and left me at the door, but when I went upstairs, Mama was in a panic. Hysterical. She had called the cops. They were out looking for me.

Whack. Where were you? *Whack.*

Ma, I got lost.

Whack. I told you to come straight home. Always to come straight home. *Whack.* Who were you playing with? What did they do to you?

I wasn't playing. Stop hitting me, Ma. I got lost. My teacher found me and took me home.

Mama's rage subsided with the magic word, "teacher." That's when I learned that a tiny fib can cure a little girl's troubles.

JULY 1970

"'I'm writing a novel," she told him. "That's what I really do in life—at least on the days I'm not subbing. I thought you should know, in case you have an aversion to lady writers." She gave him a fast look. They were strolling along the Coney Island boardwalk. Neither of them had been to Coney since high school.

20

"I'm impressed. Nothing could get me to sit at a typewriter except when I had a term paper, and then I tried to find some guy to write it for me for a couple of bucks. Want to tell me what it's about?"

"I don't think I should say. There's a theory that if you talk about it, you won't write it."

"Suit yourself. A novel by Judith Winograd? Let me guess. It's about a girl from Brooklyn who crosses the big bridge into Manhattan, gets a job as a substitute teacher to support her writing habit, and then picks up this guy at a street fair in Greenwich Village—"

"Goddamn you, Barry Kantor."

"Was I close?"

"No. Yes. Well, it *is* about a girl from Brooklyn who becomes a teacher, but it's not autobiographical. I mean, you have to write about what you know," she finished lamely.

"*A Tree Grows in Brooklyn.*"

"She didn't become a teacher. She worked in an office, but you get the idea she kept on writing."

"Total recall, huh?" He was silent for a while. "Remember when Francie and Neeley get the Christmas tree thrown on them?"

"Barry, that was my favorite scene in the entire book!"

"Yeah, it was a lot of people's favorite scene."

"What else did you read when you were a kid?"

"You mean, what else that really impressed me? Let me think for a minute."

"I know what you're going to say."

"What?"

"*Catcher in the Rye.*"

"I was going to say *The Amboy Dukes.*"

"Oh," she breathed. "I loved it."

"Sure, another Brooklyn book."

She poked him playfully on the arm. "So you like the idea that I'm a writer?"

21

He grabbed her wrist and pinned it behind her back. It hurt, but she didn't want to let on. Finally she squealed and he let go.

"Okay, here's the choice," he said. "A frankfurter at Nathan's or a knish at Mrs. Stahl's."

"Do you think Mrs. Stahl's is still there?" she said. "Can you find it?"

"Wanna bet?"

He led her unerringly back the way they came. Across the street from the entrance to the elevated tracks they found Mrs. Stahl's. He ordered a hot potato knish, and just to be different, she ordered hers with kasha.

"Next time we do this," she said as she watched him finish her knish, "we do it up proper and go to Lundy's. My treat."

"Go where?"

"Lundy's," she repeated. "You never went to F. W. I. L. Lundy's, named for the four brothers? The waiters were all light-skinned blacks, we used to call them 'colored.' We went there for Sunday dinner. We sat in the big dining room and had the bluefish special, but the real action was in the clam bar, where the Irish and Italians ate lobster and steamers. You never went to Lundy's? Oh, you poor deprived little Jewish boy from the Bronx."

AUGUST 1970

Barry had a one-bedroom apartment on Waverly Place near Washington Square Park in a beautiful old brownstone that was still under rent control, a wonderful find. Originally the apartment belonged to a client, Judith was hazy about the details. When she asked about Barry's clients, he usually changed the subject. He had this lawyer thing about privileged communication, it was a very principled position and she respected him for it. First he had been on a long sublet, he told her, and then he negotiated a new lease with the landlord at no increase at all. He was very clever that way. She was paying double what he paid for her twelve-by-fourteen-foot studio, with an increase every two years.

New York. Sometimes she thought she wasn't tough enough for New York, but with Barry she felt she could run up the Empire State Building two steps at a time.

He was such a doer. He was the only man she knew who kept a car in the city, a cute little VW bug. It delighted her to see him park in one of those restricted zones she hadn't even known existed. A friend in the Motor Vehicles Department had finagled him journalist's license plates so he could park the bug almost anywhere, like a foreign diplomat. She couldn't even drive, girls who grew up in Brooklyn usually didn't, and then with her terrible sense of direction, if she ever did learn, she knew she'd never remember where she left the car from one day to the next.

Barry knew the subways better than she did, too. He'd point her toward an entrance and say, "Take the A to Fifty-ninth and grab the D from there, you'll save ten minutes," or "Take the Flushing line at Forty-second Street, it's faster than the shuttle." He always kept an eye out for shortcuts. When she came over to his house, he'd have her pick up his suit at the dry cleaner on the way. No wasted motions, no duplicated effort, just pure efficiency. A lesson she had to learn if she was going to keep up with him. Oh, did she have a tiger by the tail.

BB, she had dated boys, that was the difference. Barry was a *man*, a man who took command of his life. Maybe he would bring some order and direction to hers.

He is telling her his life story. When they get together at his place, they smoke a joint, break open a bottle of wine, and Barry talks. She could listen to him for hours.

Morris Avenue, she sees it so clearly. Except for the hills it could be Avenue U.

The little boy on the shiny roller skates. "Honest, Mommy, honest, I won them in a fight."

"Don't tell your father. You'll get killed."

Friday night Mr. Kantor comes home early for Shabbas, climbing the Morris Avenue hill. There is Barry skating down, can't stop. He whizzes by his father on wheels of silver.

"Come back here, you little *momser,* where did you steal those skates? I'll beat you, I'll beat you within an inch of your life."

Barry crouches under the stairwell. He sneaks into the boiler room, he sleeps near the dumbwaiter. He hides for two days. The superintendent brings him a sandwich. The neighbors come and go, they see but they don't tell. They are enjoying the joke. The big *macher* on the fifth floor, the hotshot accountant with the clubhouse connections, he can't control his *meshuganah* son.

Finally a neighbor tells Abe Kantor, "Your son the holy terror is right under your nose." This is a big laugh in the Carlton Gardens, but not in Apartment 5-C.

"Lily, get the belt."

The next day Mrs. Kantor marches Barry to the Hebrew Orphan Home on the Grand Concourse. "I want to turn in a child, he's no good."

Barry is screaming, "Mommy, Mommy, take me home, I'll be good."

24

Mrs. Kantor relents. Barry is allowed to go home. But every week she marches him past the orphan home to remind him what happens to no-good children. Sometimes for good measure she takes him to the big white stone courthouse at 161st. This is what'll happen when you're older, she tells him, this is where the juvenile delinquents wind up.

OCTOBER 10, 1970

Every story Barry has told her about the Bronx ends with a leather belt or a wooden coat hanger.

"Which hurt you more?" she asks. They are lying in bed.

"What? Come off it, Judith."

"No, I need to know."

"The belt hurt more, but I got the wood hanger every day. What are you doing, taking notes for your novel?"

"Barry!" How could he think she was pumping him for details so she could put them on paper? He had no idea who she was, he had never known a loyal woman. "I'm not writing about you, Barry."

"You better not be." He reaches over and turns off the TV.

"Barry—"

"Go to sleep, Judith. If we're not at Bear Mountain by nine a.m., forget it."

She lies there without speaking for ten minutes.

"Barry, did anybody, your mother, a neighbor or somebody, try to interfere?"

"Are you still awake?"

"I can't sleep after what you told me."

"It happened a long time ago, Judith. It doesn't make any difference anymore." He rolls over on his other side, away from her. "My mother was terrified of him, and the

25

neighbors had their hands full with their own children."

"Nobody tried to stop him?"

"Stop him?" The question seems to puzzle him. "Yeah, my aunt Rose."

Aunt Rose. Judith sifts through her mental file of Barry's aunts and uncles and cousins. "Your cousin Howie's mother?"

She gets no answer. He is snoring.

OCTOBER 11, 1970

Judith looked down at her new sandals. They were caked with mud, utterly ruined. He had told her to wear sneakers if she didn't have hiking boots. Why did she decide that this was the day she was going to show her independence? The last hour had been a miserable trek uphill. If they'd passed any interesting scenery, she wouldn't have known. All she'd been able to do was put one foot in front of the other, trying to keep him in sight.

"Barry!" He turned around, impatient. "I've got to rest."

"There's a picnic table a couple of miles ahead."

"Barry, I've got to stop now."

"I'll wait for you up ahead." He was gone.

Judith sat down on a rock and examined her left heel. The beginnings of a blister, and the strap on her sandal was coming loose. A couple of miles? She'd never make it. She got up wearily and started trudging, looking for that familiar figure in the plaid shirt, shoulders hunched forward under the weight of the backpack. He was carrying the canteen, their lunch sandwiches, his camera, and her extra sweater. All she had to carry was herself. Come on, Judith, she told herself grimly. One, two, one, two, establish a rhythm. She had told him she loved the outdoors. What a lie. He had taken one look at her sandals and known she'd never gone hiking before. Well, she was game, he had to grant her that.

She turned a bend in the trail, and there he was.

"What took you so long?"

"Barry!" She ran to him with her last ounce of strength and threw her arms around his middle. "I thought I was lost."

"You can't get lost, Judith. You just follow the markers."

After they finished lunch he was ready to move.

"Give me a break," she said. "I need another five minutes."

He took off his pack and flung it on the ground.

"Tell me about your aunt Rose. She was Howie's mother, right?"

"Jesus, Judith, you're obsessive, you know that? You never let a thing go."

"I want to know about Aunt Rose."

"There's nothing to tell." He lit up a joint.

"We'll trade. I'll tell you about my aunt Evelyn." Judith spoke in a rush. "Aunt Evelyn was my maiden aunt who lived with my grandmother Winograd in Canarsie. She was a salesclerk at Gimbel's and brought me nice presents, but she always pinched my cheek till it hurt. When my father saw me with my nose stuck in a book, he'd tease that if I didn't watch out, I'd grow up to be Aunt Evelyn. That meant I wouldn't get married."

She was sorry she'd said that. Why had she mentioned marriage?

"Maybe you won't get married."

"Maybe I won't."

"Does the possibility scare you?"

"Nothing scares me, Barry, not even you."

He gave her a funny look that caused her to lower her eyes. Everything scared her, who was she trying to fool? She sat there feeling naked. What scared her most was the deep untapped well of her own anger. Sometimes she was afraid that if she started screaming, she'd never stop. But of course he knew that—he knew everything about her without even asking.

"Aunt Rose," she prompted.

"Yeah. She had nice hair. My mother's younger sister. She came to the house with Howie every Saturday morning. The two of them sat in the kitchen hocking each other over evaporated milk and coffee. They switched into Yiddish for the parts we weren't supposed to hear. Two women telling their secrets. 'Go play,' they'd tell us. 'Go play.' So Howie and I played tag in the hall, and I'd throttle the kid every chance I got."

"And?"

"And? My father would come home and hear the racket. He'd come running with the wood hanger. 'I'll break every bone in your body.' I'd try to duck, but he was pretty fast. When he really got going, it used to upset Aunt Rose. She'd scream, 'Stop it, Abe, he'll get a soft head.'"

"Yes?"

"What yes? Howie would whimper and hide in the closet, Aunt Rose and my mother would grab each other for dear life, and I'd get the rest of my beating."

"That's all?"

"I told you there was nothing to tell." He hoisted the backpack onto his shoulders and started down the trail.

Judith

Yiddish was dirty jokes and curse words, punchlines and epithets. The rest of that colorful language had been jettisoned before we were born, when the sisters Leah and Rivka became Lily and Rose, and in another part of the city my aunt Yetta restyled herself Evelyn and took a job selling moderate-priced lingerie at Gimbel's.

But at home among themselves things could remain the same. In the Bronx, Barry's father called him *momser,* bastard, when he got out the belt. For other occasions it was *shmendrik. Hey, shmendrik.* That's what Barry answered to. *Shmendrik* means hapless little fuckup with your head screwed on loose, but it sounds more final in the mother tongue. The variation was *putz,* literally translated as penis, as in the expression *Hey, putz, show me your wee-wee.* In Brooklyn, when I spilled my milk or wet my pants, I got a smack and *Ich hab dir in drerd.* I'll have you in hell. When I did something awful like throw up in Uncle Joe's car or grind my crayons into the rug, or—this was the height, the absolute extent, of my insurrection— when I hid the bottle of Argyrol nose drops behind the sofa, she'd wail, *Aiii, livergut!* That's how I heard it. Livergut. A bloody bruised squirming sickening purple mass of innards. *Aiii, livergut!* Me. The ugliest sound in my childhood, the destiny I fought against, the life sentence I resisted. I'd lie next to the radiator crying my eyes out with the dreadful syllables pounding my ears. *I'm not a livergut, I'm not a livergut. I'll show them.*

One day after we were living together I told Barry about *livergut.* He scratched his head. "Something's wrong. You heard it wrong."

He made me repeat it several times. I said it in a whisper, feeling my shame. Suddenly he snapped his fingers. "*Lieber Gott!* She was saying, *Aiii, lieber Gott. Dear God.* You heard it wrong all those years."

We were, as they say, a transitional generation.

NOVEMBER 1970

"Jap," he said out of nowhere. They were lying in bed after sex, sharing a cigarette. "You're waiting for me to get you the ashtray."

She looked around, reluctantly disengaging her fingers from his mop of curly dark hair. The ashtray was always in its familiar spot on his nightstand. Well, it wasn't now. She got out of bed and went through the apartment on an ashtray hunt. Finally she located a saucer in the kitchen and brought it to him.

"That's not an ashtray, Judith."

"Barry, I didn't see any other ashtray."

"Where did you look?" He stormed into the bathroom, slamming the door. She heard the sound of running water. His shower.

Barry used the shower to punctuate the different episodes of his day. What they had just shared in bed was being washed away, he was readying himself for the next item on the agenda. Dinner. She wondered if she would be included. He hadn't said anything about dinner when he'd called a few hours ago and asked what she was doing. What had she been doing? Waiting for his call, of course.

After five months of seeing Barry Kantor, she still didn't know where she stood. One minute they were lying there so peacefully, communicating with their hands and mouths without saying a word, and the next minute he was up and agitated, finding fault with her for some minor infraction of a rule she hadn't been told about. Breathe deeply, she told herself, breathe deeply. When she was with Barry, sometimes she forgot to breathe.

He came out of the shower with a towel wrapped around his hips. God, he was gorgeous.

"Make it snappy," he said, rubbing his scalp. "Fun's over. Got a pile of work." He jerked his thumb toward the bathroom.

She was being dismissed. *No, she would not be dismissed.* "You've got to have dinner sometime, Barry. You might as well have it with me."

"I'll grab something later. I need to be alone now, Judith." He was prowling through his underwear drawer.

30

"It won't take long."

He relented. "A quick bite, then you go home."

He put on his pants and grabbed Thor's leash.

At the waffle shop on Eighth Street he let her have it. "You make me feel closed in, Judith. Sometimes I think you're all I ever wanted in a girl, and then you go Jappy on me. You're a *nudge* and a slob. You expect everyone to pick up after you."

"That's not true. I don't."

"Don't argue with me. You buy expensive clothes and your place is a mess."

Sometimes I think you're all I ever wanted in a girl. He'd actually said it, he said it. He was so wrong about the Jewish American Princess thing. Nothing in her background was Jappy, he knew that. It was just his fear of a permanent relationship because things had gone wrong the first time with that cold bitch he'd married when he was stationed at Fort Jackson.

"I thought you liked the way I dress."

He motioned to the waitress. She was being dismissed again. Judith reminded herself to breathe.

"I thought you liked the way I dress, Barry."

"You're *nudging* me again." She saw the look in his eyes that said back off.

Outside the restaurant, he untied the patient dog and fed it a piece of waffle soggy with melted ice cream. "I'll give you a call later in the week."

She'd lost. Okay. It was only a skirmish. She wasn't a quitter, he'd figure that out soon.

DECEMBER 1970

Carol takes Judith to a friend's apartment for a meeting of something called the Women's Liberation Movement. Eight women about their age are sitting in a

31

sparsely furnished living room, talking about their abortions.

Judith stares at a spot on the floor. Carol picks at an imaginary piece of lint on the arm of the sofa. The two friends, usually so glib when they talk about sex, are conspicuous in their silence. Plus, they are dressed differently. Carol and Judith are wearing skirts.

Afterward Carol asks Judith, "What did you think?"

Judith considers. "I think they're a bunch of dykes."

Carol laughs. "A totally lousy way to meet new men."

Judith

When I was thirteen Mama took me to the doctor. I hadn't gotten my period yet, and my chest was as flat as a pancake. He told her not to worry, some girls just develop later than others.

A year later we were back in his office. I was no further along in the menstrual department, although my breasts had made some visible progress. Not enough to warrant a brassiere, but enough to make Dr. Juriansky tweak them happily while I cringed on the examination table.

So I was going to look like a female after all.

At seventeen we had a false alarm. One night I took off my underpants and saw a beautiful red stain. "It's come, it's come!" I ran into Mama's bedroom waving my red-and-white flag. We hugged each other, one of the few times . . .

This is very painful to think about.

We hugged each other. I can't remember a happier moment in Mama's house. Her Judy was normal. I wasn't a fraud, I wasn't a failure, I was just like everyone else only it took me a little longer to get there.

The bleeding stopped the next day.

32

Okay, it's called irregular ovulation. Lots of women have it, I understand that now. A thyroid deficiency or something. I went on medication and everything straightened out, but it left me wondering what was wrong with me—why wasn't I like everybody else? After I met Barry I stopped thinking about whether I could get pregnant, because he told me it didn't matter to him.

Barry is the first person besides my parents to know my secret.

JANUARY 1971

Shelley List and her three eight-year-old assistants taped a roll of white paper to the rear wall of the classroom. Today she was going to start the third-graders on a mural.

The art teacher handed out the boxes of tempera paints and brushes, and sent Roberto, her favorite, to fill some jars with water from the drinking fountain in the hall. Next she divided the class into teams of five and assigned them to their work stations.

"Okay, children," she announced, "we're doing a big scenic picture of New York in winter. Put in whatever you like, even words if you want to, and don't be afraid to use your imagination."

Murals were always a winner. The kids dove right in, and you never knew what they'd come up with. She patrolled the wall with satisfaction as recognizable trees and buildings began to take shape. Is this how Michelangelo felt? she wondered.

"Miss List, there's no red paint."

"Miss List, I can't find no red paint either."

Shelley cursed under her breath. "Roberto," she said, "go next door to Room 108 and ask Mrs. Mandel if she'd please let you borrow the box of paints from her locker."

She resumed her patrol, offering encouragement to one team and advice to another. Roberto was taking an awfully long time on his errand. What was the matter with him today?

"Miss List, I can't go on without my red."

"Try using orange, sweetheart."

"Oh, no, that'll mess up my picture."

Roberto came back sheepish and empty-handed. "I couldn't get in the door."

"What do you mean?"

"They've got the door locked or something. I couldn't get in."

Shelley did not believe him, but this was not the moment to show her irritation. She appointed Roberto class monitor and left the room to see what the story was.

The door of 108 did appear to be locked, and the noise inside spelled out a simple message. Classroom out of control.

"Open up in there, you're all going to be reported." She banged on the door until it gave way.

Thirty giggling children were whooping around the room like little Indians, erasers and spitballs flying.

"Stop that this instant. Everyone, back in your seats, I'm giving you three seconds. One . . . two . . . *You*—close that window!"

Shelley was barking out commands in her best no-nonsense voice when she noticed the substitute teacher sitting frozen at her desk.

"Why didn't you stop them?" she hissed in the sub's direction.

"I didn't know how," the woman whispered.

Shelley told the story in the teachers' lounge that afternoon.

"What the hell is that sub's name, the one who was in

for Mandel today? I forced open the door, and it was absolute chaos. She's sitting there in her long skirt and boots with a shawl draped around her fancy white blouse. Paralyzed! The kids were holding her hostage."

"Oh, Winograd, you must mean Judy Winograd."

"She doesn't belong in a school like this."

"I'm sure she'd agree with you, but what can we do?"

Judith

He found a Kama Sutra chart somewhere, one of those things showing fifty positions, most of them so extraordinarily contorted that I couldn't imagine how two people could possibly get into, let alone hold, the pose, even if they were yoga masters. But he was entranced and said he wanted to try every one of the fifty positions in 1971, that was his New Year's resolution. He tacked the chart up on the wall near the bed for reference.

I am so incredibly orgasmic with him, it doesn't matter which way he turns me or what he does. He has unlocked something deep inside me, liberated a part of me I did not know existed. Maybe it's the pot, I don't know. We always get stoned before we have sex, or rather, I get stoned. I never see any change in him. That is part of the excitement for both of us, I think. He is so cool and detached, and I am like jelly.

"Put your right leg over my left shoulder."

"Like this?"

"Yeah. Now reach around and grab my balls with your right hand."

"Like this?"

I come every which way, over and over.

"Stand up against the wall, facing me. No, face the wall. That's better. How does it feel?"

It felt so fine I couldn't answer.

"Now get down on the floor and put your legs up over your head."

"I can't breathe."

"Shut up and do it."

I came that way too.

"You know what?" he said one evening. "I just look at you and you come. You come so easily it's no challenge. You ought to go into the record book, sweetheart."

FEBRUARY 1971

Barry and Judith drove to Stowe practically nonstop, with the car radio tuned to a basketball game most of the way. They had gotten a late start because of a foul-up at the ski rental place. For an awful forty-five minutes she thought they might not be able to go at all because the shop didn't have a pair of boots that was right for Barry. Three hours into the trip she asked him to pull over at a rest area, but he didn't want to lose his momentum. Judith tried to keep her mind off her bladder for the next fifty miles, but she thought she was going to burst before he announced it was time to gas up. He was a maniac on the road, absolutely single-minded. "The only way to get there is to get there," he muttered, punching the radio buttons to get some scores.

The directions to the ski house were very exact. His friends were asleep when they arrived, but a block-lettered message on the kitchen table said, "Sack out in living room. Brown couch opens into double bed. See you on the slopes. Roger and Sue." They fell asleep, exhausted.

Everyone in the house was up and out before they woke up except for Roger, who had stayed behind to show them the drill. Neither of them had skied before. Barry put on his old jeans and a down vest. He laughed when Judith came out of the bathroom in a powder blue ski suit she had bought at Saks.

Roger took them to a beginners' slope and showed them the basics. Judith had trouble coordinating her poles and skis, and kept falling down. When she brushed off the snow for the tenth time and looked around for Barry, he was gliding down a small hill like he'd been skiing all his life.

After lunch at the ski lodge, the three of them went back to the beginners' slope. She could tell that Barry was disappointed in her. Roger told her to practice snowplowing while he took Barry to the rope tow. When the two men returned an hour later, Barry was grinning and breathing hard. "Boy, is he a natural!" Roger exclaimed.

"Listen, Judith," Barry said, his breath forming puffs of white. "We're gonna try the chair lift. Roger says I can handle a trail. We'll meet you back here in a couple of hours." She felt bereft.

Back at the house that evening, she was introduced to the others. All the talk at dinner was about lift tickets and waiting times and what a natural skier Barry Kantor had turned out to be.

The next morning the six of them piled into one car. She was deposited at the beginners' slope with a cheery wave. Sue suggested she might want to hire an instructor, there were lots of ski bums hanging around. "You'll be okay on your own for lunch?" Barry asked her. Of course she said yes.

Judith practiced her snowplowing until she felt confident enough to try the rope tow. She stood in line and took her turn, but each time she grasped the rope it slipped out of her hands and she landed on her backside. She was mortified when the people behind her yelled, "Hey, out of the way!"

On her fourth try she heard a voice behind her say, "Mind if I help?" By wrapping his arms around hers, the fellow got her up the hill. He skied with her for the rest of the afternoon, and once she even managed to hang on to the rope tow by herself. "You don't have much strength in your hands," he told her. "You'll catch on, though." His name was Skip Anderson, and he was a student at the University of Vermont. A really nice kid who enjoyed giving snow bunnies free lessons. Snow bunnies wore fancy ski suits and didn't know the first thing about skiing. She was a snow bunny all right.

She was practicing stem turns with Skip and relaxing—even enjoying herself—for the first time that weekend when she saw Barry and Roger. She waved at them happily and explained to Skip that these were the people she had come with. He nodded and skied off with a "See you on the slopes."

When they got back to the house, Barry said, "Judith, step outside. I want to ask you something."

They stood facing each other. His voice was low. "Who was that guy you were batting your eyes at?"

"What guy? You mean the student who was helping me on the rope tow—"

Without warning, he clapped her ears in one violent motion. "Don't ever do that to me again."

"Barry—"

Her ears were buzzing. She swallowed hard.

"You deliberately made a fool of me, Judith, in front of my friends." He raised his hand to hit her again. She stared at him, her mouth open. Tears stung her eyes.

"Barry, you don't understand. I love you."

He turned on his heel and walked back into the house. A few minutes later she followed.

Barry was unusually animated at the dinner table, but Judith was silent. Theirs was the first car to leave for the long trek back to the city.

"A mouse," Sue said to Roger as she helped him with the ski rack. "Barry's got himself a drab little mouse. How long do you think she'll last?"

Judith

He is going through a terrible emotional crisis. Only two or three people are aware of it, he keeps it all bottled up inside. The best I can do is hang on. Last month Thor, his beautiful Great Dane, had to be put away, and then two weeks ago Barry's father died. I did not have the opportunity to meet Mr. Kantor, but I know there was an ugly scandal when Barry was in high school. Something about a state liquor authority investigation. The Bronx politicians folded their arms and let Abe Kantor take the rap. Barry's father didn't go to prison, but there was a hearing and a reprimand, and they took away his CPA license.

Last night was the second time I've seen Barry explode. He had made all the arrangements for his father's funeral and spent a lot of time with his mother, but he hadn't allowed any emotion to surface. I wanted to draw him out. We were walking down West Fourth Street, coming home from a restaurant, and I said—I didn't mean to be flippant—"I can see where it might be liberating to lose a parent, sort of the final stage of growing up."

He grabbed me by the shoulders and shoved. I fell backward, banging my head against a brick wall.

We stood there panting, like each of us had seen a monster. I began to tremble. The back of my head hurt, but it didn't matter. What mattered was the powerful current flooding between us. I felt so alert, so alive.

"Don't talk about my father in that tone of voice again, Judith," he said, "unless you want me to walk out of your life."

I had done a terrible thing. I had showed my lack of

39

respect for his father. But he had told me those awful stories, the beatings with the leather belt! I hadn't understood that he loved the old man too.

He didn't mean to bang my head against the wall. It was an accident. We misunderstood each other—like the weekend in Stowe when he thought I was flirting on the slopes.

This is a man who cares so deeply, who feels so much pain.

Nosy New Yorkers! There was this woman walking her dog who must have seen the whole thing, because she was rooted to the sidewalk about ten feet away.

"What are you staring at, lady?" I said. She hustled off quickly. Good. That was my way of telling Barry that what happened hadn't been his fault.

There is so much I don't understand about Barry, but there is one thing I do understand. We have connected. I have reached him. And I'm not going to let him walk out of my life. Not ever.

MARCH 1971

Kathy Novawicki Norton, one of the women who had been at the ski house, called Roger to ask about Barry Kantor.

Roger laughed. "He's the kind of guy who pours cheap scotch into a Chivas Regal bottle for a BYO party."

"Oh, come on, Roger, we've all done that at one time or another."

"I'm sort of pissed with him right now. Sue's friend Doris wanted to come up to Stowe that weekend, so I had her call him to arrange a ride. He told her it would cost an extra twenty round-trip for her baby, so she didn't come. Sue's mad as hell at me."

"Is he a good lawyer? That's what I'm asking."

"Oh, as a lawyer, you mean. Sure. Why not? He graduated from NYU."

"I want a legal separation from Ron. Something amicable but on the road toward final. Life with an intern at Sloan-Kettering isn't all it's cracked up to be, maybe I'll get back into modeling."

"Gee, I'm sorry to hear that. What has it been—a year? He seemed like a nice fellow the one time I met him. Yeah, Barry's done matrimonials, if that's what you're asking. I thought you were expressing a personal interest."

Kathy arrived at Barry Kantor's office promptly at three o'clock.

"Hey, did you catch the guy who just walked out?" he asked. "A top-flight forger, one of the best in the business." He made a big point of buzzing his secretary to bring in some coffee, although Kathy told him she had just finished lunch and didn't want a thing.

She glanced at the dirty cream walls in need of a paint job.

"I could have joined a big downtown firm after law school," he told her, "but who needs those phonies with their fake wood paneling and wall-to-wall carpets? I'm making twice what a third-year associate makes in one of those firms." He pulled open his client file and showed her the names on the folders. She nodded politely.

"Connected," he said, "I'm very connected," giving her a broad wink behind his glasses. She stared at the unfamiliar names, not certain what he was driving at.

After the coffee arrived, he took out a legal pad and asked her for a list of Ron's assets. She mentioned the Mercedes, the Sutton Place co-op that had been a wedding gift from his parents, and the stock portfolio his father had started for him, with the blue-chip IBM he wasn't supposed to touch and the Xerox that kept splitting. His eyes lit up. Then he told her to clear out their savings and joint checking account before Ron beat her to it. "The deal is, I get one-third of the settlement. We'll put him through the washing machine."

Kathy said she'd think it over. She wanted an amicable separation, not an announcement of open warfare.

Kantor sent her a bill for two hundred dollars, his fee for a first consultation. Kathy almost wasn't going to pay it, but she was afraid she'd wind up in small-claims court, so what the hell—it had been an experience.

Later, when she consulted another attorney, she found out it was much more usual to be charged an hourly rate.

She and Ron decided to stick it out for another year. All it had cost her was the two hundred to Kantor and sixty to the other lawyer. She figured she had gotten away cheap.

APRIL 1971

Judith entered a list of Barry's strengths and vulnerabilities in her journal. Under "Vulnerabilities" she wrote:

> *Glasses. Very sensitive about having to wear them but won't try contacts. GO WITH HIM TO GET DESIGNER FRAMES. Tortoise shell?*

She giggled and made another entry.

> *Teeth. Probably genetic. Hates to go to the dentist. Who doesn't?*

42

After considerable thought she composed her third entry.

> *Anger. Big unresolved problem from childhood—*
> *Find out what happened in the army— Likes to*
> *con the system as a way of getting even. See*
> *Strengths.*

Following the section marked "Barry" she wrote, "Judith." Under "Strengths" she wrote:

> *Good eyes.*
> *Good teeth.*
> *Calm (comparatively).*

Under "Vulnerabilities" she wrote, *See elsewhere in this journal*, then crossed that out and wrote, *Barry Kantor.*

She closed the book.

MAY 3, 1971

Barry cleared space in the living room for her desk and typewriter table. He told her she could pile her books and clothes in the bedroom where he kept his storage boxes. The two of them worked all Saturday and Sunday hauling her things. He was so generous that way. Of course it made sense. She was still paying rent on her Perry Street studio, but she hadn't been there in ages except to collect more clothes, so she had to agree that keeping a separate apartment was a terrible waste of money. They had never actually said it formally, but they were living together. The closet space was ridiculous, so most of her stuff was still in shopping bags, but that didn't bother her. The main problem was that she needed a place to work on her novel on those precious free days when she wasn't doing the substitute teaching, but now that had been solved.

Carol, who she was beginning to think was not such a reliable friend after all, didn't think the new arrangement was a good idea.

"Why should he marry you if you're living with him already?"

"Jesus, Carol, you sound like my mother." They were gabbing on the phone, something they hadn't done for a while. She wanted to keep in touch with Carol, catch up on her latest romances and all that, but lately she hadn't had much time.

"So what are you going to tell your mother?"

"Well, obviously she knows something is up. I'm never at the Perry Street number when she calls. Listen, she adores him. He knows how to wrap little old Jewish ladies around his pinky. He sounds like a yeshiva *bucher* with her—the way he gives her that little-boy grin and bats his long lashes, really it's hysterical."

"Whatever you do, don't give up your apartment. It's your ace in the hole."

"Carol, I am not playing poker. I'm living with a man I happen to love. There is a thing called commitment, and that's what we have between us. It doesn't require a wedding ring. Look around you, people are shacking up all over the place. If you can't accept it, then why don't you admit you're a hopeless square?"

The conversation was beginning to bore her. Judith looked at her watch. The evening was half over and she hadn't gotten to the typewriter yet. Soon Barry would be home, and she swore she'd have a couple of pages to show him. Carol had a ninny quality—where had she gotten that word "ninny"? oh, probably from Barry—that might be contagious if she was exposed to it in large doses. She held the receiver away from her ear and reached into the drawer where she kept her carton of cigarettes. The idea

44

of a close girlfriend for heart-to-hearts was appealing, but the truth was she preferred the company of men, always had.

"Uh-huh." Carol was still talking. Good. If she responded with an appropriate uh-huh every now and then, Carol would never notice that she had tuned out. Ya-tata, ya-tata, a perfect ninny. She should try to work Carol into her novel. Better yet, make her a short story. Call it "A Perfect Ninny." Sounds like a *New Yorker* piece, doesn't it? "A Perfect Ninny," by Judith Winograd. Maybe just "The Ninny," by J. Winograd. They were into minimalism these days. She could do it Dorothy Parker–style. Get a tape recorder and run one of Carol's monologues verbatim, taking out her occasional uh-huhs. No, leaving in the uh-huhs, to break up the page.

"Uh, listen, Carol. Got to go. Barry's coming home soon, and I've got a few things to do."

Free at last. She looked at the clock. Eleven p.m. Where was he?

JUNE 1971

Mrs. Laemmerle opened her door when she heard footsteps coming down the stairs. "Oh, it's you," she said. "I thought it might be the new gal on your floor." Marianna nodded curtly and tried to brush by her, but Mrs. Laemmerle was not a woman one brushed by with equanimity, even if one was late for work. "Do you know if her name is Wino-, Wino-something? I can't really see without my glasses. This was in my mailbox, but I think it's for her. From Lord and Taylor. When you see the window, you know it's a bill."

Marianna glanced at the envelope and then at Mrs. Laemmerle in her floral housecoat, ready for a full-dress conversation. How the hell do I know who it's for, she

45

thought crossly, and why does this busybody always open her door when she hears a creak on the stairs? "Give it back to the postman, Mrs. Laemmerle. That's what I would do." She tossed her mane of blond hair and was out the front door before Mrs. Laemmerle could get in another word.

Marianna Buchanan was in a foul mood all the way uptown on the bus. When friends oohed and aahed over her charming Village apartment on such a quaint tree-lined street, she quickly countered that living in a reno-vated brownstone townhouse had disadvantages that had never crossed her mind before she moved from her door-man-and-elevator building on the Upper East Side. The bricked-in fireplace that took up almost an entire wall of her living room, not enough heat on the coldest days of winter, the part-time superintendent who lived two blocks away and was never available on weekends. And then there was Mrs. Laemmerle, who lived on the ground floor and acted like a concierge.

So the next-door neighbor had acquired a live-in. That must have been the racket she'd heard in the hallway last month just before her trip to Virginia. Moving in furni-ture. Wasn't his place crowded enough already? Not that she'd ever been invited in to see her neighbor's apart-ment, or he hers, for that matter. When she first moved into the building, she had had a ridiculous hallway flirta-tion with Barry Kantor. Once they'd halfheartedly set up a dinner date, but she'd canceled the day before when an out-of-town assignment came through, and he didn't seem inclined to set up another. The casual chumminess came to an end when she got fed up with the parade of females going in and out of 3-A. One of his bimbos had actually rung her bell at two in the morning, trying to get into the building.

Marianna put her Waverly Place neighbors out of her

mind and concentrated on the day's work ahead of her. Try and set up the interview with Balanchine. Convince the PR people that a piece on the new ballet absolutely won't work without a sound bite from the great master and some footage of him with Farrell. See what the researcher has come up with on the hunger-in-Appalachia piece. Plead with the desk that she be allowed to produce the Panthers story since her contacts in Oakland were better than the San Francisco bureau's.

All in all, Marianna thought, she was having a good year. She had given up hope of being on-camera—all that money wasted on the voice coach, trying to inject some life into her flat Midwestern delivery—but she had proved to the desk she was a damn good field producer, and her career had taken a big leap forward. Of course the women's suit at the network had helped a lot, but the series she did on congressional wives—with no help at all from the Washington bureau—had really put her on the map. She'd made it from local to network. In a few years she'd be doing hard-news documentaries or have the Paris bureau for sure.

SEPTEMBER 1971

Mr. and Mrs. Winograd climbed the three flights of stairs with the box of cookies they had picked up at Sutter's. Judith's mother paused on the landing with her hand on her heart, composing herself before she spoke.

"I notice he doesn't even put your name on the doorbell?"

The opening salvo, before she had entered the apartment! Judith involuntarily tensed her shoulders. Her parents could slice under her skin and expose a raw nerve in two seconds flat. If she didn't watch it, they'd be scream-

47

ing at each other before Barry came home. He'd left a little blue pill on the bed table this morning, a ten-milligram Valium. For insurance, he said. She'd never taken more than a five before.

"It's a protection against the landlord, Ma. Barry's going to write him a letter after he signs the new lease in November."

"November." Her mother sighed. "This is not what I expected when I came to see my daughter in her . . . her new home." She choked on "home." Judith remembered she'd had the same exact catch in her voice when she first visited Perry Street. *This is not what I expected.* What the hell did she expect? A wedding in some hired hall on Kings Highway, attended by the Cleveland cousins she'd never met? Her mother would never forgive her for denying the Cleveland cousins their big opportunity to come to New York.

"A nice house from the outside," her father the peacemaker chimed in. "Substantial. I was imagining worse. So what sort of people live in such a building, Judith?" He pronounced her name "Juditt." She was nearly thirty and it still drove her crazy that they had given her a name that defied his tongue.

"Homos and perverts, Daddy, is that what you mean?"

"Feh." He failed to catch her irony, but her wily mother wouldn't let the moment slide.

"She's making fun of us, Max. Our sophisticated daughter thinks her parents are a couple of ignoramuses because we don't speak good the way she does. We weren't born yesterday, kiddo. I always say you make your bed and you lie in it. Someday when it's too late you'll realize we were only looking after your interests."

Judith left her mother in the front room to mouth the rest of her homilies to the four walls and the fireplace, and trailed down the hall after her father, who was pushing open the French doors to the bedroom. Their Fibber

McGee closet. The rest of the apartment was as neat as a pin. What primeval instinct led him to make a beeline to the place where she and Barry threw their junk?

Emboldened by her mother, her father worked himself into one of his melodramatic stands. "This is the way you let a lawyer keep his books and his clothes? A lawyer?" He shook his head.

"They happen to be my books, Daddy."

He didn't hear. "Some way to keep house. This you didn't learn from your mother."

Remarkable, the disordered room was all her fault. Her father had that awed Old World respect for professionals, they were royalty who did not mix with the likes of him and his kin. The big shots. If Max Winograd's daughter had hooked up with a potential big shot by some peculiar happenstance he couldn't fathom, the relationship had to be destined for failure. Already he'd sniffed out the ominous signs.

So she had disappointed him again, or rather, she had confirmed his suspicions. She could never resolve in her mind which was worse, her mother's constant, sharp belittling or her father's ingrained defeatism—or were they one and the same?

Her mother had opened the box of cookies and was arranging them on a plate in the kitchen.

"Motherrrr, before dinner? I made a reservation at the Coach House." Her mother gestured at her father, who had a sheepish look on his face.

"Max had a sandwich before we came up."

"Why, *why*? I told you we were all going to have dinner together when Barry came home." She could hear her voice rising.

"Max forgot."

"Don't worry about me, Judith. I'll have a plate of soup and some crackers."

"I don't believe this. I don't believe this." She was

screaming. "You did this deliberately." They stared at her, not comprehending. Her rages, like sudden squalls, erupted from nowhere. Their daughter. The parents stood there embarrassed.

Judith heard the turn of the key in the lock. "Barry." She flew to the door and kissed him hard on the mouth. He looked past her and took in the scene.

"Goldie, Max. Looking good! You been here long? I'll grab a shower and be with you in a minute. Judith got reservations at the best restaurant in the Village. Did she tell you?"

Her parents smiled up at him. The savior had arrived.

JUNE 1972–OCTOBER 1973

Judith joined a writers' group that met once a week on the Lower East Side. She was not a joiner by nature, but Barry said give it a try, it might help her get over her block.

She enjoyed the sessions, part group therapy, part criticism, although she dreaded the evening when she would have to read aloud from her work in progress. That night she panicked and didn't show up. God bless them, they called her at home and made her promise that she'd come back the following week. The truth was, she didn't have any work in progress. She had abandoned the novel about the teacher after she read *Up the Down Staircase*, and the short stories she'd started and worked on fitfully before she met Barry seemed so terribly thin when she read them over that she threw them out. The only writing she had managed for the last year and a half was an occasional entry in her journal.

The group agreed she could stay for six months even if she didn't read, and then they'd reconsider her status.

There were four men who came regularly and three other occasional members, including a red-haired woman she detested on sight, who showed up in overalls and handed out flyers for poetry readings and antiwar demonstrations.

She avoided the poetry readings but went with Barry to one of the demos—a big one down on Whitehall Street with barricades and police horses—but it wasn't their thing. Barry was so spontaneous and irrepressible they were both afraid he'd wind up getting arrested, not a good move for a lawyer.

The group was of several minds about Judith. Was she a serious person or not? Most of them thought not, but Larry and Mark agreed she had a fragile, vulnerable quality beneath her brittle exterior that turned them on.

"It's all in the eye makeup," scoffed Pam, the woman in overalls. Larry and Mark privately wished that Pam would go back to eye makeup, but you didn't say that to chicks anymore, they'd blow their stack. The anger of chicks these days was astonishing.

Art Houseman, who was writing a four-generation family saga and always had something to bring to the group, thought Judith dragged down their professional level. But he conceded that she was a good listener who laughed in the right places when he read his stuff. He agreed with Larry and Mark that she wasn't a libber. "Maybe that's her problem. She ought to be in a consciousness-raising group if she's looking for community. That's not what we're about."

Bob Rothman, who was writing a play about Vietnam and went to his street theater collective on Thursdays, felt Judith suffered from the same problem he saw in other women writers. "They don't get a chance to rack up experience, they're left out of the major events of history, all the earthshaking adventures. I'm not saying she's *not* a writer, however," he said to Art. "Maybe she'll fool us. Grace Paley stunned the shit out of a lot of folks in the antiwar movement who just knew her from demonstrations. I mean, bam, there she was in the *New Yorker*. Writers develop at different paces. Isn't that what our group is about?"

Larry nodded. "Yeah. I had a friend at Cornell who took a survey course with Nabokov before *Lolita*. He had no idea the guy was writing fiction."

The thought cheered them up. Not everyone came on like Hemingway and Mailer.

One evening Bob asked Judith if she'd ever thought of writing a children's book. She hadn't.

"I've got a friend who's an editor at Scholastic," he told her. "They're always looking for new talent, it's a wide-open market. Of course they exploit authors horrendously in children's books, and the royalties are pathetic, but it's a way to work up a steady income. You knock 'em out, they stay in print, and if you're a fast writer, you can sort of build up an annuity over the years."

"I'm not a fast writer. I labor over each sentence like I'm engraving it in stone."

"Well, think of it this way. With children's books the sentences are short and you don't have to write so many words."

"I'll keep that in mind," she laughed. She knew he was being generous, but she felt somewhat slighted, like he wasn't taking her ambitions as seriously as he took the others'. She'd have to screw up her courage and bring the group something she'd written, even if it was only a fragment from her journal, a couple of disjointed pages. Then they'd see the sort of work she was capable of.

Everything was going to fall into place once she found

her subject. What was the Pirandello play? *Six Characters in Search of an Author.* She was an author in search of six characters, a setting, and a plot. Nothing seriously amiss, just a case of a few missing pieces.

She liked Bob a lot, and thought he was probably gay but didn't know it. That was okay with her. She felt very comfortable with gay men. She could talk to him about Barry.

Maybe.

Bob didn't let the subject drop. They were sharing a joint and listening to the new Stones album at her place —Barry was out of town.

"I'm serious, Jude. First time you get published you'll be over your block. That's what happened to me when the *Voice* printed my piece on the street theater collective." He got up to flip over the record.

Judith lurched toward the turntable. "Please, I'll do it —he doesn't like people fooling with his stereo." She had moved a bit too urgently. Bob gave her a funny look. "He just replaced the cartridge last month. You know how men are about equipment."

"Yeah, heavy. Pride of ownership. A big bourgeois hangup."

They let the music take over and followed where it led them. No need to talk. Finally Bob stirred on the couch. "Whew, Barry has the best grass in town, doesn't he?"

"Yeah. Pride of ownership." They giggled. Bob was her friend. She owed him an explanation, but it was hard to do stoned. She concentrated and made the effort. "Dust. He's fanatic about dust."

"About dust?"

"Dust on the stereo." They giggled again. Was that what she meant to say? What had she meant to say? Something about fear. She felt a chill.

53

"Not to change the subject, or rather, to go back to the original subject."

It took her a moment to catch his drift. Oh, that subject. "Bob, I work with kids all day long. I do other things on my own time."

"But that's the point, you know the stuff a kid can handle. You've got a leg up."

The image of a leg up convulsed her.

JANUARY 1974

She was exempted from the visits to the Bronx. Barry's mother still lived in the old apartment on Morris Avenue. Nothing could get her to move, and Barry went up to have dinner with her once a month. She had gone with him a couple of times after his father's funeral, but Mrs. Kantor had taken such a strong dislike to her that she and Barry agreed it would be better if she stayed away.

His mother still dusted his old room every day, Barry told her. Her hair had gone white and her eyesight was failing, but she still kept up a stream of vituperation about the inferior sturgeon at Daitch's, the crazy woman who lived next door, and what Morris Avenue was coming to now that the *shvartzes* were moving in.

Seeing Barry in his mother's house had been a revelation. The apartment was dark and gloomy, with nothing growing in it except for a tired rubber plant on the windowsill. It was hard to believe that this ailing, corseted figure in a black dress and elastic stockings had once cowered in this very room while her husband used a wooden hanger as an extension of his right arm.

Apparently his mother had forgotten those days too. "Such a good boy," she'd said to Judith. "The apple of his father's eye." When Judith walked down the dark

54

hallway to use the bathroom, his mother had said something in Yiddish she didn't understand, but the words after that came through loud and clear. "Is she feeding you hot meals?" Judith was livid, but she didn't let on she'd heard.

It was fine with her that Barry preferred to execute his filial obligations without involving her, but he always came back from the Bronx in such a grump that Judith wished his mother would take the big plunge and move to Miami. Barry had made her a standing offer, he told her he'd pay for a condo any time she was ready, but the old lady wouldn't budge.

FEBRUARY 14, 1974

Carol and her new guy, Jonathan, were into their second bottle of wine when they heard the downstairs buzzer. "It's me. Judith. I'm coming up, but I'm alone."

"Weird," Carol muttered.

"That our dinner guests?" Jonathan said from the couch. "Not that I think we will ever be having our dinner. No dinner tonight."

"One of them. Just Judith." She went to the door, trying to get her anger under control.

Judith came in, running her fingers through her kinky hair. "Carol, I'm sorry. I'm really sorry. Barry had to work late. He's still at the office."

"Couldn't you call? You're two hours late."

"I am? I didn't know what time it was. Barry was working, he thought he could get away."

"How could you do this to me, Judith?"

"Look, I'll leave. I'm sorry I came."

She looked so woeful that Jonathan sprang to attention. "Take off your coat, Judith. Glad you could make it. Carol started her paella too early, that's all." He put his arms

55

around Carol and hugged her waist. "Just serve it, honey, it'll be great."

Carol went into the kitchen and slammed the door. Judith looked ready to bolt.

"Hey, come on, girls," Jonathan said. "I'm hungry."

Judith pulled a bottle of wine from her totebag and laid it on the table.

"Good, you're staying. I'm Jonathan Altman, Carol's intended."

They ate the dried-out paella by candlelight. Carol had pulled out all the stops, Judith noticed with sour glee. Her mother's silver candlesticks and a white damask tablecloth that probably came from her hope chest. Carol really was very bourgeois, they had nothing in common when you got right down to it. So this was her "intended." That was the word he had actually used. God, people could delude themselves. He wouldn't be around in six months; she knew Carol's pattern.

"Carol tells me you're a schoolteacher, Judith."

"Me? I work in the New York City school system, yes, but that's not how I define myself." She poured more wine into her glass. Why hadn't she brought a stick of Barry's pot? She could be smoking it now in the bathroom.

"How do you define yourself?"

"Well, not as a substitute teacher. I'm a writer." There was always a thudding silence when she said that to people. Funny, you don't look like a writer. Come off it, honey, we all thought we were going to be writers, but most of us grew up. Have you written anything I might have read?

Jonathan was preparing to speak. "Have you written anything I might have read?"

The sixty-four-dollar question. Why is it all the assholes of the world know how to ask the sixty-four-dollar question? She'd bring this up at the next meeting of the group.

Carol rushed into the breach. "I don't see anything insignificant about being a schoolteacher. It's more socially useful than what I do."

"That's so very kind of you," Judith replied with an icy glare, "but subbing is not what I see as the central focus of my life." She waved her hand to emphasize her point and knocked over her wineglass. The three of them watched for one paralyzed moment as the wet spot spread on the tablecloth.

"Don't worry about it. White wine doesn't stain." Jonathan mopped the spill with his cloth napkin.

What an idiot thing to do, tip over the glass. She was so jittery lately.

Carol came back from the kitchen with a frosted cake decorated with a lumpy red heart. "Ta-da! Happy Valentine's Day, lovers. I made it myself." Jonathan applauded. Judith managed a weak smile.

She left as soon as she could make a decent getaway. Carol wrapped up a piece of cake for her to take home to Barry.

"I thought your friend was a little hostile," Jonathan said as he cleared the dishes.

"A little hostile? She was so incredibly rude to you I couldn't believe it. And all her conversation was about Barry."

"Do you think she didn't catch on when I said I was your intended?" He nuzzled her neck as they moved toward the bedroom.

"I don't know what she caught or didn't catch, and I'm not sure she's my friend anymore either. I have a feeling that if I never called her again, Miss Judith Winograd wouldn't even notice. She wouldn't care if I fell off the face of the earth."

57

"What's Barry like?"

"El Mysterioso, the hotshot attorney? I've never met him. Every time we're supposed to get together he's out of town or working late. I don't think she wants me to meet him. At first I thought she was afraid I'd steal him out from under her or something. You know, girlfriends are like that—I mean women, we're supposed to say women now."

"You're my woman now."

"Cute. But I'm beginning to think it's something else. Judith thinks I'm too square to pass muster."

"Maybe he doesn't exist."

"Oh, he exists all right. I've seen the signs. The bruises. He's the kind of man who likes to leave his mark." She snapped off the light.

"To each his own," Jonathan murmured as he reached for her breast.

Barry was smoking a joint and watching TV in the darkened bedroom when Judith got home.

"What took you so long? You missed a great flick."

She could never understand his passion for television. The set was on all the time now, the sound low and muted unless there was something that grabbed his attention. They went to sleep with it and woke up to it in the morning. At the beginning when he brought home the big twenty-four-inch set she had checked the nightly listings and marked off the programs she thought they might like to watch together, but nothing she chose ever met with his approval, so she had given up trying. One show was as good as another to her, and Barry was at his sweetest when he had an old movie to hold his interest. Otherwise he'd flick the dials, back and forth, back and forth. Trouble.

"I don't think I'm going to see Carol again."

"Good."

"Both of them, she and her boyfriend, asked where you were."

"I told you to tell them I was working."

"I did. She set a place for you at the table." It came out like an accusation, but that wasn't what she meant, she was only reporting on her dreadful evening. Judith gave Barry a quick look. He was watching a Carson monologue, deeply engrossed. Maybe he hadn't heard. She heaved a sigh of relief and crawled into bed.

"Did you lock the front door?"

A moment of panic tightened her stomach. Why was it she never remembered the door? Barry wanted her to get into an orderly routine. Come into the apartment, lock the door behind you. So simple. But no use, it was one of her weak sides, her usual forgetfulness. Both of them used to laugh about it at first, but now that she was living in his space it wasn't so funny. She got out of bed and double-latched the door. Then she remembered the piece of cake with the Valentine heart. She wrapped it securely in extra foil and stuck it in the refrigerator. Then she took it out again and found a label. Barry liked a neat, organized refrigerator with everything labeled. How should she label the cake? She drew a heart to remind her of the lumpy Valentine. That ought to do it. When she came back to the bedroom he was flicking the channels. A bad sign.

"What are you standing there for like a ninny? Get into bed."

She crawled under the covers, staying well over on her side. Barry hated to be touched when he was in one of his moods.

She closed her eyes. The drone from the tube was having its effect, she was getting drowsy.

Peace.

"Judith!"

Barry was in the kitchen slamming cupboards and drawers. Judith scrambled out of bed and looked at the clock. Seven-forty, she had slept through the alarm. She'd be late for work. *Barry's court case.* He'd be late for court.

"Judith!" He was bellowing with rage.

The kitchen had been turned upside down. Flour, sugar, instant coffee, cornflakes—the mess lay an inch deep on the linoleum floor. Barry was tugging at the silverware drawer. With a yell he wrenched it free. Knives and forks clattered onto the heap.

What had she done? She had put away the dishes and wiped the counters thoroughly last night before they went to bed, and there was plenty of milk for his morning coffee. The coffeepot! No, she had filled it last night, she knew she had.

He kicked the stove. "A roach. I didn't have roaches before you moved in. You're turning this place into a fucking pigsty."

He started on the refrigerator, methodically dumping bowls and containers. Last night's leftovers, which she had carefully stored.

"What's this shit?" He hurled a package of sliced bread across the room. "How many times do I have to tell you —*don't leave the garbage overnight.*"

No, she couldn't have! Oh no, oh no, she had forgotten to take down the garbage.

"I'm sorry."

"I'm sorry, I'm sorry," he mimicked. "When was the last time you cleaned out the refrigerator? Do I have to do everything myself? Get rid of this stuff, just get rid of it. Get a big trash bag and pile it in. Hurry up, you're making me late for court."

She hunted through the debris for the box of trash bags. "I'll call the exterminator."

"You do that." He was still pulling things out of the refrigerator and tossing them behind him. A solitary egg smashed against the wall.

"What the fucking hell is this?" He was holding a crushed foil wad in his hand. From where she stood she could see her hand-drawn label. A heart. The Valentine cake from Carol's dinner. "How long has this been in the refrigerator, Judith?"

Was it four days or three? Barry hated imprecise answers. She stood there numbly, trying to count.

"Answer me, Judith. How long?"

What had he told her to say if she didn't know the answer? I don't know. That was it—the truth—that's what he wanted.

"I don't know."

"You don't know, Judith?" His voice was deadly quiet. "What kind of imbecile am I living with?"

She started to cry. Great big tears that wet her cheeks. It was so unfair. She had given him a truthful answer.

He stalked out of the kitchen. She heard him rummaging in the hall closet. She got down on her knees to pick up the silverware, she'd have to wash and dry every piece before it went back in the drawer. It was sort of like pickup sticks, her favorite childhood game. The trick was to take one stick without jarring the others. If another stick moved, you were out. Barry was right. She *was* an imbecile. The Valentine's dinner had been on the fourteenth. This was the nineteenth, it was marked on her calendar, the day Barry was defending the Puerto Rican bomber. She was so proud he had taken the case, but now she had messed up his concentration by her stupidity and carelessness.

The garbage should have gone out the night before. *Imbecile, imbecile.* Now, how long had the cake been in the refrigerator? Five days, the answer was five days. She'd go to him with the correct answer and apologize.

Too late. She heard him slam the front door.

Judith looked around the ruined kitchen. She'd clean up the mess and call the exterminator, and then when he came home they'd forget about the morning's ugliness.

School. She was subbing in Bay Ridge this week. What time was it? She looked at the clock. If she got to the subway in fifteen minutes and a train came . . . but she wasn't even dressed yet. Her face was probably puffy from crying. Call the school, that's what she should do, call the school and say . . . say what? Say an emergency has come up. A fire. A fire in the kitchen. Firemen still here, can't leave. Water damage. Need a full day to clean up the kitchen. *Don't tell them that.* Buy a couple of cans of roach spray and attack the whole apartment, the exterminators never do a thorough job anyway.

Judith got on the phone and spoke to the school administrator. That made her feel a lot better. Barry always teased that she was a dolt on the telephone, but he'd have been proud to hear the way she piled on the agony this morning. Utterly convincing.

NOVEMBER 1974

Barry and a lawyer named Ed Meegan teamed up and rented a suite of offices on lower Broadway for two thousand a month. They had space for a third person. Ed knew a guy from law school, Steve Tobias, who was shopping around for a partnership arrangement. The three lawyers met for lunch at Forlini's, behind the criminal court building on Centre Street. The waiters in Forlini's were famous for their good manners. Every customer in a dark business suit was called "your honor" so they wouldn't inadvertently slight some judge.

Barry dominated the conversation while he cased the room, pointing out Judge Saypol in the corner and Judge Greenfield at a banquette. He explained to Steve Tobias that he was hot to trot, he wanted to make up for lost time —the years he had spent in the army before finishing up at NYU. He outlined his plans for a multiservice law firm that would do criminal work, tax cases, matrimonials, personal injury, incorporations, the works.

"Once we get 'em in the shop we keep 'em." He reached over with his fork and speared a succulent piece of veal from Steve's plate. "We'll let you handle the trial work," he said, waving the fork. "I'm a settler and a pleader. When I figure out what Ed is good for, I'll let you know."

The next day Steve Tobias called Ed Meegan and said, "Count me out. I can't see going into partnership with a guy who grabs food off my plate and talks with his mouth full of manicotti."

Ed said that was unkind, he ought to have a better reason.

"Okay, I didn't like the way he made a weak pass at the check and then stuck you with it. If you don't think that says something about how the guy practices law, you're crazy."

Four months later Ed Meegan got out of his deal with Barry Kantor and went in with another lawyer. He called Steve Tobias to give him his new number.

"I'll be paying two rents for the rest of the year, but Jesus, it's worth it to be free of that cheapskate, that

. . . that *hornswoggler*. That guy Kantor will nickel-and-dime anybody, it doesn't matter if it's a cup of coffee or five grand."

"What did I tell you?" Tobias roared. "Manicotti!"

APRIL 1975

Judith called Bob Rothman and met him for lunch near the Flatiron building, where he edited a chemical industry magazine.

Since the writers' group had broken up they hadn't seen each other much. She had heard from Mark when they met by chance at the movies that Bob was now out of the closet, except at work, where his bosses were real conservative types. She understood exactly. Never trust the straight world with the intimate details of your personal life, Barry had drummed into her, they'll only use it against you at the first opportunity. When Barry appeared in criminal court in his business suit, he looked establishment all the way. She had managed to fool the New York City school system for seven years. God, when she thought about it—staggering into class the morning after an all-night acid trip, that was a trip and a half. Smoking a joint in the faculty lounge between classes, well, lots of people smoked dope. She and Barry still liked a good toke, but they didn't do psychedelics anymore. They were moving into a new phase.

After the how's-tricks and how's-by-you, she came to the point. Did he still think she could get into the children's book field, and what could he do to help her?

"I've had it with teaching, Bob," she said with an earnest shake of her head, hoping he'd notice her fashionable new frizz. "Barry's earning so much loot I'm ready to play Sadie Married Lady."

That was a slight fib. They were always short of cash.

She didn't wish to tell him her absence record was so atrocious this past semester that the Board of Ed had taken her off the list of active subs.

Bob said he'd make a couple of calls. His friend at Scholastic had moved to Doubleday, so that was a possibility, and Random House was coming out with a new kiddie line, he'd just read about that in *Publishers Weekly*. There was Simon and Schuster, but the person he knew there had just been assigned to cookbooks. "Cookbooks aren't for you," he mused, "although they *can* make a mint."

"Let's stay with the children's book idea," she laughed. She was feeling better than she had felt in months. The new haircut was a great lift—she never thought she'd live to see the day when naturally kinky hair was in fashion. "I'd like to try my hand at illustrating too."

"I didn't know you could draw."

"There's a lot about me you don't know." They looked at each other for a long moment. We've each got secrets, don't we, she thought. "Actually I wanted to be an artist before I wanted to write. I won all the prizes in school."

"Slow down," Bob said. "One thing at a time. Get your foot in the door first. Come up with a list of your concepts and I'll get you together with Tom Houghton, who'll have some ideas of his own."

She was pleased to hear that his editor friend was a man. She always did better with men.

Bob paid for the lunch with his credit card. After all, he said, they had discussed business.

JULY 1975

Tom Houghton couldn't give her a contract since she hadn't published a thing in her life, but as a favor to Bob he looked at her list and showed her some of the in-house ideas he'd been trying to find an author for. He told her to choose one and he'd reserve it for her for a couple of months. Then she was to come in and show him her pages, and if it looked like she knew what she was doing, it might be the start of a beautiful relationship. When she left his office she was loaded down with juvenile books to study.

"Formula," he told her. "Figure out the formula and do it. Better advice than that I cannot give you."

She chose *Vegetables That Grow Underground* for the five-to-eight-year-old market.

Barry and she played Vegetables That Grow Underground. She said, "Beets!" and he yelled, "Carrots!" She clapped her hands crying, "Rutabaga, rutabaga!" and skipped around the living room. He caught her by the arm and wrestled her onto the rug. When he had her pinned down he breathed, "Onions!" They both shouted, "Potatoes!" but he claimed he had spit it out first.

They hadn't laughed so hard in years. Barry said, "Yeah, good coke," and put down another couple of lines.

She told Barry she wanted to do the illustrations herself.

"Babe, I have great faith in you," he said. "We're gonna make you the Dr. Seuss of the five-to-eight-year-old market."

"Dr. Seuss always does his own drawings. Too cartoony for my taste, I don't see what's so special. I know what I'd do. I'd do watercolor washes on rice paper in strong primary colors."

"See? You're gaining on him already."

She loved it when he teased her like that. Why couldn't he be this sweet and gentle all the time? The rages in Barry were a puzzle to her. The slightest spark could touch them off, but blessing of blessings, they lifted just as

66

suddenly, and then their relationship was bathed in glorious sunshine again. She loved him more than ever, and she knew he loved her. What they had was more than love. He needed her. The hurt look that came over him when he saw the bruise under her eye the other day—she would carry that memory for the rest of her life. If he didn't know what he was doing sometimes, that was because he felt everything so keenly. She'd shoulder the burden of his pain and sensitivity, she'd make him whole again.

"Babe, don't fix dinner. Let's order in Chinese."

"Great idea."

"Don't call yet, hon. Let's do another toot." He shaved a sliver off the crystal and pulverized it into white dust on her mirror. "Listen, babe, it was brilliant of you to get the seed catalogues. You saved yourself a shitload of time."

Brilliant. He said that. She hugged herself in delight.

"You're gonna knock out a whole series of these how-do-they-grow books. Vegetables that grow aboveground, fruits that grow on bushes, fruits that grow on trees. The exciting new series by Judith Winograd. City kids don't know any of this stuff, Jude. I grew up thinking carrots and peas came in a can."

"Barry, I have to do the first one first." He was always eight steps ahead of her. It was one of the things she loved him for. "Bob says if they like this one, I should get an agent."

"I'll take a look at your contract when it comes in."

"I was hoping you would." He was such a genius at contracts, spotting the loopholes nobody else saw, untangling the legalese. She wouldn't need an agent if she had Barry.

They were a team.

A wave of euphoria spread over her. She was beginning to see what he saw in coke.

Judith turned in *Vegetables That Grow Underground* with a set of her own watercolor illustrations. A new editor had replaced Tom Houghton. They met for lunch. Marcia Rosen informed her as gently as she could that the art department was farming out her manuscript to a professional illustrator, someone who knew all about specs and other technical matters.

"We'll do a good job. Don't worry."

Judith tried to put up a brave front.

"For a first time out, you did very well. We're scheduling it for next spring, if all goes well with the artwork."

Next spring. A year away. She picked at her food. Barry had told her to talk about a second book. Okay.

"I conceived of *Vegetables That Grow* as part of a series."

"So did we," Marcia nodded vigorously. "In fact, we're moving *Vegetables That Grow on Vines* into production before yours. Stringbeans, cucumbers, squash, peas, tomatoes. The author came up with quite a basket." She chuckled.

"Somehow I thought of it as my series."

The new editor shrugged. She couldn't be more than twenty-four years old. "Well, you weren't exactly speedy on delivery. Look, let's see how this one goes, and then we'll talk about other projects. In the meantime, I have a note here somewhere—oh, yes. We were wondering why you forgot to include turnips."

Judith stiffened. "A rutabaga is a kind of turnip." Oh, how she had slaved over her rutabaga illustration.

"A kind of turnip. Ah. Well, let's go with the generic, shall we? Write me a turnip page and we'll scratch the rutabagas. And Judith, we believe it's most important that somewhere, either in 'Turnips' or 'Parsnips,' you distinguish between the two."

Marcia Rosen tucked the restaurant receipt into her wallet. Authors and their deathless prose, how they hated the nuts and bolts of the editorial process. This one looked like she was going to cry. "It shouldn't take you long," she said brightly. "And keep in mind how much you're learning."

SEPTEMBER 1976

After several tries, Judith got a call-back from Marcia Rosen, who apologized profusely for being so swamped. Yes, she had gotten the new turnip and parsnip pages, and they looked fine.

Vegetables That Grow Underground was being pushed back to the fall 1977 list. A logjam in the production department. She'd ask accounting about Judith's check.

JANUARY 1977

Barry's practice had really taken off since the Betts case. He was handling drug busts routinely now, although he still did matrimonials and negligence cases and an occasional real estate deal. Her man was not one to box himself into a narrow specialty. He loved putting deals together, but the excitement of criminal work was in his blood.

Betts was his lucky break. None of his pals had seen any future in the drug cases, but when Legal Aid threw him Betts, Barry jumped at the chance. She had never seen him work so hard, studying the precedents in Vermont and California. He brought up constitutional issues in

Betts that hadn't been tried in New York State before, and he won flat out on entrapment. A reporter for the *Daily News* happened to be in court the last day of the trial, and his feature story, HUBBY AND WIFE BEAT DRUG RAP, while a little fanciful on the facts, had spelled the name Barry Kantor correctly.

"Win a reputation for getting up early and you can sleep late the rest of your life," he told her.

There was an interesting angle to the druggies. They paid his retainer in cash.

AUGUST 26, 1977

Judith got an advance copy of *Vegetables That Grow Underground* in time to have a wonderful surprise for Barry's birthday. She had been tiptoeing around the house, keeping her secret to herself. He tended to get in a funk on holidays and birthdays. What had gone wrong last year on his thirty-fifth? She couldn't remember.

Three months ago she'd had a drag-out fight with her publisher about putting in a dedication page. The production people informed her she was too late, she should have sent in the dedication when she returned her proofread galleys, but Marcia Rosen went to bat for her and got the page inserted.

"To Barry, the star in my constellation." It was his book as much as it was hers. She'd never have pulled it off without him.

SEPTEMBER 5, 1977

Barry came home from the Bronx in a dark mood. To save the situation, they snorted most of a half-gram of coke between them.

Thank God for the white stuff. That had become her prayer.

SEPTEMBER 6, 1977

He grabbed for the little glass vial when he woke up.

Wexley. He had to get an adjournment. Ask the judge. Get down on his hands and knees. That tough bastard Clynes never granted adjournments.

He needed a shot of courage.

SEPTEMBER 7, 1977

He made a fool of himself and lost every motion he presented. Called the state's witness by the wrong name twice. The twirp assistant DA Kleinfeld had actually smirked.

The max. He had gotten his client the max. "Bad break, we'll win on appeal," he told Wexley's father as he buckled his briefcase, avoiding the man's eyes.

Judith was in the kitchen when Barry came home. The odor of baking lasagna made him retch. He saw the set table and the small wrapped package that lay on his plate. He went into the bedroom and slammed the door.

An hour later he emerged and closeted himself in the bathroom.

She was giving him a wide berth, the bitch. Good, at least he had taught her something.

He left the apartment without saying a word.

71

SEPTEMBER 8, 1977, 3:00 A.M.

He grabbed her by the hair and slammed her head against the bedpost. Judith awoke on impact.

"You went to sleep with the oven on."

Her head hit the post again. "The oven, you crazy bitch, you left it on full blast." His other hand gripped her neck. She clawed at his fingers.

Suddenly he released her. "I could have come home to an inferno."

She lay there panting, feeling no pain. The pain would come later. For now it was over. She cried tears of relief.

JULY 1978

Jeff Kellerman, who was sharing office space with Barry in the Cubby Building on West Forty-fourth Street near the Bar Association, invited them out to Fire Island for the weekend. Barry almost canceled at the last minute, but his curiosity about Jeff's house won out over his usual reluctance to go anywhere during the summer. Judith packed two large suitcases because she wasn't sure how dressy people got on the Island. When Barry came home and saw the luggage, he flew into a rage. He made her take everything apart and repacked their things himself in the smaller of the cases. That made them so late they got stalled in the worst of the Friday evening traffic on the Brooklyn-Queens Expressway. Barry wanted to turn around and go home, but she managed to calm him down, and they got to the Ocean Bay Park ferry one minute before the last boat of the night pulled away from the dock.

Jeff and his girlfriend Cindy met their boat on the other side. Jeff hoisted their suitcase into a little red children's wagon, along with the two bottles of Jack Daniels Barry had brought as a present, and led the procession down a narrow concrete path. It turned out Jeff had a house near the ocean that he and Cindy shared with two other couples, but one of them had stayed in town to go to a wedding, so Barry and Judith had a bedroom to themselves.

That night the four of them went to a place called Flynn's for drinks and a late dinner. The boisterous bar and restaurant was on the bay side of the Island, near where the ferry had landed. Judith tried to adjust to the decibel level. They all ordered clam chowder and lobsters. Barry kept craning his neck, saying everybody in the place looked like someone he knew. Jeff gave them a rundown of Island sociology, reeling off names of communities and their salient descriptions: Irish, Jewish, Wasp, family, singles, gay. Ocean Bay Park apparently had a good mix. A lot of the Flynn's crowd were boaters, he told them. The men did most of the talking. They congratulated themselves on getting prime office space at such a good price—Barry had done the bargaining. Jeff explained to Judith and Cindy what a coup it was to be across from the Bar Association and have access to a complete law library.

On Saturday morning the men played volleyball. Cindy and the other woman were going to walk down to the Sunken Forest, but Judith declined their invitation to come along because she felt she wasn't really wanted. She took a long walk on the beach by herself. When she returned to the house, the men were drinking on the deck and the women were unloading the stuff they had bought for dinner. Barry motioned to her to go in and help them,

73

but she took out a novel and curled up in the living room. She was reading Erica Jong's *Fear of Flying,* a book she'd been avoiding for some time.

"Oh, you're reading Jong," Cindy said in passing when she went through the living room an hour later. "Like the poetry, don't much care for the novels." The screen door slammed behind her. People in this house are always going in and out, Judith thought to herself, and stayed put. She begged off when the others went for a late afternoon swim.

Dinner didn't get off the ground until eleven p.m., and by that time nobody much cared. They had finished the Jack Daniels, two huge bottles of Soave, and all the coke Barry had brought with him. Judith overcame her shyness with new people sufficiently to have an honest conversation with Cindy, in which they agreed that they detested Jong for writing a book they wished they'd written, and would have if they'd thought of it, but she had and they hadn't, so they had every right to hate her guts.

Vicki—she had finally learned the other woman's name —said, "Oh, I know Erica. She's absolutely like her novels." Cindy gave Judith a wink, which Judith interpreted as "Vicki always says she knows everybody," and started an elaborate story filled with esoteric gossip about the newspaper where she worked. Tony and Vicki were in advertising and soon had them all discussing the latest changes at Della Femina, even Barry, who was speaking knowledgeably about "Jerry" the way Vicki had been talking about "Erica" an hour before. When the conversation lulled, Barry volunteered that Judith had written a children's book.

"No kidding?" Cindy exclaimed in genuine surprise. "That's the sort of information I'd lead with if I were you."

"Do you have children of your own, Janey?" Vicki asked.

"Her name is Judy, dumbo," said Tony. "One book? What happened to the second one?"

Judith gave Barry a beseeching look that said "Bail me out." The second book had died aborning, and she'd been doing temp work and thinking about her novel again. It was nothing she cared to confide to these glib, interrogating strangers. Barry changed the subject by bringing up one of his drug cases. Ramirez.

"The damndest case I ever handled. Did I tell you about Hector Ramirez, Jeff?" He addressed the others in a smoky voice overlaid with childlike wonder. "When my client was busted, the house was absolutely clean. A very clever fellow. Ramirez had gone to the trouble of stowing a decoy under a loose floorboard, a very obvious loose floorboard. A stack of glassine packets filled with pure Domino sugar. One hundred percent sugar. Talk about confidence! I waited for those sweet lab reports to get a 'case dismissed on insufficient,' but they flummoxed us both. Guess what the lab reported? You got it. Twelve percent heroin. Goodbye, Ramirez."

Everybody roared. On that note they retired to their bedrooms saying they'd deal with the dishes in the morning.

When Barry saw the overcast sky at eight a.m., he told Judith to pack up and find them a ferry schedule. He was hot to get on the road and beat the Sunday night traffic. Cindy asked if she could hitch a ride with them to the city. A warning bell went off in Judith's head—had Cindy and Barry been exchanging signals she had missed?—but Jeff explained that Cindy worked the Sunday evening shift at her paper and they were hoping all weekend that Barry could give her a ride.

The two women sat next to each other on the ferry crossing back to Bayshore while Barry paced the upper deck.

"He doesn't sit still for long, does he?" Cindy observed.

"No, I'm afraid not," Judith answered. She never felt comfortable discussing Barry with anyone, particularly not with other women.

"He clobbered the guys on the volleyball court. He was spiking everything that came over the net. Men and their machismo." Cindy laughed. "Saturday morning volleyball is the highlight of the week for Jeff and Tony, but they felt rather upstaged by Barry. Listen," she said, tugging at Judith's arm, "my sister's head of children's books at Claridge and Palmer. They just got swallowed by that German conglomerate with the unpronounceable name, but she says the krauts are pouring in fresh money. It wouldn't hurt if you gave her a call. Use my name." She wrote out the information, and Judith stuck the piece of paper in her pocket.

After they dropped Cindy off, Barry wanted to know what the two women had been gabbing about on the ferry. Judith pulled out the piece of paper.

"Joanne Owens, Claridge and Palmer. Cindy's sister works there."

"You gonna call?"

"I might."

SEPTEMBER 1978

Judith spent the Labor Day weekend composing a short, elegant note to the editor at Claridge and Palmer whose name had been pinned up on her bulletin board for two months. Cindy was prominently featured, and so was *Vegetables That Grow Underground*. She followed her letter up with a telephone call and got through on her second try. Joanne Owens asked if she was absolutely wedded to writing children's books or if other things were more compelling to her. Judith admitted that she saw herself as a writer of adult fiction primarily, but until a few years ago most of her work experience had been with children, teaching in the city system. That impressed Ms. Owens, who said she had been a high school teacher herself before she switched over to publishing. And what, she asked, was Judith doing now to earn a living? When she heard temporary secretarial work, Ms. Owens got positively friendly. She inquired if Judith had ever thought about working at the other end of a manuscript. Judith hadn't, but she promised to send a full résumé with a copy of her book.

Three weeks later Joanne Owens offered Judith a job as a sort of glorified secretary with the chance of being made an assistant editor if things worked out. The pay was peanuts, but Barry told her to take it. "Connections," he said. "Your problem is lack of connections. Once you're in the door of Claridge and Palmer, you'll psych out the publishing business and take it from there."

NOVEMBER 1978

The offices of Claridge and Palmer occupied several floors in one of those imposing old granite skyscrapers near Rockefeller Center that Judith had walked past hurriedly without really seeing since her teens, when she first discovered the wonders and glories of the Fifth Avenue department stores. Who knew, she thought, she might reacquaint herself with the stores on her lunch hours. She had stopped paying attention to fashion a few years ago, just when the rest of the world had begun to take a renewed interest in it. Was she behind the times or ahead of the times? She didn't know.

Children's Books at her august new place of employment was a backwater of tiny windowless cubicles off a long, narrow corridor that was one left turn and three right turns past the elevators and carpeted reception area on the fourteenth floor. With her terrible sense of direction, Judith managed to get lost twice while trying to find the ladies' room during her first week on the job. One right turn and three lefts had taken her into Travel. Two lefts and two rights took her back to Reception. There was a circularity to the corridor arrangements on fourteen that she never quite mastered. The power arrangements at Claridge were easier to grasp. Trade Books and Sales were on eleven and twelve, that was where the important people in the publishing house got on and off the elevator.

But, she told Barry, she had to admit that working for Claridge, even in the least significant division of the most prestigious house in the business, was a vast improvement over her office jobs as a temp. For one thing, her chronic morning lateness didn't seem to faze anybody, and the office practically shut down between twelve and two-thirty, although she was expected to be back at her desk and covering the phones by two. There was a relaxed atmosphere in her department that she hadn't known was possible in an office. In fact, she hadn't known that sophisticated, collegial jobs like this existed when she was at Brooklyn studying ed. Her years of teaching had been a mistake. But the choices back then had seemed so narrow —teaching or merchandising, and the idea of working in the garment center had turned her stomach. She had assumed all along that you needed a Seven Sisters diploma to get into publishing. Well, that was still largely true. All the superbly confident young things who roamed the halls in designer pants seemed straight out of Smith, Radcliffe, or Wellesley.

The work wasn't taxing, but it wasn't stretching her capacities either. Occasionally she'd be asked to retype an author's manuscript after the senior editors had done their number on it, but mainly she handled the slush pile for Joanne Owens. She read the unsolicited manuscripts that came into the house, rejected the impossible ones outright, and wrote a reader's report on the rare few with a spark of something—originality, whimsy, an as yet untried theme—that caught her fancy. The decent manuscripts were "agented," she explained to Barry, and went directly to Joanne or her three associate editors. She didn't mind dealing with the slush, and nobody bothered her much at Claridge. It was fine not having someone look over her shoulder, but she did not have the feeling that she was on a career track either.

APRIL 1979

Barry had a drink with Jeff Kellerman at Val's after court. They liked the policemen's bar, it was a good place to schmooze and grouse about judges. Income tax time had rolled around again, but this year the two lawyers were feeling chipper. They had figured out that the way to make their nut without sweating was to take a bunch of 18-B cases. Assigned-counsel work for indigent defendants was the bottom of the barrel, but it got them in front of a lot of different judges, and come hell or high water, the City of New York made good on the vouchers.

"Cheers," Barry said, clinking Jeff's glass. "Next year we double the load."

Later that evening Barry and Judith met Jeff and Cindy at O'Henry's for dinner. Afterward they all went to the Vanguard to hear some music.

On the way home, Barry told Judith he didn't want her to get chummy with Cindy Owens. "I have a professional relationship with Jeff," he explained. "You two women have a catfight or something, it can wreck us."

Judith liked Cindy and felt grateful for the steer to Claridge and Palmer, but she instantly understood Barry's point.

MAY 1979

Martha Harris from the art department invited Judith and a few other people at Claridge to the opening of Ten Downtown. She had a couple of her large acrylic canvases in the biennial group show.

The reception was packed with the usual assortment of artists, family, and friends. Martha counted three Japanese performance artists in stone-colored jumpsuits, long black scarves, and running shoes. What would an opening in Soho be without them?

Judith arrived at the gallery with the man she lived with. He picked an argument with Martha about her work two minutes after he was introduced, backing her against the buffet table while he wolfed the hors d'oeuvres. When Martha tried to change the subject, he jabbed his index finger at her and said, "You're shifting your ground." Judith just stood there smiling.

What did Judith's friend think he was doing—giving her the third-degree in a police station?

"Excuse me," Martha put in finally, "I really should circulate around the room."

Judith stiffened. "Barry knows a lot about art," she said with a hurt look on her face.

When Martha looked back, Judith and her man were walking out the door.

SEPTEMBER 1979

As a favor to Barry, Jeff Kellerman represented one of his clients at the Parking Violations Bureau. The guy had about two thousand dollars' worth of tickets outstanding, and Jeff got the PVB to settle for eight hundred and fifty. The grateful client gave him three hundred in cash, not bad for a half-hour's work.

Barry was grinning when Jeff got back to the office. "Where is it, where's the loot? Don't get cute with me, Kellerman. Gimme."

Jeff was so startled he handed over the three bills. He felt like a chump for the rest of the day. Kantor would lean on a gorilla if the gorilla was carrying cash, he said to himself.

APRIL 14, 1980

Barry checked the 1099 from the Department of Finance against the green FISA forms in his folder. He double-checked his vouchers and scratched his head. Last year he had volunteered for thirty-five cases under the assigned-counsel plan. A fistful of plea bargains, but they added up. "Too much reportable income," he muttered as he worked over the numbers. "Who needs it?"

He did a quick toot and rechecked the numbers. He decided to file for an extension.

OCTOBER 1980

Judith was given the title of associate editor along with a twenty-five-dollar raise. A manuscript she had rescued from the slush pile had won a Newbery Medal, one of the biggest honors in the children's book field. She was now an acquiring editor with authors of her own. Her specialty was science—it had fallen to her by default—and there was talk at Claridge that she might be named senior editor for their newly expanded textbook division. Her department was expected to move to larger quarters on another floor within the year, but in the meantime she still worked at her old desk.

One of the first people she called when she got her promotion was Bob Rothman. Her old friend from the Lower East Side writers' group had fallen into a rut on the chemical industry journal, his hopes for becoming the Arthur Miller of his generation having faded with the memory of his unfinished play on Vietnam. She signed him up to write a book on toxic waste for the grade school level. With the material that crossed his desk every day at the magazine, it was going to be a snap. They both had a laugh when he told her he might have to publish under an assumed name.

"Shouldn't I get an agent?" he asked her. "Not that I don't trust you, Jude, but we're older now, and we have to think about things like money."

"Bob! I know I work for Claridge and Palmer, and Claridge works for an international conglomerate, but it's my authors I care about. Why don't you let Barry vet the contract for you? He'll follow the Authors Guild recommendations, I'll get it through our legal department, and he'll only charge you ten percent. The agents are upping their fees to fifteen."

Ten percent sounded good to Bob, although the idea of getting his advance money and royalty checks through Barry Kantor was a little peculiar. He had never liked the guy Judith lived with, not since that time in their apartment on Waverly Place when he saw Judith was terrified to touch his stereo equipment. What was that story he'd heard about Kantor? Oh, yeah, he was handling porno cases for the Mob. Penny-ante stuff, nothing that made the papers, just your typical, routine bust on Times Square. Not that obscenity laws weren't a crock of shit—

he himself was a First Amendment man all the way—but everybody knew that the Mafia controlled the grunge flow in the city. So if Barry was representing these fellows in court on the awkward occasions when they got busted, he must be in pretty thick with them.

Bob mulled over his new situation. A book on toxic waste and its effect on the environment, and a Mafia lawyer to vet the contract. Quit exaggerating, Rothman, he told himself. If Barry was really Mafia, why would he want to handle your two-bit deal? And wasn't a smut merchant, a polluter of the environment in his own smarmy way, entitled to legal representation?

Judith

We are basing now. Changing the water-soluble flake back to an oily base so it can burn.

An advanced high school chemistry lesson called freeing the base. They sell the kits in head shops for twenty-five dollars, with three pages of typed instructions and an underlined warning to keep away from sources of heat. Add ether and ammonia to the cocaine hydrochloride and shake. Take off the cap, let the impurities settle. Siphon off the top layer, dry on glass. That is the mysterious process.

Then we smoke the beautiful crystals.

And Barry talks.

"I told my mother we got married." He sucked in the vapor till the glowing crystals blackened and melted. "In Hawaii." He exhaled with a long, pronounced sigh and handed me the glass pipe. "Said we sent her a picture postcard, must have gotten lost in the mail."

"Any particular part of Hawaii?"

"Hold it in! Yeah, Lahaina. A fishing port on Maui. Bone up on it, she might ask you some questions."

"That's where we spent our honeymoon?"

"Don't you remember?" He scooped some more crystals onto the screen. "Turn off the overhead light in the hall, babe, it's too bright. And babe? While you're up, bring me a cup of coffee."

I came back and sat next to him on the sofa, folding my legs so my skirt grazed his thigh. His pupils were dilated behind his glasses; he absently fingered his mustache. I felt cold.

"Tell me about Maui."

"What? Oh, yeah. I was actually there once, with another lady. Before I met you. Ever smoke any Maui Wowie?"

"Barry, you're making that up!"

"That's your problem, Judith. You're Little Miss Know-It-All. Anything they don't talk about at Claridge and Palmer doesn't exist. It just so happens there was a brief minute in the unwritten history of the lesser Schedule One controlled substances when Maui Wowie was top of the line, almost on a par with Thai stick."

"I'll bring it up tomorrow at the editorial meeting."

"Make sure you credit the source."

"I don't talk about you at work, Barry. You're a mystery man as far as they're concerned."

"Yeah? Well, keep it that way."

"Maui. Tell me about Maui."

He told me about the island. Lava rocks, volcanoes, waterfalls, green rain forest, white sand.

"I liked Maui a lot," I said. "Tell me more."

He was lava running down a mountainside, a hot stream of words flowing faster, faster, gathering speed. I was under the waterfall, wading through jets of white mist.

His voice rose and fell, the musical cadence of flowing lava, a baritone saxophone, improvised riffs. We sat close together on the rain-forest floor. I was the tourist, the sightseer. He was my guide. I strained to decipher the language, a singsong dialect of offbeat stresses, unfinished phrases, ellipses, slurs.

"Barry, slow down. I'm not following—"

"You want me to translate? Since you got the fucking promotion, you lost the capacity to understand adult speech."

"That's not fair. You were speaking so fast."

"I'm not gonna slow down my mind for you, that's a drag. The whole point is to free up the thinking process. Right now I'm verbalizing maybe one-tenth of what's in my head. Pay attention, you're a bright lady, you'll follow."

He put the glass pipe in my hand and held the flame. The crystals glowed. I was the captured princess, chosen to appease the angry gods. He was the last aboriginal, practicing his ancient rite. He carried me up the gravel mountain to the glowing crater. I stood in the path of the molten lava. I was encircled by lava, I craved its warmth. I crawled on my knees through the gravel toward the molten source, stretching my hands, my tongue, toward the heat. I was enveloped in lava, I spoke the language, the torrent of words came faster. And then it veered.

He stood up and stretched. "What time is it? I'm going to sleep."

MARCH 1981

Mary Ann Collado missed her period again. "Mother of God," she whispered. "Please." It wasn't much of a prayer, but Mary Ann did not have the words to say the terrible things she was thinking.

She came home from her after-school job at the hardware store and went up to her room. No one was in the house, but she locked her door anyway, put a chair against it for good measure, and pulled down the shades. She lay on her bed for two hours, until she heard her mother calling her for dinner. Before she collected herself to go downstairs, she went into the bathroom and checked her pants again. Nothing. The box of Junior Modess was in the white cabinet above the toilet. Mary Ann took a fresh napkin and pinned it in place, methodically shredding and flushing the one she had put on that morning. Maybe tonight, while she slept. It had happened before. She'd wake up and feel the drip before she swung her legs out of bed. This way she'd be prepared.

Mary Ann washed her hands, avoiding her reflection in the mirror above the sink. "Please," she whispered. "Mother of God, help me."

APRIL 1981

Barry convinced Jeff Kellerman to go in with him on a boat, a twenty-one-foot Boston Whaler, brand-new, with a two-hundred-horsepower outboard. He could get a good price on it if they moved swiftly. Jeff had been saying for years that Fire Island would be this side of paradise if he owned a boat and could tootle up and down the shoreline of Great South Bay. Were Barry and Judith going to buy a place on the Island? He asked and got an evasive answer.

"People usually buy the summer house first, Barry, and then they get the boat. You don't even like Fire Island."

"Yeah, but I know a deal when I see one, and this boat's

a honey. The guy has to sell fast, he'll take eight grand. They go for ten."

Jeff got the distinct impression that the guy who had to sell fast was one of Barry's clients. Still, a boat. They could moor it at Ocean Bay Park in Flynn's Marina. Once they got the hang of it—he supposed there were things to learn about channels and navigation—they could go to the Pines and Cherry Grove for dinner. What a blast.

"When can we see it, hotshot?"

"Tomorrow. It's over on City Island."

"That's a different body of water, wise guy. Long Island Sound."

Barry's eyes blinked rapidly behind his glasses. One of his mannerisms. "Yeah, well, that's where it is. Whaddya want, door-to-door delivery?"

The two men went in Barry's R.V.-7 to look at the Whaler. Barry closed the deal on the spot for fifteen hundred less than the guy's asking price. They agreed to pay cash. Jeff had to admit that the boat was a beauty and the price was fantastic. He said he'd draw up the papers and get the registration certificate.

That had been two months ago. Their Boston Whaler was still sitting in its berth on City Island. Jeff visited it a couple of times, and Barry took it out for some short spins. Neither man knew enough about boating to run the Whaler clear around Manhattan into the Atlantic and over to Great South Bay. And Barry hadn't bought a place on Fire Island after all.

"Typical Kantor maneuver," Jeff fumed to Cindy. "I share office space with this guy, you'd think I'd be onto his scams. He never intended to bring that boat to Fire Island."

"Can't you get a trailer and move it by land?"

"Yeah, sure. I guess so. But Kantor's going to split the cost with me."

Cindy got the idea that Jeff was expecting trouble.

Barry got a blast of sour breath when Grabinoff leaned over to break the bad news. "Your gums are in lousy shape, my friend. The rate you're going, you're gonna need a partial on the bottom and a full plate on top."

So his teeth had let him down. No surprise. The payback for years of avoiding the chair.

Grabinoff tapped a rotting molar. "This one better come out today."

"Yeah, okay. Make it snappy. With gas."

The dentist started to hum. A dumb schmuck who hummed when he did extractions—well, he couldn't complain, the work was free. He had represented Harold Grabinoff a while back on a little case of med mal. The dentist had been peeing in his pants before the plaintiff agreed to settle. He was so happy to be cleared of the malpractice charge that he offered to do Barry's platework without sending a bill.

The gas was starting to take effect. Barry nodded and gripped the armrest. A couple of yanks and Grabinoff had wrested the molar. He held it up for his patient's inspection.

"Sit there for a minute," Grabinoff instructed. Barry fought off a wave of nausea.

"I have a proposition to make you," the dentist said as he cleaned his tools. "Or rather, my brother does. He'd like for the two of you to get together. You remember my telling you about my older brother, the bright one in the family who went into ob-gyn and wasted his life on a crazy broad who only knew from cars and clothes? He got married again and settled down in Rockville Center. Bought a general practice, a little of this, a little of that. Still does obstetrics when the calls come his way."

Grabinoff babbled on about his brother the doctor, whose second wife was apparently as crazy as the first one. The story didn't seem to be going anywhere. Barry was tuning out until he heard the words "white babies."

He sat up straight in the chair.

JUNE 6, 1981

Mary Ann thumbed through the worn directory until she found "Physicians and Surgeons." Rockville Center was two towns over from hers on the Long Island Railroad. That was the first thing in its favor—she didn't know a soul who lived there. The second was that the Center part sounded large and impersonal, like it would have a big downtown district with lots of doctors who didn't ask too many questions. She wanted a foreign name in an unfamiliar town. The one her finger rested on she couldn't even pronounce. K-r-z and then a peculiar mess of letters.

She dialed the number from the phone booth at the station. When the receptionist answered, Mary Ann blurted out, "Does the doctor do pregnancy tests?"

The voice at the other end suppressed a giggle. "Not as a rule. You're calling an ear, nose, and throat doctor."

Mary Ann hung up. She consulted the directory again and fished in her purse for more change. This time she got a recorded message saying that the doctor's office hours were from twelve-thirty to three on Monday and Thursday. On her third call she hit pay dirt. The voice at the other end asked where she was calling from and said, "Come right over." Mary Ann's heart gave a small leap. She took down the directions on a scrap of paper she tore out of the telephone book.

The doctor's office was a short walk from the train station. Mary Ann filled out the two-page form the receptionist handed her on a clipboard, leaving a blank space under "Recommended by" and "Medical Plan." Under "Reason for Visit" she started to write "Pregnant" but crossed it out and printed "Missed period" followed by three question marks. It seemed more polite. She wrote down her real name but fudged a little on her address. The receptionist took the clipboard from her, glanced at it briefly, and wrote something on a card she took into the doctor's examining room. She was back in a minute. Mary Ann returned to her armchair and leafed through a *Good Housekeeping* and a back issue of *Cosmopolitan* while a man with his arm in a cast kidded with the receptionist about going to the racetrack with him. A woman and a small boy who were seated on a black leather sofa when she arrived had their names called out and were told to go into the examining room. When they came out, the man with the cast went in. The woman spoke to the receptionist about making another appointment for the boy. Mary Ann got up and moved to the black leather sofa. Fifteen minutes later the man with the cast came out and started kidding around with the receptionist again. Mary Ann pretended not to listen, which was hard to do.

"The doctor will see you now," the receptionist said with a bright smile.

JUNE 11, 1981

Sheldon Grabinoff—there was no mistaking the sallow complexion and balding dome of his dentist's brother—met Barry at 5:45 in a glitzed-up bar on Thirty-third Street across from Penn Station. Happy Hour. Barry winced at the term. Junior execs and secretaries swigging their doubles before they caught their trains to nowhere.

He munched on a bowl of peanuts at the lilliputian cocktail table while Grabinoff the elder danced around the edges of his proposition.

"It breaks my heart," Grabinoff said in a low voice. "All these desperate young couples who could provide such a nice home, making their hopeless rounds of the agencies, putting their names down on lists." He shook his head. "Going off on a wild goose chase to Peru or Mexico, wherever they hear of a lead, working through these religious groups in the underdeveloped countries, taking a chance on congenital diseases and God knows what genetic mishmash." Grabinoff leaned in close. "And then what I see at my end of the merry-go-round! The poor dumb cows who get themselves into a pickle the first time they get laid behind the bleachers at the football stadium! I tell you, there's no justice in the world, Barry. Them that want don't get. Mother Nature plays dirty tricks."

"Uh-huh." Barry gobbled another handful of peanuts. Who's got the fish on the line? he wondered. Let Grabinoff do the reeling in. That would strengthen his own position.

"A smart young lawyer like you," Grabinoff went on. "My brother thinks the world of you, you know that. The circles you travel in, you probably run across many of these unfortunate young couples. Couples who are desperate to adopt a healthy white infant at any price. Who won't ask too many questions as long as they get the answer to their prayers."

Barry nodded without speaking. Out with it, Grabinoff, out with it. Put your cards on the table.

The doctor finished his drink and motioned for another. "Sometimes the poor girls come in too late for an abortion, sometimes they tell me they have religious scruples. My practice is on Long Island, but I can arrange for beds at two New York hospitals. I've kept my affiliations."

Barry was impressed. The old phoney had been doing

91

his homework, thinking ahead. Maybe this wasn't his first
go-round. The trick was not to show interest. He leaned
back in his chair and worked a piece of peanut out of the
hole that used to be his molar. Grabinoff got ready to play
his card.

"You line up the prospective customers, I steer the
business your way, we split fifty-fifty."

Barry sprang into action. This was the part he liked. "No
deal. The risk is ninety percent on my side. Either the cut
reflects it or we're wasting each other's time."

The dashed look on Grabinoff's face told him he'd won
the round.

JUNE 12, 1981

Barry scooped up the papers at the big newsstand on
West Forty-second Street, the Nassau and Suffolk week-
lies that carried the personal ads he was looking for. A
couple of Westchester papers caught his eye, and he
threw them in for good measure.

As long as he was in the vicinity, he decided to amuse
himself by ducking into the Palace of Wet Dreams, one of
his clients. The hole-in-the-wall bookstore had three customers browsing at the racks at eleven in the morning,
middle-aged men in raincoats poring over magazines
with titles like *Ebony Tits, Gestapo Gash, Yellow Cherry.*
The manager shuffled out of the back room to greet him.

"Mr. Kantor, what a nice surprise."

"How's business?"

The man shrugged and pointed to a colorful display
near the cash register. "Taiwan."

Barry stared. It was a March of Dimes–style condom
rack, each fully extended rubber tipped by what appeared to be a garish trout fly. He supposed it was some-

one's idea of a French tickler. His eye moved on to an eight-inch pink plastic dildo, battery not included, a hangman's mask in black leather, and a pair of manacles with silver studs. Something for everyone.

Two doors down from the Palace of Wet Dreams he passed the Pussy Peep Arcade, known as the cleanest shop on the street. He had to hand it to the owner, whoever he was. Four rows of wood stalls that could be mistaken for outhouses or Porto-San toilets. Inside the booths, the clientele jerked off to bestiality films on a loop, one minute of *German Shepherd Humps Gidget* for a twenty-five-cent token. Two dollars usually did it, he'd heard. The coin-operated peeps were a cinch to run. One attendant sat in a high chair and made the change. Whenever there was a lull in business, the attendant climbed down from his perch and emptied the slots of their tokens. When the Pussy Peep first opened, they got hit with summonses on a daily basis—the sprays of dried cum on the walls and the wadded up tissues on the floor were a health violation. So the owner had hired a crippled black guy to swab out the booths with a bucket of disinfectant on a continuous cycle. Apparently the patrons were immune to the overpowering smell of Lysol.

He crossed the street, glancing up by habit at three grimy windows covered with Mylar. A modest sign read ESCORTS, DAY AND NIGHT. The oldest established permanent floating brothel in New York. He'd been one of a team of lawyers representing the place two years ago. The case was thrown out of court, and the stationary escorts were back on the job the next day. He had a standing offer to try out the service anytime he liked, whenever he felt the urge. But the problem was that these days he didn't feel much of an urge, and hadn't felt much of an urge in a long time.

Back in his office, he opened one of the suburban papers

93

and scanned the classifieds and personal columns. It didn't take long to find what he was looking for.

> Larchmont couple with everything in the world except God's bundle of joy looking to adopt. Will pay all maternity costs and legal fees. Prefer infant, either sex, but will gladly open our hearts to any dear wonderful healthy Caucasian child two years or younger. No questions asked. Box 472.

He tore out the page. The next thin tabloid-size newspaper also carried the Larchmont couple's personal ad and two additional items. One read:

> Professionals, P and RC mixed marriage. Nursery empty for five years while we search for you. Please do not give up hope. Answer this ad. Confidential. Box XY.

The other personal notice was so piteous in its description of the years of longing and frustrated hope that Barry wondered if it might be a plant. Most of the weekly newspapers yielded a nugget or two, with a few duplications. Grabinoff had been right about the treasure trove of yearning that lay in these pages. A need he could fill.

He took a quick snort of the white stuff and pecked out the draft of his letter on his old Underwood standard. He still had the same machine his mother had bought for him when he entered law school.

"I am a lawyer specializing in private adoptions here and abroad," he typed. What next? Maybe a new beginning.

"A client of mine who wishes to remain anonymous at this time, for reasons I'm sure you understand . . ." No, the first version was better.

94

He thought about the new legal temp who was sitting in the outer office typing one of Kellerman's briefs. She took his phone messages and ordered from the deli for him. He could probably get her to drop her work for Jeff and run off ten letters. But he didn't have the last sentence.

"I believe I can provide the . . ." Judith. Judith would know how to hit the right tone. She could bat out the copies in her office.

He made up a folder with the personal notices and a supply of his letterhead and envelopes, marked it "Judith," and slipped it in his briefcase.

It was time to go to the gym and work out.

JULY 10–12, 1981

Judith went off on a tennis weekend with Sally Milton, one of the senior editors in her office. The tennis camp in Accord, New York, was run by a pro who Sally said had played at Wimbledon twenty years ago.

She and Sally shared a room, but Sally was in the intermediate class and Judith was one of those perpetual beginners. A duffer, Sally teased. Her problem was her serve. It was soft. The instructor worked with her on her grip and tried to get her to charge the net during rallies, but she felt more comfortable staying in the backcourt. He told her she lacked the killer instinct.

Sally got the idea that Judith was taking tennis lessons to please the guy she lived with. To hear her tell it, he was an amazing athlete. He was spending the weekend alone on his boat, Judith said. By Sunday evening Sally Milton was sick and tired of hearing about this super athlete Barry Kantor.

Mary Ann told her mother she had found a good full-time job for the summer in Rockville Center, where her high school placement department had connections with a medical clinic. She'd be taking care of the doctor's files and stuff like that. If she liked it, maybe she'd apply to nursing school next fall. The doctor's receptionist had a spare room in her house that she rented out to the summer trainees for next to nothing. She'd be sharing the room with another girl from school.

Her mother thought a change of scenery might be a good idea. Mary Ann had been moping around the house and putting on weight all spring. The girl never went out anymore, something must have happened to the boy she was stuck on last year. Well, she had warned her daughter she was too young to go steady. Just look at her own life. Married at seventeen and three kids before she was twenty. Well, that was water under the bridge. He brought home his paycheck every Friday, went to mass with her on Sunday. They owned their own house and had three lovely children.

She found her daughter crying in her room when she went upstairs with the blue suitcase from the basement. Mary Ann was her oldest, she had never been away from them before. "If you're not happy, you just leave that job and come home," she told her. Mary Ann nodded.

The clothes her daughter was planning to take were laid out on her bed. Just a few blouses and skirts. Nothing else fit. She'd have to buy some new things or go on a diet. Kids were always bingeing or dieting these days. She blamed it on the junk food, the tacos and pizzas and gyros. Wherever you turned they were opening a new stand.

96

She took down the telephone number Mary Ann gave her. It was only for emergencies. Mary Ann promised she'd call home every Friday evening at six p.m. She almost went teary herself when she saw Mary Ann put the raggedy old teddy bear in the suitcase. In some ways her solemn, quiet daughter was still just a child.

SEPTEMBER 3, 1981

The Feds had a search warrant, so there was nothing Don and Ellie Hethington could do except match their politeness and try to stay cool. The bastards knew exactly where to look. They went straight to the cornfield behind the house like they had a map of the fucking place. The sweet little plants that Don and Ellie had tended so lovingly all summer were ripped out one by one.

Corn was the perfect camouflage, everyone agreed. Their partner, Joe Fricks, who gave them the Afghani seeds, had assured Don that helicopters would have a helluva time spotting their crop from the air. They had followed his advice to the letter. "Don't be greedy," Joe warned them. "A few plants tucked here and there and you'll make your forty thou easy."

The Hethingtons had bought the rundown old farm in Vermont's Northeast Kingdom thinking they could make a go of marketing organic produce so that Don could paint to his heart's content in the barn and gain the confidence to show his work. Ellie's father had advanced them the mortgage money. But the growing season was so short in Vermont, and their land was so hilly. Don's friend Joe Fricks convinced them the only way to turn a profit was to grow sinsemilla from very good seed. This was going to be their first crop.

Ellie had slaved all summer over the little darlings.

Rooting out the males and pinching the females to make them bushy was labor-intensive work, a lot more demanding than nursing her strawberry patch. The idea was to encourage the production of resinous flowers. Resin was the whole ball of wax. "To resin," Don had toasted her just last night.

It had to have been an informer, but who? There'd be plenty of time to figure it out, but first they needed a lawyer. Maybe two lawyers. Don wasn't going to let Ellie take the rap. He shuddered. Ellie would make a ruckus, but they'd have to tell her father. He'd find out anyway. Don was sure the old man would spring for a good lawyer. In the meantime, they needed to call a neighbor, someone to mind Ellie's kids while they went with these very polite gentlemen to the arraignment in Burlington.

SEPTEMBER 4, 1981

Dr. Sheldon Grabinoff left a message with Jeff Kellerman's legal temp that he'd like a call-back from Mr. Kantor. When Barry phoned, the obstetrician told him he'd scheduled a delivery for the tenth of September.

SEPTEMBER 6, 1981

The Hethingtons came to New York to see Ellie's father and meet their lawyer. Barry Kantor had come well recommended by a friend of Joe Fricks' who said he'd represented some people he knew and had gotten them a good deal. The friends of Joe's friend had made every mistake in the book. They came into Kennedy on a direct flight from Cartagena with a shitload of coke packed in aerosol shaving cans and were picked off at Customs one by one.

Three guys and their girlfriends, their first attempt to score. Kantor worked out a deal so the girlfriends got off with suspended sentences and the guys got four to seven, which meant they'd be out in two and a half.

What the Hethingtons liked best about the Cartagena-JFK story was that a fourth couple had come in undetected by way of Miami later in the day. Since they were all in it together, the fourth couple agreed it was only fair that the stuff they brought through belonged to all of them and should be used for the defense. Before they could find a buyer, Kantor said why go through the trouble, he would take part of his retainer in blow. A hip guy!

It was important to them to have a hip lawyer, someone who dug their lifestyle, not one of the stiff-assed attorneys Ellie's father wanted to get them, who'd look down his nose at Don and probably try to make time with Ellie on the side.

The first thing Kantor said over the phone was "Money up front." That had thrown Don a little, but Kantor explained that this wasn't like a personal injury case where the attorney stood to make a bundle from a settlement at the other end. Don laughed, and that cleared the air. When Don said that he was broke but Ellie's father had loot, Kantor asked a lot of questions about their relationship and about the farm. Don said he supposed the farm could be used as collateral for a loan. Then Kantor asked how they felt about Northern Italian and suggested they meet for dinner at a place in the Village on Hudson Street. He wanted Ellie's father to come along, but Ellie said nix.

They liked the idea of meeting their lawyer for dinner. None of that "me right side, you wrong side of the law" kind of shit. Kantor brought along the woman he lived with, who he said did some of his legal research. She didn't contribute much to the conversation. The Hethingtons had the impression she was just getting over an illness. She looked washed out. Ellie suggested that she come up to Vermont sometime and visit them on the farm. The woman brightened and mentioned a book she had written about vegetables.

Kantor told them not to worry, he'd be glad to represent both of them, though it might look better if he brought in a partner to represent Ellie as sort of a passive stand-in for him. But he doubted that Ellie would have to stand trial. He was pretty sure he could work out a deal for Ellie long before the trial date, or maybe during the trial—sometimes it was better to do it that way. Don would get off with maybe six months to a year because it was his first offense. He'd see to it that they came before a certain judge—he couldn't say the name there in the restaurant, but he hinted the fix was as good as in. It would cost them, he wanted that understood. Don and Ellie practically hugged him across the table.

Then Kantor said his fortieth birthday was coming up and did they know where he could find some good blow. Don gave Ellie a wink and said they had some in the car all wrapped up for him, and if he liked the quality they'd bring down more when they delivered the first chunk of the retainer. "Cash," he reminded them. They nodded, and Ellie picked up the check. She didn't want their lawyer to think they were expecting a free dinner.

Ellie said afterward she got good vibes from Kantor. He was someone she could relate to, very up front about his needs. Now, she told Don, she had to work on her father.

SEPTEMBER 10, 1981

They wheeled the gurney into the delivery room. Everyone's so busy, Mary Ann thought. Who are all these people? A lot of green masks. She tried to make out her

100

doctor, but the overhead light was too strong. Things were moving so fast. Someone pressed her stomach. It must be him.

"Do you understand the procedure, Mary Ann?" the man said. "I induced the labor. You're fully dilated. It won't be long now."

"Push, honey, push." A woman's voice. "Bear down hard."

The white light was blinding. They had shot her up with something to bring it off. How long ago? Minutes? Hours? She couldn't remember. Her head was spinning. Get me out of here, she thought. Get it over with. Push. The slow, rhythmic jackhammer inside her body was driving her down, down. She was going to be torn in two. Push.

The light was brilliant. A beautiful lady in a long white dress floated toward her with outstretched arms. "Mary Ann, Mary Ann," she said softly. "You are not alone." Mary Ann breathed in short, rapid gasps. The jackhammer pressed against her bowels. "I brought some friends to help you. Look, Mary Ann, look." Two more beautiful ladies in evening gowns danced through the sky, gyrating their hips. Dolly. Cher. She wanted to call out their names, but Cher touched a long red polished fingernail to her lips.

"All together now, girls," said Dolly. "One-two-three, push."

Mary Ann grunted.

"Good girl," said a faraway voice. "You did it."

SEPTEMBER 12, 1981

Barry sat in his parked car and waited. Grabinoff's receptionist would be walking out the side entrance with the bundle in a half-hour or so. She'd put it in the front seat between them, and then he'd slip her a hundred for

101

her trouble. She'd make a fuss and say she felt funny taking his money for something she did out of the kindness of her heart for God's unfortunate souls, but he'd say, Go on, I know you picked up some incidental expenses. Use the rest to buy yourself a new hat. Did women wear hats anymore? He hadn't seen a woman in a hat in ten or fifteen years, but the phrase had become a code between them. She'd say, Oh, Mr. Kantor, and take the bill. It was important that she take the bill. A cheap way to seal her mouth. He understood human nature. If she ever had second thoughts down the line, she'd remember the hundred and wonder how she'd explain it to—what was the word they used in newspapers? The authorities. If you had your suspicions, why didn't you go to the authorities?

He was sweating. That was okay. This was his third transfer in three months, and the others had gone off like clockwork. He was working a new angle this time. He had two prospective customers down to the wire. Each had guaranteed him fifty and put down a deposit. Delivery date imminent, he told them, but you never know, sometimes they decide to keep it. As soon as he got out of here with the bundle, he'd make a call. Tell the first client something's come through but there's been a slight hitch, he's got an offer for seventy-five. If they went for it, cool, if not he had his ace in the hole. Jesus, people were gullible when they were needy, but he hadn't run into a customer yet who didn't initially balk at the price. They all wanted a healthy bundle with no strings attached. A clean, honest birth certificate and a waiver of all claims from the natural mother. But that didn't stop them from trying to haggle when he told them the facts of life. That was okay too. If they couldn't meet his terms he'd tell them to call Spence-Chapin and put their names on the list. They knew what that meant, they'd gone that route already. Then they were ready to talk business.

The cows were something else. They expected to be treated like dirt in payment for their sin. Throw enough dirt at them and they felt they were on the road to salvation. He didn't spend much time with the cows, they were Grabinoff's responsibility. He met them once before they went into the hospital, and got them to sign a general release. They blinked when they saw the Blumberg form with its fancy typefaces. An official document that was going to give them their legal absolution. One of them had hesitated for a moment before signing and asked if her baby was going to go to a good Roman Catholic home. She wanted to be able to tell that to the priest someday if the burden she was carrying grew too heavy to bear. She meant the burden of guilt, not her swollen belly. He looked her in the eye and said, If that's what you want, then you have my promise.

Why not? The cows never considered the financial aspects of the arrangement. They wanted to serve their sentence and put it behind them. He thought of the fifteen-year-old, his youngest to date, who checked into the hospital with her mother. The mother nabbed him in the maternity ward visitors' lounge. Between puffs of her cigarette she said she wanted his assurance that this terrible calamity would never come back to haunt them. It was hard enough keeping the thing from the girl's father— she'd sent her to a sister in Wantagh to wait out her term —and she still didn't know how she would handle the neighbors. The father and the neighbors. The girls and their mothers lived in terror of both. The fifteen-year-old's mother had been in such a panic about being found out that he told her he needed five hundred dollars as a binder on the contract. She paid it without a murmur. Had the traveler's checks in her purse.

The kid in there now. Collado. A charity case. Been hiding out with the receptionist and working part-time in Grabinoff's office to pay for her keep. Couldn't be more than seventeen, and still keeping mum on the father. He told Grabinoff's gal to put down "Father unknown," make up a next of kin, and use his own name and address as legal guardian on the admittance form. One thing about these private hospitals, they were so understaffed at the clerical end that he could risk a few inconsistencies in the records. He'd paid the full bill on this one already. That was always a good move. Pay in advance. Don't want some administrator to start checking up when the forms go through Social Services and Accounting.

Grabinoff's receptionist pushed sideways through the revolving glass doors. The bundle was cradled in her arms. She was followed by a hospital nurse with a carryall.

He honked the horn twice and opened the car door.

When Judith came home, Barry was talking to someone on the phone in the bedroom, a loud, unpleasant argument, from what she could make out.

It was unlike him to be home at this hour. She hung up her jacket, stacked his mail on the dining room table, and tiptoed down the hallway, uncertain whether he wanted privacy or not.

A baby was lying on their bed. It took up so little room, that was her first thought.

Judith

Something had gone very, very wrong. One of the clients backed down at the last moment, and the husband of the other couple was away on a business trip to Bahrain.

He'd be gone for a month, and the wife didn't feel she could handle the arrangements on her own.

Barry said he'd make another connection in a couple of days, the thing was not to panic. If the client at the other end sensed he was desperate to unload, they'd drive the price down, and this one had come with extra freight to begin with. So he was going to play it cool, take all the time he needed, and collect the full fee.

"In the meantime," he said, looking at me with a glum little-boy grin, "we've got a problem. Tell them at work you have to take a few days off, okay?" He sat down gingerly on the end of the bed, careful not to disturb the sleeping infant. I'd never seen him look so vulnerable. "We're in this together, Jude." Of course we are in it together!

We call her The Surprise. I was afraid to go near her the first night, I thought I'd do something wrong, but Barry said, "She won't break, Judith. Look." He picked up her tiny little bowed leg by the foot. "See?" He was fearless. I moved a little closer. The tiniest foot and the tiniest little nails I had ever seen. He put his pinky in her fist. She gripped it.

Barry was handling her like he'd been doing it all his life, and I was hovering around the edge of the bed like a visitor from Mars. He gave me a list of instructions. Bring him the big plastic laundry basket, some towels and a sheet, he was going to make a bassinet for her so she could spend the night on the floor on his side of the bed. I could barely function, but I went through the motions.

"What's your problem, Judith?" he said. "Didn't you ever bring home a kitten when you were a kid? Pretend it's a kitten if that'll help."

He was beginning to enjoy himself, he had a new challenge to master. The less I was able to manage, the more confident he became. He seemed to know exactly how to handle The Surprise. "Listen, kiddo," he said. "This is a fifty- to seventy-five-thousand investment. We've got to keep it clean and happy." I nodded. "She came with a box of her own formula and a feeding schedule. Go down to the drugstore and get some disposable bottles and handy wipes, a rubber sheet, and infant Pampers. Babies are leaky."

It took me a while to get all the items. When I came back to the apartment, he was on the floor next to the laundry basket tickling The Surprise. She looked so shriveled. "Doesn't she cry?" I asked.

"She'll cry," he said. "They all cry sooner or later."

SEPTEMBER 14, 1981

Judith called Claridge and Palmer the first thing in the morning and told Harvey Erickson, the new executive editor, that she needed to take a few days off. A huge, unexpected personal problem that she couldn't discuss. Thursday, she might be in on Thursday. All her projects were under control, if anything came up they could call her at home.

Barry stayed home too. Grabinoff lost his temper when he called him in Rockville Center to explain about the slight hitch, but then he calmed down and offered the name of a trustworthy pediatrician in case the baby came down with colic or diarrhea. Dr. Michael Rochette had a practice on West Twelfth Street, a good name to have in his files.

Grabinoff was antsy, he wasn't sure he wanted to take on any more cases. Barry said they'd discuss it further when this contract was successfully concluded, but if it was the money he was worried about, they'd settle now.

106

Grabinoff said it wasn't the money, he just wanted out. He was thinking of retiring anyway, moving to Florida.

It was remarkable, Barry said to Judith, how people lost their grip when things didn't go according to schedule. Then he sent her out to the Jefferson Market Library to get a book on infant care. He told her if she didn't come by it naturally, maybe she could pick up some pointers from reading. Judith said she'd check out a copy of Spock if they had one on the shelf, but it was a pity she hadn't had a premonition last Friday. Claridge had a raft of new childcare books in the office.

Barry was a wonder. Judith marveled at him. "Look at this, Judith," he commanded. He dangled the baby by the armpits, and its little legs churned on the wood floor as if it were walking.

He handled the feeding and changing himself. He carried the baby all around the apartment, dipping it down, hoisting it up, introducing it to the kitchen—hello, refrigerator—the bathroom, even the hall closet. He carried it to the front windows and showed it the green plants. Infants need a lot of stimulation, he told her. The human touch. He put the baby in her arms and had her hold it for a minute.

"Am I doing it right?" she asked.

"What's right is what feels comfortable," he told her. "Get a grip on her behind and cradle her head, don't let it wobble."

She felt the warmth from the baby's body. Somehow she hadn't been prepared for the warmth.

"Rock her a little." She tried, but her arms felt stiff. He sensed she was feeling anxious and took the baby back from her.

That night after dinner, instead of watching TV, Barry moved The Surprise into the living room. He put the plastic laundry basket on the coffee table and stared into it for hours while the baby slept. When the phone rang, he told Judith not to answer, let the answering machine pick up.

It was a mutual fund salesman trying for a telephone solicitation. They listened over the speaker as the flustered salesman made an abbreviated pitch, left his number, and hung up.

Barry went back to his staring while Judith pretended to be absorbed in a book. She looked up from time to time, waiting for him to break the silence. The only sound she heard was the door slamming across the hall when their neighbor came home. Finally he stirred and shook himself out of his trance.

"Mollie or Melinda," he said. Then he carried the laundry basket into the bedroom.

Judith

He'd been brooding about his fortieth birthday all month, feeling he'd passed a significant milestone but what had he accomplished? The baby appeared to be an answer. He said it was like winning the lottery when he'd forgotten he bought a ticket.

For me, too. When I was younger I always assumed there would be a child in my life someday, but it was always way off in the future, after I'd published a novel and won the Pulitzer Prize. I'd think, If I ever get pregnant that's when we'll get married, and I'll quit smoking cigarettes and start taking an exercise class in earnest. I'd make up names for the children Barry and I were going to have, and scribble them over and over on a piece of paper. Brian and Kimberly, Pete and Patricia, Jason and Dru. I saw myself walking through Washington Square Park with the carriage. I rehearsed the interview I'd grant

the reporter from *Vogue*. People Are Talking About
. . . Prize-Winning Author Judith Winograd, her brilliant
lawyer husband, and their two adorable children.

When I turned thirty-nine I had a moment of revela-
tion. If it hadn't happened so far, it probably wasn't going
to happen. Novels and babies were both out of my reach.
Marriage was a forbidden subject between us, something
Barry did not care to discuss. And then he brought home
Melinda.

I moved like a zombie during those first few weeks. It
was unreal. Sometimes when he sent me out to the store,
I came back half expecting not to find her in the apartment. I thought, I'll open the door and he'll be sitting
there alone on the sofa smoking a joint, with the Talking
Heads on the tape deck. He'll say, Hey, Jude, the deal
came through, or Hey, Jude, they picked her up while you
were out.

Or is that what I hoped?

Once or twice during that first month I think he did try
to place her with a client. There were some mysterious
telephone conversations I wasn't supposed to hear. He'd
bundle her up with one of her rattles and tell me he'd be
back in a couple of hours.

But they always came back together.

SEPTEMBER 21, 1981

Topic A around the coffee wagon at Claridge and
Palmer that Monday morning was that Judith Winograd
and the guy she lives with have adopted a baby.

"Rather sudden, don't you think?" Harvey Erickson
said to his boss, Joanne Owens, as he bit into a Danish.

Joanne shook her head. "Can you believe it? I'm

stunned. How does a single woman get to adopt a child in this city? There's a waiting list a mile long for married couples."

"It's gotta be Vietnamese, Korean, or black," Sally Milton said with her usual authority as she poured in her cream and sugar. "Did she volunteer what color, or did you avoid delving into specifics out of your disgusting liberal politesse?"

Harvey, who had taken the call, admitted he was lousy on the who, what, and why. Asking direct questions wasn't his bag, otherwise he might still be working for the Associated Press.

Sally snapped her fingers like she'd solved the entire mystery and it wasn't even ten a.m. "A single friend of mine adopted a black kid two years ago. A sweet little four-year-old girl with a heart murmur who'd been living in foster homes since birth. Nobody else would take her, so my friend Sheila got lucky. But the Department of Social Services gave her hell until they approved the papers. They made her go through these demeaning home visits. Proving she had a separate room for the kid was the least of it, they wanted to know if she ever had men sleeping over."

They kidded Harvey that at least he got the sex right. A girl named Melinda. No one in the office could remember Judith ever saying she wanted a baby, that was one of the oddest things about it.

"I always said she was secretive," Joanne agreed, "and I'm the one who hired her."

"Do you think she'll come back?" Harvey asked.

"Of course she will," said Joanne. "That's hardly an issue these days, is it? What I'm wondering is, what's the protocol on the baby shower? Do we take her to lunch at Giambelli's, or do I call Dean and DeLuca and cater it at my house with spouses and significant others?"

110

They grew quiet at the thought of spending another awkward evening at Joanne's Gramercy Park apartment with the people they were close to in personal life. Their ebullient office chatter would fall flat, and their nearest and dearest would stand around the crystal punch bowl looking grim. It happened every Christmas. Once a year was enough.

Sally suggested an easy alternative. Why didn't they all chip in and buy one major gift, like a collapsible playpen or a really fantastic six-foot giraffe from F. A. O. Schwarz? She was willing to take up the collection.

SEPTEMBER 23, 1981

Gunther Heald couldn't wait to tell his lover the news. He'd only been living with Jim for two months, but they'd settled into a beautiful, stable routine. This was his night to do the cooking, so he'd gone to Balducci's for some fiddlehead ferns, thinking he'd sauté them lightly in butter and serve them with breast of chicken. Just chicken and ferns, *très élégant*. But the ferns were out of season, so he had to settle for leeks. He supposed that when their relationship matured he'd be able to admit to Jim that he really preferred steak and potatoes, but it was fun to play around with nouvelle cuisine and surprise each other every night with something exotic. After all, they'd met over food, when he had served Jim's table at Odeon.

His luck was turning. Two months ago he had been an unemployed actor waiting tables and sharing a hovel on Eldridge Street with a painter and a male model. Now he was up for a good part in an off-Broadway show, and living in a beautiful townhouse in the Village with a man who adored him. Jim was twenty years older than

111

Gunther, and into monogamy. His lover put on a dark pinstripe suit every morning to face his insurance company job as an actuary, but the apartment expressed who he really was. He'd done the whole thing by himself, without a decorator, in French Provincial with fabulous pieces from Pierre Deux and other antique shops on that incredible stretch of Bleecker Street that he and Gunther loved to explore.

But the fly in Jim's ointment, and consequently in Gunther's—although he had difficulty sharing Jim's sense of outrage after a year on Eldridge Street—was noise. The woman below them practiced scales on her baby grand every night at eleven p.m.—Jim said you could set your watch by her—and the man across the hall in 2-B had recently acquired an Akita puppy that growled at the door whenever Jim or Gunther came home.

And then there was 3-A. The couple upstairs had monthly scraps and set-tos that sounded like they were throwing the furniture from one end of the apartment to the other. "There they go, they're at it again. Maggie and Jiggs," Jim fussed and fumed late one evening shortly after Gunther moved in. He snapped on the stereo and turned up the volume on Mahler's Eighth Symphony. When Gunther said, "Maggie and *who*?" Jim told him about the comic strip in the Sunday papers when he was a boy, how Maggie chased Jiggs around the house with a rolling pin.

Gunther's news was about these upstairs neighbors. He'd run into the woman in Balducci's, and she told him they'd adopted a baby. He knew what Jim would say when he reported the glad tidings, and considered beating him to it. Gunther practiced a campy swagger in front of the mirror, using Jim's inflection.

"Keep your fingers crossed, sweetheart. Maggie and Jiggs may be moving to a larger apartment."

SEPTEMBER 24, 1981

Mr. and Mrs. Winograd got a call from Barry. He put Judith on the line.

"It's true," she said. "We've named her Melinda. *Melinda.* It's too soon to tell, but we think her hair is going to be blond. Yes, it was very sudden. *What?* Last week."

Goldie said she couldn't understand why Judith's voice was so faint.

"I'm exhausted, Ma. I'm very tired."

Her mother said she'd come into the city tomorrow, but Judith said no. "Barry's worried she might catch a bug. We'll let you know when it's all right."

SEPTEMBER 26, 1981

Marianna had invited her boss and his wife for dinner. She was doing a whole poached salmon in a court bouillon, to be served lukewarm with a green sauce of fresh basil and dill from Julia Child. Bill and Maria Laughlin, her old standbys, were picking up a chocolate torte from Sarabeth, the bakeshop that decorated so inventively with fresh flowers. "Not to worry," Maria assured her. "You're getting real violets, not candies." On the spur of the moment she'd invited her ex-lover Ken Angiers to round out the guest list, and was already regretting it. But Ken was her classiest name, and he'd supply some delightful Hollywood gossip—this had to be a numero uno classy evening. If she played her cards right, she'd wind up with the China assignment.

113

She was climbing the stairs with an armload of groceries for the third time that Saturday morning when she bumped into her next-door neighbor coming down. He had a baby strapped in a denim carrier on his chest.

"Taking her out for an airing," he said as he passed her on the second-floor landing.

She put down her packages and stared.

He paused halfway down the flight of stairs and turned around. "Some people produce television shows, and some people produce babies. You ought to knock on the door and say congratulations to Judith."

Marianna boiled with rage for the rest of the morning. Of all the sly innuendos about career women and biological clocks, that one took the cake. She had no intention of going in to say anything to the ding-a-ling next door. They hadn't exchanged a civil word since she moved in.

So Mrs. Laemmerle was right, as usual. There *was* a baby in 3-A. Next they'd be knocking on her door, wondering if she could sit for them in a pinch. Another good reason to keep her distance.

Judith

I was sterilizing bottles of Enfamil the afternoon Bob Rothman came over to see Melinda. Barry had showed me how much cheaper it was to use powdered formula, and he wanted me to mix up a fresh batch every day, but the joke was on me. Grade-school-level science was my specialty at Claridge and Palmer, and I could freebase cocaine, but I lived in terror that I'd get the proportions of water to formula wrong.

I had bottles boiling on the stove and was hunting

through my storage boxes for one of my silver demitasse spoons to use for measuring when I heard the downstairs buzzer. Bob looked at the sleeping baby and at the mess in the kitchen and shook his head. He said, "Some women are born mothers, some achieve motherhood, and some have motherhood thrust upon them. Judith, you've got to go back to the office. ASAP. Hire a daytime nurse and give the kid quality time."

When I told that to Barry, he wouldn't hear of it. He wanted the baby to bond to us, not to a nurse, and he didn't want my mother sticking her nose into our lives on a regular basis either. I stayed home with Melinda for six weeks on full-pay maternity leave. Now I take her to the office with me every day in a taxi.

Claridge and Palmer doesn't have daycare facilities, but Joanne and Harvey agreed that it would be bad form for the children's book department not to accommodate a real child. I keep her near my desk in the collapsible playpen they gave us. Barry doesn't want the playpen in the house, he says it's a prison. At first everyone trooped in and out to take a look at Melinda, but now they're used to her being there, and so am I. The secretaries—this year from Vassar and Bennington—have made her an office project. They don't mind changing her, and they take turns giving her the bottle.

Sally Milton attached a mobile of circus animals to the playpen, and it was Harvey, of all people, who came back from lunch one day with a pacifier after Melinda had been on a crying jag all morning.

Melinda thrives on all the attention. She is a good baby, she likes her pacifier, and she saves her really bad spells of crying for nighttime, as if she knows she has to be on her best behavior at work.

And when she breaks into a smile she wins everybody's heart.

The Hethingtons arrived at their lawyer's house with ten thousand in cash, a large bag of coke, and a bottle of Dom Perignon to celebrate the new baby. Barry said, "Let's start the party right now," and uncorked the bottle.

Ellie saw Judith give Barry a fearful look. Something was wrong, but she couldn't figure out what.

Melinda was a dream. A sunny, friendly baby with strawberry blond hair. Barry put her through her paces while the Hethingtons clucked and cooed.

When the men went into the kitchen to play chemist, Ellie told Judith about her own two children. They were six and eight, and they called Don "Papa Don." Papa John, their real father, had moved to Wyoming.

Before the bust, Ellie confided, Don had been thinking of adopting them formally, but they supposed that would have to wait. Barry called out from the kitchen that he'd handle the adoption papers for them when they were ready. "Adoption's a cinch, isn't it, Judith?" he said.

Barry was wonderful with the baby. Don admitted he was very impressed. Ellie said Melinda was some lucky kid. It was obvious as all get-out that she was going to be one spoiled little princess.

When they heard about the collapsible playpen that had come from Judith's office and had gone back there, the Hethingtons agreed with Barry that playpens were prisons and could retard a baby's development.

"The floor is perfectly safe for them," Ellie told Judith as she looked around, "so long as you babyproof the entire apartment. Mine never even slept in cribs. I put down a sleeping bag for one and a futon for the other."

Judith said that's what they were thinking. All that stuff

116

people said you should buy! Nothing but consumer hype. What a baby needed was love and attention.

Barry brought out his new glass pipe. Between tokes they finished off the champagne. The Hethingtons said they were sorry they'd brought only one bottle. Barry said, "Are you kidding? This is New York. Anything you want is a phone call away."

He called the liquor store, ordered two more chilled bottles, and had them throw in a fifth of Sambuca. The delivery arrived in nothing flat.

Ellie had a personal rule against mixing her stimulants, but Don tried to match Barry hit for hit and glass for glass. Judith was very quiet. A hard person to draw out, Ellie knew the type. Judith preferred to let her man dominate the conversation.

Barry didn't want to talk about their case. Instead he bent their ear with some elaborate stories about intelligence work in Germany when he was stationed there during the Vietnam War. The way he told it, you'd think he'd single-handedly kept the country from going Communist by finding out in advance when the radical students were going to stage a demonstration. Then when he came back to New York to finish law school, he'd been in the thick of the draft resistance movement, to hear him talk. His stories didn't quite link up, but Ellie supposed that was the combined effect of the dope and the booze.

The four of them had planned to go out to dinner at a neighborhood place, but it seemed a pity to wake up the baby and take her out in the cold. Judith ordered in pizza, and Barry insisted on paying.

Melinda woke up when the pizza arrived. Ellie picked her up and soothed her while Judith put the plates and napkins on the table. The baby had a full load in her diaper.

"I'll change her. Where do you keep the Pampers?" Ellie asked.

"She'll do it," Barry said.

"No, really, I don't mind at all. It's been a long time since I changed a kid's diapers. I sort of miss it."

"Let the editor do it," Barry snapped in a harsh voice.

Ellie stopped in her tracks. Don looked at her in confusion.

"Judith is one of the top children's book editors at Claridge and Palmer," Barry announced in sarcastic tones. "Did you know that? One of the top. Her books win prizes. Let's see how long it takes her to change a diaper."

It was not a good moment. At Barry's insistence, Don and Ellie sat down at the dining table under the Tiffany lamp and helped themselves to pizza while Judith changed Melinda in the other room.

Barry urged them to go ahead and eat. "She's used to it cold," he told them.

Don and Ellie took a walk around the block to clear their heads before they drove uptown to Ellie's father's apartment.

"Boy, his personality changed fast after a couple of hits," Ellie said. "I didn't like that at all."

"It's got to be a big adjustment for both of them, having a baby. He was terrific with Melinda."

"Yeah, but he was so overbearing with his lady. Ordering her around like that in front of us."

"That's how you interpreted it. She didn't seem to mind."

"Oh, come on, Don! She jumped like a scared rabbit. I think she's afraid of him. And imagine, she's an editor at Claridge and Palmer. Did I tell you I saw a look of absolute panic on her face when he gulped the champagne from the bottle?"

"That's 'cause she recognized the label. She knew he was chugalugging expensive stuff. Listen, this may have been the first chance he had to relax since the baby came into the house. So he overdid it a little. That's all. We'll make sure there's no Dom Perignon around when he goes into court. It's coke he wants, anyway."

"You saw how they didn't have any booze in the house? They had to send out for it. I bet he beats up on her after he's downed a couple."

"Aren't you hanging the guy based on your experience with your first husband?"

"Probably."

"Well, do me a favor. Don't analyze it to death, okay? He got a little wasted and already you're calling him a wife beater."

She had to admit she was jumping to conclusions. That's why Don was so good for her. Nothing upset him. He was steady as a rock, especially when she got on her paranoid trip.

FEBRUARY 1982

Goldie couldn't get over her changeable daughter. One minute she blew hot, another minute she blew cold. Judith never had time to bring the baby to the Winograds' new garden apartment in Bayonne, and she found something negative to say about every item of clothing or toy they bought for Melinda. But when Max offhandedly mentioned the nice synagogue they had joined, and how last Saturday morning after the service the rabbi invited the entire congregation to a *kiddush* for a newborn, suddenly Judith was all ears.

Then Mr. Barry himself called up. He said that he and Judith wanted to have some sort of Jewish ceremony to welcome Melinda into the fold. Did they think that would be a problem for the temple? He asked for the name of the rabbi and said he'd give him a call. A half-hour later he rang back and said the synagogue was very amenable to the idea. There was a new liturgical practice called a naming ceremony, there was a date open in February, but the Winograds had to make the arrangements with the rabbi's office because they were the members.

A donation was in order, he told them. He'd be more than happy to give a little extra besides. All Max and Goldie had to do was nail down the date and make sure about the scroll. He was very particular about the scroll. He wanted something in calligraphy that looked official, so they could frame it, he said. "Don't say we're not married," he added. "It's an unnecessary complication."

The Winograds were delighted. Since her Sunday school lessons at the New Parkway Jewish Center, Judith had shown no interest in the Jewish faith. Having a baby, even a little *shiksa* who slept in a basket, must have made the two of them more conscious of their roots. Next maybe they'd want a wedding under the *chuppah*, with printed invitations.

The day of the naming ceremony Barry and Judith brought Melinda to Bayonne bright and early in the morning. Then they all drove to the temple in Barry's new Volvo.

After the reading of the Torah, the parents and grandparents were called to the altar. Barry wore a *yarmulke* and carried a squirming Melinda in his arms. At five months she was getting very active. The young reform rabbi intoned the name Melinda Winograd-Kantor, and then her Hebrew name, Shoshana. He said a few words about the next generation, that opportunities were open to Melinda and other girls as yet unborn that had been unthinkable in earlier times. Then he handed Judith the calligraphic scroll. She kissed her mother and father. Goldie cried.

The *kiddush* was held downstairs in a meeting room. According to custom, the Winograds provided the cakes and wine. Several members of the congregation came over to shake their hands. Melinda babbled happily in her carrier seat, and Judith fed her some mashed banana. Everyone said she was a beauty. Out of the rabbi's earshot, Max grumbled that the ceremony smacked of a *goyishe* christening to him, but Goldie told him he was just old-fashioned. The only tense moment came when Barry lit a cigarette and the rabbi came over to say that smoking was prohibited on the Sabbath. He went outside and finished it there.

Judith

Barry said that the scroll would never stand up in a court of law, but it would probably satisfy a school or any other institution down the line that needed some proof of adoption. A piece of paper, he said. How easily they're fooled by an official-looking piece of paper.

He told me from the beginning that we could never legally adopt Melinda in the state of New York. There was no point even trying to file a petition. Right off the bat we would stand to lose because the natural mother was Roman Catholic and the courts felt strongly about raising the child in the mother's religion. If we ever got over that hurdle, they'd get us on the other stuff. We weren't married, I worked full-time, we didn't have a large enough

121

apartment, and our lifestyle could never withstand the scrutiny of home visits from the city's Department of Social Services.

"Do you want them prying into our lives?" he asked. "What for? Can you bend yourself to fit the moralistic rules and regulations of a hypocritical bureaucracy? The law is an ass, Judith. Believe me, I work with the assholes all day long. When I defend a client in court, do you think they pay me to present the truth? They don't. My job is to present a plausible scenario that *sounds* like it *could* be the truth. Reasonable doubt, the basis of American jurisprudence. Now, turn that around. 'Hello, everybody, come see our beautiful adopted baby, her name is Melinda.' Think about it. Would it be reasonable for anyone to doubt that she's legally adopted?"

For the clincher, he reminded me of his custody work. He had won custody for two fathers in divorce proceedings by arguing that the mother's unconventional sexual habits made her unfit to keep her children. One had become a lesbian, the other lived in an arrangement similar to ours.

"Were they unfit mothers?" I asked.

He laughed. "They were in the eyes of the judge when I got through with them. I told you, the law is an ass. You'd be a sitting duck on the witness stand, Judith."

Fitness wasn't the point, he added. In custody cases the point was alimony and child-support payments. "The bitches got zilch," he said, rubbing his hands. "That made my clients very happy."

MARCH 6, 1982

Barry strapped Melinda into her carrier seat while Judith put a few of her toys and her bottle of juice in a totebag. Judith had always dreaded Barry's trips to the

122

Bronx, and the baby hadn't changed things any. He never failed to come back silent and edgy.

She knew she was in for it this time. The tension between them had been building since the day after the naming ceremony in Bayonne. *Why?* She had tried so hard to keep things peaceful. The service in the silly temple had gone so well, they had gotten the precious scroll with the wording they needed. And her parents had arranged it beautifully. They had done everything Barry asked for, down to giving the calligrapher the exact text he dictated.

Why? Why was he starting in on her again?

Maybe he was having trouble with one of his clients. Some of them were deadbeats, she knew that. Or maybe it was Jeff Kellerman. Something had gone wrong between him and Jeff. They were fighting over the boat. Jeff said he wasn't getting enough access to it. And Barry had told her they were quarreling over the rent they were paying for their hole-in-the-wall in the Cubby Building. Jeff had just signed a new lease without consulting Barry. How could Jeff have done that? Of course Barry got angry when Jeff told him just like that he'd have to fork over another three hundred a month. If Barry had negotiated the new lease instead of Jeff, they wouldn't be having a problem.

Old lady Kantor. Barry had wanted his mother to witness the ceremony, he said it was only right. Judith knew it *was* only right, but it was also wrong, wrong, wrong. She had used all her powers of persuasion to convince him that it was better for everyone, including Melinda, if Grandmother Kantor was kept in the dark about the service in Bayonne. Between his mother and her mother there was sure to be an explosion, and they both knew that things had to go smoothly that day. And they had, hadn't they?

But he hadn't let up ever since.

Last night she had pleaded with him to skip the visit to Morris Avenue. Melinda had a slight cold, she'd be runny and cranky all day. She was into a phase where she suddenly got fearful when she left the house. The childcare books said it was a normal development. Melinda would act up, she might even throw up in the car, the day would be a disaster.

And she'd get it when he came home. She always did. She couldn't remember a single time he had been to visit his mother when he hadn't come back in a leaden fury. He knew it and she knew it, but she could never stop him from going.

This morning she tried one last time, approaching him cautiously in the kitchen. "Barry, it's going to rain. Melinda shouldn't be—"

"Out of my way," he snapped.

The force of his arm threw her off balance, and she stumbled against the cabinet. She steadied herself and retreated into the bedroom. No use getting the baby upset.

MARCH 8, 1982

Sally Milton happened to be standing at the fourteenth-floor reception desk that Monday morning when Judith wheeled Melinda off the elevator in her stroller. The first peculiar thing Sally noticed was that Judith was wearing dark glasses. Then she saw her swollen lip.

Judith tried to wheel Melinda past her quickly, but Sally blurted out without thinking, "What happened to *you*?"

Her co-worker turned her head the other way and pushed the stroller down the hall. Sally followed to Judith's office.

"What happened? You look like you ran into a truck."

"I tripped over one of Melinda's toys," Judith said curtly.

Sally marched into Joanne's office and closed the door. "I just saw Judith Winograd come in with Melinda. Her lip was out to there, and I think she has a beaut of a shiner. She was wearing dark glasses."

"Again?"

"Again."

Joanne sighed. The two women exchanged a knowing look. "What did she say this time?"

"She mumbled something about tripping over Melinda's toys. Then she closed the door on me, very pointedly. What could I do?"

"How was the baby?"

"Fine. At least I think she was fine. Now I'm getting even more upset—no, I would have noticed if there was a bruise on Melinda."

Joanne buzzed her secretary and told her to hold all her calls. "Sally, there's no way you can talk to her, I've tried. She's absolutely unapproachable."

"I don't agree with you, Joanne. There's got to be something we can do. He's going to do her serious bodily damage one day—*what am I saying?* He's already done her serious harm. The first time someone took a swing at me he'd be out of the house so fast—I wouldn't put up with it for a second. What is this, the fourth or fifth time she's crept in here after he's beaten her black and blue, and we're afraid to confront her on it?"

She was raising her voice. Joanne motioned her to be quiet. "She needs our support, I agree, but I'm not so sure the best way to go about it is to speak to her directly."

"What do you suggest we do? Find her a shrink and tell her it's on the house, the latest employee benefit at Claridge?"

"That's not such a bad idea."

"Are you kidding? She'd never go."

The two women had reached an impasse. Sally got up from her chair. "I'm not going to be able to work today, I just know it," she said as she left Joanne's office.

Joanne placed a call to her sister at the paper. Cindy was out on assignment, but the desk said they'd give her the message. It was important to check with Cindy before she went any further. Her sister wasn't living with Jeff Kellerman anymore, but they were still fairly close. Jeff would have some idea what was going on with the man Judith was involved with. As she recalled, they weren't partners, but they shared office space. Yes, it would be wise to have a discreet conversation with Jeff. Maybe the three of them, she, Cindy, and Jeff, could have dinner. Then she'd have a better sense of how to proceed.

She thought of Judith sitting in her office down the hall. It would be so easy to drop in on her, or better yet, dial her extension and invite her in to discuss a manuscript. Normally they did this several times a week. But today! Judith would be instantly on guard, and besides, it would be a cruel thing to do. It must have taken great courage for her to walk into Claridge and Palmer this morning. Perhaps the most humane policy after all was to pretend that nothing was wrong.

Sally. She was such an excitable personality. It was holding her back from a promotion, and she didn't even know it. Last week the art department had been in an uproar over one of Sally's "We need it now, we needed it yesterday" tantrums. That wasn't the way things worked in Children's Books. Not that she considered Sally an alarmist, she was a very talented editor—so was Judith—but she did have a tendency to go off half-cocked. Judith, on the other hand, did her work efficiently and never asked art or production for special favors. She was really an ideal employee.

Joanne forced herself to recall Judith's unexplained absences and the lame excuses and flustered evasions when she came back to the office. It dawned on her finally that she had been subliminally aware of Judith's problem for three years. Not the specific nature of the problem, but her subconscious had known all along that the isolated incidents were part of a pattern.

A pattern of what? She supposed the clinical term for it was sadomasochism. That was where she differed from someone like Sally. Where Sally saw a one-way street of male violence against women, she saw the subtle colorations of a complex psychological relationship between two people. Why was Sally so certain that Judith wanted to extricate herself from her particular situation?

Game playing in bed wasn't exactly Joanne's cup of tea either—she blushed to think of the starched white coverlet on the canopied single bed in her Gramercy Park apartment—but she prided herself on her tolerant attitude toward others. Her department functioned as well as it did because she was not the kind of boss who delved into the private affairs of her subordinates. She thought of the monosyllabic black jazz musician Sally brought to her last Christmas party, and the young man Harvey had in tow, who said he was with the New York City Ballet and spent the evening flexing his ankle. Lord, if everyone at Claridge and Palmer was held accountable for his or her private peccadilloes . . .

Peccadilloes? Joanne was a very precise editor. If an author of hers used "peccadillo" in this context, she'd blue-pencil it immediately.

What was the correct word? Joanne was stymied. It was very unlike her to be at a loss when it came to the English language.

127

APRIL 3, 1982

When Judith took Melinda to Dr. Michael Rochette for her checkup, she asked if he could give her a Valium prescription. She said she was under a lot of pressure at work and was having trouble sleeping.

The pediatrician agreed that while Melinda was gaining weight nicely, Judith looked exhausted. When Judith started to describe her other symptoms—the pain in her lower back that always seemed worse when she got out of bed in the morning, the mid-afternoon fatigue that made her gobble a doughnut and two cups of coffee at her desk —he said it sounded like a classic case of new-mother anxiety and tension.

He wrote out the prescription for her and suggested that she take no more than half a pill at bedtime. She went straight from his office to a pharmacy on Eighth Avenue, one that she had never been in before. The other Valium prescription she had cadged that month had been filled at a cut-rate drugstore near her office.

APRIL 13, 1982

Judith was alert as soon as she heard the key in the lock. He was home too early. A bad sign. He never came home this early on poker night.

Melinda breathed rhythmically in her sleep. Judith held her breath in the darkened bedroom, straining for every sound. She heard him in the kitchen, slamming the refrigerator and banging plates. Pounding, pounding, her heart was pounding.

Suddenly the bedroom was ablaze with light.

"Get out of bed, you dumb cunt." Melinda started to cry.

"Barry, the baby!"

He pulled her out of bed by the arm and dragged her into the kitchen, twisting her elbow behind her back. With his free hand he opened the refrigerator door and shoved. Her forehead struck the metal rim of a shelf.

"What do you see in there, cunt?" He kicked her in the small of the back. She slumped to the floor.

"Get up, jackass, I'm not through with you yet." He pulled her up by the hair and smacked her across the face. She fell against the sink and cowered.

"I'm hungry. Make me something to eat," he snarled. "Go ahead."

Her eyes darted frantically around the kitchen.

"Move it!" He grabbed her shoulders and threw her against the stove.

She crouched where she fell and whimpered.

"Whatsa matter? No ideas? The busy little editor forgot to go shopping?"

Melinda was wailing in the bedroom. He opened cupboard doors at random, sweeping the contents off the shelves. Momentarily forgotten, she crawled toward the hallway, but he was too quick for her. He dragged her back by her feet, grabbed for her neck, and banged her head against the oven.

This is it, she thought. He is killing me. She tried to scream, but nothing came out. Somehow he got the oven door open and shoved her head and shoulders inside. *Nooooooo, I am going to be burned alive.* She kicked backward with her bare feet, wrenched out of his grip, and rolled over, protecting her face with her hands.

"Kicks you want? Kicks." The heel of his shoe slammed into her crotch.

She lay there and took the blows. She was past caring. He was stomping on her pubic bone when she passed out.

APRIL 14, 1982, 3:00 A.M.

The paramedics hooked up the IV in the ambulance. One drew a blood sample from Judith's arm, the other pressed in on her pelvic girdle. It was soft.

"Forget the MAST trousers. Call the ER."

The driver got the emergency room on the cellular phone. "Forty-year-old female coming in. Assault to the pelvic area. Fast pulse. She's diaphoretic."

It came over the loudspeaker as Code Blue. St. Vincent's trauma team was gowned up and waiting in the emergency room when the paramedics wheeled in the gurney.

"Get X-Ray. We need a portable stat."

"Put a Foley catheter in."

The blood sample went to a nurse. "Save this for type and cross."

Ten minutes later they had the stats. The patient had a fractured pelvis. Her bladder wasn't ruptured, and her vital signs were normal. The trauma team relaxed.

"Admit her for bed rest and rapid mobilization."

APRIL 14, 1982, 9:00 A.M.

Barry called the Hethingtons in Vermont. No, it wasn't about their case, he still didn't have a trial date. This was a personal matter. Judith was in the hospital. Nothing serious, a mild case of pneumonia. Could Don and Ellie take Melinda for a couple of weeks? He could drive up and be there late tonight.

130

APRIL 15, 1982, 4:00 P.M.

Sally Milton finally reached Barry on the phone. Judith hadn't been in to work for two days, and she was worried. He said he was surprised she hadn't heard. A slipup somewhere. Judith was in St. Vincent's. She'd taken a bad fall in the bathtub and fractured her pelvis. One of those freak accidents. He was on his way to the hospital right now.

APRIL 15, 1982, 4:30 P.M.

Judith opened her eyes and shut them again. She was dreaming of Hansel and Gretel and the wicked witch. The witch was dressed in black and was trying to push her head in the oven. But when she opened her eyes the witch was still there.

APRIL 15, 1982, 5:00 P.M.

When Sally called Patient Information, she was told that Judith Winograd had been moved to a private room, 408, but had not requested a phone. Visiting hours were normally from two to eight, but there was a note on her record that the patient did not want visitors just yet.

APRIL 16, 1982, 6:00 P.M.

Joanne and Sally arrived at the visitors' entrance and were told that the visitors' cards for Winograd were al-

131

ready in use. They would have to wait downstairs or come back later.

Sally said, "Come on," and took Joanne around to the hospital's Eleventh Street entrance. The two women marched through the lobby, boarded an elevator, and got off on the fourth floor.

"Pretend you know where you're going," Sally murmured to Joanne under her breath. They walked briskly through several swinging doors, checking the room numbers until they reached Judith's wing.

Sally gave a friendly, professional nod in the direction of the nurses' station and opened the door to 408.

Judith was awake, lying propped up on pillows. She stared at them vacantly and then turned her head and started to cry.

The visitors stayed only a few minutes. Neither could think of a cheery thing to say except that everybody in the office wished her a speedy recovery and that it was unnaturally quiet on the fourteenth floor without Melinda.

"She's with friends in Vermont. Such a stupid accident," Judith said dully.

Even Sally didn't have the heart to contradict her. They said they'd check in on her again tomorrow. Now that they knew where she was, probably some of the others would want to visit.

"No," she said. "Please."

They closed the door securely behind them. Sally caught the attention of someone at the nurses' station and asked where they could find the social worker on the floor.

Ms. Prathia Ferry, as her nameplate identified her, was on the phone in her tiny office, trying to track down a Medicaid application. She motioned them to have a seat. Ms. Ferry was a black woman who appeared to be in her late fifties. She was wearing a white nylon blouse with a big bow at the neck, under a boxy suit with braided trim that Joanne and Sally expertly appraised as a second- or third-generation knockoff Chanel. The designer's classic lines and good cut had been lost in translation. The Claridge and Palmer women were attuned to New York's subtle frictions of race and class: Prathia Ferry, they instinctively knew, had fought hard to attain her professional status. She would perceive them as interlopers from another world. She would not welcome their intrusion into her tiny domain; she would not unbend.

When she got off the phone, they told her they were there to speak privately about Judith Winograd in 408. The social worker pursed her lips and riffled through a file of manila folders on her desk.

"Are you family or friends?" she asked.

"We work with her," Joanne explained in her best executive voice. "At Claridge and Palmer, the publishers. She's one of our senior editors." Ms. Ferry looked surprised.

Joanne took a deep breath. "Would you say that her injuries are consonant with an accident or not?"

"I'm afraid that's a question you'll have to ask her doctor."

"Well, we'll tell you," Sally broke in sharply. "It wasn't an accident. This is a pattern of abuse that has been going on for years."

Ms. Ferry widened her eyes and made some notes on a piece of paper. "Have you spoken with members of her family?" she asked. "I believe they're in the visitors' lounge right now."

"No *thanks*." Sally spat out the words. She and the social worker bristled at each other. Sally poked Joanne and rose to go.

"Sit down a minute," Ms. Ferry said. Sally sat down. The social worker tapped a pencil on her desk. "This is a very serious and confidential matter, and one that we usually don't discuss with outsiders, particularly outsiders who come barging in here trying to tell us our business."

"You'll have to forgive Miss Milton and me," Joanne said calmly. "All of us at Claridge and Palmer are very upset. There's a child involved too."

Ms. Ferry made another notation on her paper. "I can see that you ladies are genuinely concerned. By law I don't have to tell you anything, but I want you to know that my department is well aware of the situation. Well aware. Saint Vincent's has a counseling program for battered women, but it's voluntary. They have to ask for help, do you understand what I'm saying? This is a classic case of denial. A textbook case."

"She has to get out from under him, Ms. Ferry," Sally pleaded. "He's going to kill her one of these days."

"You're a bright, educated woman," Ms. Ferry said. "I assume your friend is bright and educated too. If she can't see intellectually and emotionally that she's in a dangerous situation, what can you reasonably expect us to do?"

"So you're saying there's nothing that can be done?"

"I did not say that," Ms. Ferry replied testily. "I said she has to be ready to see it herself."

APRIL 17, 1982, MORNING

The nurse's aide brought in another basket of flowers. "Somebody sure loves you, honey," she said. She put the basket on the windowsill and gave Judith the card. *Pink peonies,* it read. *Nothing ordinary for you.*

Judith gazed around her hospital room. Vases of lush, regal peonies in shades of pink, white, and fuchsia crowded the window. A springtime basket of tulips and iris sat on her nightstand next to a bowl of blooming lilies of the valley. A giant green-leaved ficus tree shared the corner with a potted rosebush, and a lofty bouquet of silver balloons bearing the message "Get Well Soon" floated over her bed.

He had transformed the bare institutional surroundings into an arbor. For her. And she hadn't said a word to him yet.

She tucked the card under her pillow with the others and smiled.

APRIL 17, 1982, EVENING

The door opened. She was expecting the orderly with her dinner tray, but it was Barry. He stood there framed in the doorway, the tray in his hands. His curly black hair fell across his forehead, he'd forgotten to comb it. She worked the corners of her mouth to keep from smiling. He looked so woeful and uncertain, but proud of himself too. He must have tipped the orderly to let him carry in her dinner.

"Judith, may I come in?"

She nodded without speaking.

He rolled the table into position and set down the tray. "Let's see now, what have we here? Ah, tomato juice, unidentified brown meat, mashed potatoes. Applesauce! Let's hear a cheer for applesauce. What'll we try first? Tomato juice, okay?"

He handed her the juice, and she took a sip. He stared at her gravely. "Judith. You have to speak to me, Judith."

She saw him waver between sitting on her bed or a chair. He pulled up the chair. Good. He was afraid to take a liberty she hadn't offered. She took another sip of the juice and watched him over the rim of the cup. He looked so pitiful she could hardly bear it. She set down the cup and looked away.

135

"Enough juice, sweetheart? Okay, let's try the meat. Here, let me cut it for you."

He had to stand up to cut the meat. He leaned over the bed so close to her that if either of them moved an inch they'd be touching. She could feel the heat of his body.

"I'll make you a promise," he said. "Eat all of your meat and potatoes and I'll sing you a song. Would you like that?"

She nodded. If she reached up she could touch his hair.

"But you have to tell me what song to sing."

She shook her head no.

"Not ready to talk yet? Okay." He speared a piece of meat on the fork and brought it to her lips. "Good girl."

She didn't want any more of the meat, so he fed her the mashed potatoes and applesauce. Then he opened the container of milk and unwrapped the straw.

"Ready for the song?"

Was he really going to sing? The thought of him singing to her in this flower-filled hospital room made her want to giggle. Her midsection hurt, and then she remembered why they were both there.

"You tried to burn me in the oven." She had spoken. She hadn't meant to. She started to cry.

"Judith. Judith, honey."

"I passed out."

"Judith, I know. I took you to the hospital. I carried you down the stairs in my arms."

The tears were streaming down her cheeks.

"Judith, listen to me. I wouldn't do anything to hurt you. I love you, Judith. I need you."

She shook her head.

"What happened to us, Judith? I blanked out. I'm scared. We were having an argument in the kitchen, and you fell against the stove."

"You pushed me."

"Judith, help me. I'm scared. I care about you more than anything in life. If you leave me I'll go out of my mind."

She looked into his eyes. They were as wet as hers.

"You carried me down the stairs?" she said.

APRIL 18, 1982

Judith was dozing when a dark presence sat down near her bed. For a minute she thought it was the witch in her dreams, but it was Barry's mother in a black silk dress.

Mrs. Kantor was breathing heavily and mopping her face with a handkerchief. "Judith, you're awake?" she said. "I've been here every day since he called. He's a good boy, Judith, he's my only boy. He needs you."

"Is my mother here?" Judith said. "I want to see my own mother."

Mrs. Kantor got up with great effort. "She's sitting out there where she always sits. She's got her favorite chair already. It's hers. Your father's coming back this afternoon."

Judith's small, wiry mother came in with a bag of knitting and took up her position. She put on her half-frame reading glasses and set to work. The needles clicked loudly in the quiet room as mother and daughter cast about for a neutral way to begin a conversation.

"I'm making a sweater for Melinda," her mother said. "I used to make you sweaters when you were a baby."

"I remember."

"Handmade sweaters. You couldn't buy them for fifty dollars."

137

"Yes, Ma."

"You looked so pretty when I wheeled you in the carriage."

"Mama, what should I do?"

"Get well, that's what you should do." Her mother unwound some more yarn.

"He says he needs me."

"Your father never laid a hand on me in fifty years. A lawyer, he is. A lawyer. He's an animal, a Svengali."

"Don't say that, Mama. You don't know what you're talking about."

Her mother sighed. "None of the boys at college were good enough for you. You wouldn't settle. A writer you had to be, a writer. So what did it get you?"

Judith didn't answer. Her mother took out a measuring tape and measured the sleeve of the baby's sweater. "When is he bringing back Melinda? To Vermont he had to take her? She could have stayed with us in Bayonne."

"He wants to take me to the Caribbean when I get out of here, Mother. Just the two of us. A real vacation."

"You'll quit the job?"

"No. Why would I do that? They'll give me a medical leave."

"Nobody asks me, so I don't say. But if somebody asked me, I'd tell her, who needs a job if she's got a man and a baby to take care of." Mrs. Winograd put down her knitting. She gave an anxious look toward the door. "When he gets upset with you, Judith, is it because of the job?"

She stared at her mother. "I like my job."

"Headstrong. Since a child you were headstrong."

"I'm getting a raise this year."

"Maybe if you were home when he needed you, he wouldn't find fault. It's unnatural to bring a little baby like that to an office."

"I like my job, I'm good at it. You never ask what I do in the office, Ma, you never cared enough to find out. I

138

help other people all day long. I take manuscripts that are maybe a B or a B-plus and I bring them up to A's. I shape the concept and bring up the colors in a half-formed piece of writing. I sense what kids want to read about, and I give it to them, in language they understand. It keeps me connected to the world of . . ." She wanted to say "literature," but it sounded so pedantic. She could see that her mother was not impressed.

"The girls who came to visit you from the office, they do what you do?"

"One of them does. The other one, I don't know if you met her, the other one is my boss."

"They're married, the girls in your office?"

"Those two aren't."

Mrs. Winograd's clicking needles picked up speed. She had ferreted out the significant information, arrived at the bottom line, and now it was time to pronounce the homily. Judith waited for the words.

"You make your bed and you lie in it."

APRIL 19, 1982

Barry unloaded a raft of travel folders from his briefcase and spread them out on the bed. He dug out a copy of *Frommer's Guide to the Caribbean* and the Sunday *Times* travel section. "You choose the island, Judith. The choice is yours, sweetheart."

"As long as it's got scuba and snorkeling," she teased.

"This is your vacation, baby. You're gonna rest, eat, sleep, and get some sun on your pretty face. And I'm going to be there for my honey and make the sweetest love to her she's ever had in her life. What do you think, Judith? A big fancy hotel with all the trappings, or do we rent a house? There are pros and cons each way."

"I'd be happy with anything that's on the beach. So

we can step out the door and be right at the ocean."
She picked up one of the brochures. "Tortola. Where's
that?"

He checked the *Frommer's.* "British Virgin Islands. You
fly from San Juan or Saint Croix. *Hey,* it's got great dive
sites. Judith, listen to this." He read her a passage from the
travel guide.

They decided on Tortola. It seemed fated. Her hand
had gone right to that brochure as if on a Ouija board, and
if it had good reefs Barry would be happy too.

"Barry, is this going to cost a fortune?" she asked.

He kissed her gently on the forehead in answer.

APRIL 20, 1982

Sally had just enough time for a quick visit to Judith
before she met a friend for dinner in the Village. She was
startled when she walked into Room 408. Judith was sitting in a chair, wearing an embroidered peach silk ki-
mono, and her hair was brushed and shining. The listless
patient who looked so defeated two days before had been
replaced by a glowing, confident woman who couldn't
stop chattering about the holiday she was going to take as
soon as the doctor said she was well enough to travel.

APRIL 24, 1982, MORNING

Joanne and Cindy Owens liked to book their hair ap-
pointments with Michel a half-hour apart on Saturday
morning. The Madison Avenue salon was at its liveliest
then, and the two sisters frankly enjoyed their bimonthly
foray into the unreal world of applied upper-echelon chic.
It was a sociological experience par excellence, and their

haircuts were smashing. Cindy had discovered Michel last year, and since then he had become the hottest hairdresser in town, a prince among the Andrés, Gregorys, Claudes, and Philippes who were slaves to the angularity of Vidal Sassoon. This morning the whiz with the scissors was running even later than usual, so there was plenty of time for a good gossip.

"Not only did she decide to stay with him," Joanne said. "She's convinced herself by now that the whole thing was an *accident*."

"Unbelievable. Jeff says he and Barry don't even speak anymore. He can't forgive him for what he did to Judith."

"None of us can forgive him, and all of us know it's going to happen again, except Our Lady of the Fractured Pelvis—that's what Sally Milton calls her."

"They won't go for therapy?"

"No, they're going to the Caribbean. They're going to talk things out and renew their understanding in the sun and sand. Melinda's staying with friends of theirs in Vermont. Sally wants to call the state adoption agency, or whomever you call, and report that their home isn't a safe environment for a child. Who knows what Melinda saw or heard that night? It could traumatize her for the rest of her life."

"Do babies retain such memories?"

"They do if they're Freudian babies."

"Joanne. Look over there. Isn't that Bianca Jagger?"

"Where?"

"I don't want to point. Over there. Kissing Michel."

"Oh, my God, you're right." The two women tried not to stare.

"Outside of the people in your office, do you think she has any real friends of her own?"

It took Joanne half a beat to figure out that her sister was referring to Judith Winograd. "She's pretty close with

141

some of her authors. They adore her. The male authors, at any rate. She doesn't really open up to women."

"I was just wondering."

APRIL 24, 1982, AFTERNOON

Gunther Heald was coming home from a dance class when he saw the couple from upstairs. He stood there transfixed. She was making her way up the brownstone stoop one step at a time with an aluminum walker, and he was unroping what looked like a ficus tree from the open trunk of a Volvo.

It was a cowardly thing to do, but Gunther turned on his heel and walked swiftly in the opposite direction.

Twenty minutes later, when he was sure that the coast was clear, Gunther came back and knocked on Mrs. Laemmerle's door.

"You missed all the excitement," she told him. "They're back."

Gunther went upstairs to his apartment. Ten days ago when he had called 911 in the middle of the night, he imagined that the cops were going to take Barry Kantor away in handcuffs. He and Jim had listened at the door and heard all the running up and down the stairs. The last thing he had expected was to see them together again.

MAY 9–MAY 16, 1982

The cottage Barry and Judith had rented sight unseen was on a picture-postcard beach called Cane Garden Bay. It was perfect. There were more than enough coconut palms and few enough sunbathers dotting the crescent-shaped white sand cove to restore anyone's faith in an unspoiled Caribbean paradise.

At the other end of the cove was a ramshackle hotel run by local people who brought in a calypso singer to entertain at dinner. They ate all their meals at the hotel for the first couple of days because Judith didn't feel strong enough to explore the rest of the island.

Barry rented a jeep for the week. That was how people got around on the island. Tortola was verdant and mountainous in the middle, with white sand inlets along the shoreline. Neither of them had seen anything like it. They established a simple routine. Barry would set Judith up on a blanket under their favorite coconut palm in the morning, slather her face, arms, and legs with sun block, make sure she put on her hat and had a long-sleeved shirt in her bag, and leave her with a book for a couple of hours while he swam or snorkeled. Afternoons they'd get into the jeep and try one of the other coves, or just stay put. Later in the week, when she felt a lot stronger, he made dinner reservations at various hotels and restaurants on the island. If the hotel had an interesting gift shop, he'd surprise her with a new bathing suit or a colorful muumuu or an oversized T-shirt that said DIVE BVI. He left her on her own only once, to go on an all-day dive at a place called Anegada Reef. She worried that she was cramping his style, but he told her no.

Toward the end of the week he coaxed her into the water. She was afraid she'd get toppled by a wave and do herself fresh damage, but he said, "Come on, it's like a warm bathtub out there, it'll be good for you." She put on her mask and fins, and he carried her past the breakers. Then they paddled out to the reef. True to his word, a few yards from shore there were brilliantly colored parrotfish, goatfish, angelfish, and schools of blue chromis. They were entranced by one pale-bodied fish that seemed to have a dippy smile. He'd seen it before, and took the snorkel out of his mouth to tell her it was either an ocean surgeon or a doctorfish. "Propitious," Judith said, shaking the water out of her tube. When she was floating alone she saw something that scared her. It was three feet long, needle-shaped, lethargic, and a brilliant chrome yellow. It looked like a painted stick, except it moved along the bottom coral and sucked smaller fish into its mouth. She found it later in the reef book. It was a common trumpetfish in its rare yellow phase. "I'm sort of sorry I saw it," she said to Barry.

On their last evening, when they were having dinner at a charming converted sugar mill they'd read about in the guidebook, they struck up a conversation with a couple at the next table. Except for waiters, she hadn't spoken to anyone but Barry all week. The couple told them they had two children who had stayed home in Detroit with their grandma. In turn Barry told them about Melinda and said she was adopted. Judith was surprised to hear him add that they both felt strongly about not having their own children when there were so many unfortunate kids who needed a good home. He told them he had had a vasectomy. That wasn't true. She had always believed she hadn't conceived with Barry because of her irregular ovulation, but she went along with him and got so vociferous in her arguments about Zero Population Growth and starving children in Ethiopia that the couple practically apologized for bringing two more babies into the world.

They returned to their cottage. "Barry," she sighed as she eased herself into a chair. Sudden motions still gave her pain. "Why can't we stay here forever?" There was so much she wanted to say to him, but she didn't know where to begin. "I feel so close to you," she whispered as she slipped off her sandals. "Closer than ever before."

He was standing in front of her, slowly unzipping his pants.

She looked up, startled. "Barry? The doctor said absolutely no sex until my next checkup."

"Just sit there, honey. Use your mouth."

The next morning they were at the tiny airport at nine a.m. for the flight home. Her face had good color, but nothing compared to Barry's. In one week he had acquired a perfect tan. At LaGuardia he put her in a taxi, gave the driver two twenties and an extra ten, more than twice the meter charges with a big tip, and told him to take the Williamsburg Bridge and to help the lady with the luggage at the other end. "Up the stairs," he said. He was sorry to leave her that way to fend for herself, but he had to drive straight to Vermont in the Volvo for the Hethingtons' trial. He said he'd be back in a couple of days with Melinda.

MAY 17–19, 1982

The trial was held in Federal District Court in Burlington, but not before the friendly judge Barry expected. Instead they had drawn the most hard-shelled judge in the district, Ralph Haywood, an Eisenhower appointee. Paul Scorvey, the lawyer Barry had brought in to represent Ellie as passive stand-in, said he was worried.

Barry and the Hethingtons decided to make the best of a bad situation by getting good and coked up before the ordeal began. The Hethingtons were astonished by their lawyer. He was into risk-taking far more than they were. When the judge declared a brief recess during jury selection, Barry and Don went to the men's room and did a few more lines. "I'll do a better job on the *voir dire*," he said. "Coke gives me a sixth sense, I'll be able to spot the hangmen a mile off." He felt the key to their trial was a sympathetic jury, but the native Vermont farmers were throwing him off stride. He couldn't read their opaque

145

faces. Somehow he had expected to find more hippie types on the rolls. Halfway through jury selection the judge told him he had used up all his peremptory challenges.

On the afternoon of the second day he was flying. During some technical testimony from a DEA chemist that the Hethingtons' confiscated marijuana crop was indeed *Cannabis sativa,* Barry bent down under the counsel table and pretended to search through some legal papers in his briefcase. Ellie knew what he was up to. He was scrounging around for the little bag of coke they had given him. He made a great show of putting a book in front of his face in order to have a private conversation with his clients. Behind the book he took the index finger he had dipped into the coke and rubbed it along his gums. The Hethingtons went along with the joke. If their lawyer was so out-and-out brazen, what did they have to fear?

Back at the Hethingtons' farmhouse that evening, Barry told them he was sure the assistant U.S. attorney was ready to make a deal with him on Ellie if Don would plead guilty to two charges. They asked him what that would mean in terms of Don's sentence, and he said he didn't know, he hadn't worked that part out. The Hethingtons freaked. Ellie accused him of going back on his word. He told them that was the deal all along, but Ellie said no, he had promised them Don would be able to cop to one charge, not two. He said, "You're out of your mind," and pulled Don aside. He said Ellie was a royal bitch, he didn't have to take any shit from her. "She's your wife, you handle her," he fumed. Don said that wasn't fair —after all, she'd been taking care of Melinda. He felt that everything was falling apart. Maybe trying to make a deal wasn't such a hot idea. They had gotten this far, maybe they'd get an acquittal. Barry told him he needed more coke. Don said he'd see what he could do, and went to his

146

studio in the old barn to get in a couple of hours of painting.

Next day, the jury stayed out for only an hour. Ellie was found guilty on one count of cultivation, and Don was found guilty on cultivation and on a second count of conspiracy as well. There was a gasp from their friends in the courtroom. The judge ordered a presentencing report and told them to be back in his court on June 14.

Melinda was in the last row of the courtroom with one of the Hethingtons' character witnesses. Barry picked up the baby and took her out to his car. He and Paul Scorvey drove back to New York that evening.

MAY–JUNE, 1982

When Judith came back to work, everyone at Claridge and Palmer noticed the difference in her. She kept the door to her office closed and refused invitations to go out to lunch. The secretaries who used to mind Melinda felt the rebuff most keenly. Sally told them to put themselves in Judith's shoes—wouldn't they feel enormously self-conscious if they suspected that all their colleagues were secretly replaying their own version of what happened?

Privately Sally had a lot of trouble coming to terms with her own feelings. She knew her reputation as the office radical—"Mother Bloor of the fourteenth floor" Harvey had called her when she tried to organize the department in that ill-fated union attempt—and she worried that Judith might be misinterpreting her interest as another of her political projects. It was bad form at Claridge to get overly involved in people's outside lives. In many respects Sally loved the civility of the place, the superficial friendliness that kept the wheels turning while they got out the

147

work, and the fact that almost no one ever got fired as long as they kept producing, but how her co-workers could just stand by while a human tragedy unfolded before their eyes was something she couldn't fathom.

Judith had shut her out totally and completely. When she suggested it might be fun to take a couple of tennis lessons together under the rooftop bubble at Manhattan Plaza, Judith said she didn't feel ready to pick up a racket again, and when she proposed they take in the new photography show at the Modern some afternoon on their lunch hour, Judith said she couldn't bear to fight her way through the crowds at the museum, it spoiled the experience for her so badly that she'd just as soon skip it if Sally didn't mind.

Sally did mind. She burned with humiliation, and then with anger. After a while she stopped asking.

Melinda wasn't coming to the office much anymore. Now that the baby had become a fast crawler, Judith had put her into one of those cooperative neighborhood nurseries run by parents.

Sally had no argument with that, but Joanne was appalled. "Between their two incomes, can't they hire a nanny?" she said. The two editors debated the matter at lunch in the new Japanese sushi place on Forty-sixth Street they'd been meaning to try. Joanne was adamant that Melinda would be better off at home with a full-time nanny, or if they wanted to save money, perhaps with a housekeeper who had some training in childcare. Sally felt the socializing experience of being exposed to a roomful of small children at an early age was infinitely preferable to being locked into a one-on-one with some poor exploited West Indian woman who'd be crawling the walls herself after a while. Joanne said it wasn't like

148

that at all—the women watched daytime television and got plenty of fresh air when they took the babies out in their strollers, certainly more than *they* did working for Claridge, where the windows didn't open. Sally said the women were still underpaid and exploited, even if they did get fresh air—if you could possibly call New York's polluted air "fresh"—and then she reminded Joanne that she had ducked the point about socializing with peers.

Joanne changed the subject. "Did you see Judith's memo about the astrology books?"

A piece of tuna slipped from Sally's chopsticks and splattered her soy sauce. "Say *wha'*?"

"Astrology books, you heard me the first time. She sent me a lengthy memo proposing a series of astrology books for preteens. It was embarrassing. She wants me to bring it up at the next editorial meeting."

"No kidding. What did it say?"

"She'd spent a lot of time on it, that was the awful thing. She'd figured out how to illustrate some of the covers. Let me see if I can remember this correctly. For Sagittarius she had a boy showing a girl how to shoot a bow and arrow, for Libra she had a girl reading a book—well, that's an obvious one—for Aquarius there was a boy doing a jackknife off a diving board."

"For Capricorn there was a girl milking a goat."

"Milking a goat? How strange. That's exactly what Harvey said when I showed him the memo. No, she didn't have an illustration for Capricorn."

"I can see why not. Taurus would be a little difficult too, I'd imagine. The bull. Joanne, it's an atrocious idea. We would never want to encourage young minds to believe in this flaky nonsense."

"*D'accord.* But she's so vulnerable these days, I don't know how to discourage her gently."

"Tell her it's brilliantly conceived but Claridge isn't ready for it yet."

"It's still a rejection, isn't it? Shall we order more tea?"

"I can drink gallons. Do you think they have anything for dessert besides green tea ice cream?"

"No. That's why they're all so thin."

"Sumo wrestlers aren't thin."

Joanne thought that over. There might be a book in it somewhere. Styles of sporting competitions around the world. Sumo wrestlers. Tractor pulls. Demolition derbies. No, not demolition derbies, too much destructive violence. Keep it upbeat and cute. Eskimos did weird things with ear-pulling contests. They still ran the bulls in Pamplona. She supposed that Africa was rife with unusual sports events. Perhaps she'd suggest it as a project for Judith, to get her mind off the Zodiac.

JUNE 14, 1982

Barry and Paul Scorvey drove up to Vermont for the Hethingtons' sentencing. This time they stayed in a hotel in Burlington. "The welcome mat may not be out at the farm," Barry joked to Paul.

Judge Haywood announced from the bench that he saw no reason for leniency in this case and he hoped the sentence would serve as a warning to others who thought they could flout federal law. Ellie got one year in prison, and Don got four. The defendants went numb; even the clerk of the court shook his head.

Ellie's older sister was in the front row as her family's sole representative. She sobbed aloud that she didn't know what she was going to tell Ellie's kids. Barry said he'd file an appeal immediately. The sister had a twenty-thousand-dollar bank check with her for bail money. She

150

wanted Ellie out tonight. He said he'd take care of it but she'd better sign the check over to him because the bail bondsman would only accept cash.

JUNE 24, 1982

Things came to a head in late June. The sales director called Harvey Erickson to ask what happened to the info sheets they were supposed to get for the sales meeting in Puerto Rico. A lot of them were incomplete or missing. And then Matt Melcher, who was putting the fall catalogue together, burst into Harvey's office waving some proofs. "You gave me two authors' names spelled wrong, Erickson. It's L-e-w on this one, not L-o-u, and he happens to spell his last name with two *n*'s, and there's no *e* in Joffry H. Hockinson. Look at this, you sent me copy that read J-e-f-f-r-e-y! If I didn't have a secretary with two kids who reads their books to her children, we never would have caught it. Do you know what it's going to cost to reshoot the catalogue pages?"

Harvey had a sick feeling in his stomach. They were both Judith's authors. The bound galleys of the Hockinson had just come in, he remembered they were in a pile on the floor near his desk. He looked at the cover, the title page, and the copyright data. Jeffrey H. Hockensen. He'd have to scrap them all. He buzzed his secretary to ask whether the Lewis Hermann was still in production, or had it gone to the printer? She came in ten minutes later to report that production hadn't seen the manuscript. As far as they knew, it was still on Judith Winograd's desk.

Harvey walked down the hall to Judith's office. She wasn't in. He remembered he'd told her she could work at home this week and take care of Melinda, who was down with the flu. The Hermann manuscript wasn't on

151

her desk or anywhere on her bookshelves. He dialed her at home and got no answer. Harvey sat down in Judith's chair. The empty playpen with the mobile of circus animals gave him a funny feeling. He was going to do something he despised himself for even contemplating. Open her desk drawers.

In the bottom left-hand drawer he found the Hermann, just as the author must have sent it six months before, to judge from the postmark. The padded Jiffy bag was still sealed.

"How do you want to handle it?" Harvey was leaning back in Joanne's visitor's chair; the evidence he had collected was on her desk. "I'll do it if it's awkward for you."

"No, it's something I have to do myself. I hired her." Joanne composed herself and called accounting. Her voice was firm. "Draw up a severance check for Judith Winograd," she said. "Two weeks' pay for each year, plus any vacation time outstanding. I don't think she's got any vacation days coming, but you might as well look. I want this strictly according to Hoyle."

Harvey whistled. "Two weeks for each year. Generous."

Joanne narrowed her eyes. Harvey Erickson was the most valuable member of her department; she knew he was gunning for her job. He could have gone over her head on this one, but he hadn't. Still, it wouldn't do to betray the slightest sense of uncertainty in handling the Winograd matter. Joanne went into gear.

"We'll reschedule the Hermann. I'll call him and tell him the bad news, say we're repositioning him as the lead book for next fall. You handle the damage control with sales and Matt Melcher. I'll reach Judith at home and have her come in. Face to face. I owe her that."

When Harvey left her office, the first thing Joanne did was call her sister. Naturally Cindy was out on assignment, but it made Joanne feel better to touch base with someone she trusted, even if it was only through the medium of a harassed assistant city editor who hated to take a message.

JUNE 25, 1982, MORNING

Judith's face was impassive as Joanne handed her the envelope. She hates me, Joanne thought.

"I still think you're one of our best line editors, and I'd be happy to say that in a recommendation."

There was no answer from the woman who sat staring at her across the desk.

"You know how much proofreading and indexing we farm out. I'd be glad to put you at the top of the list. Why don't you drop Sally a note when you're ready to think about working again, or better yet, stop by and have a chat with her or Harvey on your way out."

"Thank you," Judith said. "I don't think I'll be working on other people's things for a while. Perhaps I'll get back to my novel."

Joanne stood up to indicate that the distasteful interview was over. Judith took her cue.

"I suppose I can't get unemployment since technically I'm resigning instead of being fired." She had started off bravely, intending to make it a little tough for Joanne, but she choked on her words when she got to "fired."

"Personnel tells me you'll have no trouble collecting. They prefer that we do it this way."

"I see."

Joanne ushered her to the door. "Take care of yourself, Judith," she said. "I'm concerned about you—we all are. Keep in touch."

153

"Oh, yes." She ignored Joanne's outstretched hand.

Well, she didn't make it easy for me, Joanne thought. Or for herself either. Harvey was right. It was better to duck these unpleasant confrontations if one possibly could.

Judith walked down the empty hall to her office. Everyone's door was closed—she could imagine the secretaries all huddled in the ladies' room. They preferred not to be present at her funeral. She supposed she ought to clean out her desk, pack up, and take home the personal stuff. It was surprising how much junk accumulated in an office in three and a half years. Her nail kit in the middle drawer, the folding umbrella, her white summer sweater to ward off the air-conditioning chills, last winter's boots with the broken zipper. Books. The ones she always meant to take home.

She had never gone in much for personalizing her work space, thank God. Claridge and Palmer was the first and only steady office job she'd ever had; she was amazed how the others dug in and built their retreats, like bowerbirds. Harvey's desk featured a precise arrangement of antique toys that he'd collected on his travels, Sally had her changing gallery of political posters—her recent addition, a Sandinista with a rifle, had inspired some comment—and Joanne, of course, had her crystal bowl of flowers on a low coffee table in front of the executive sofa with the needlepoint throw pillows. At least Joanne had the decency not to make her sit on the sofa while she made her speech about editorial responsibility. A firing squad is a firing squad, better to take it in a straight-backed chair. She should have asked for a blindfold. That would have thrown Joanne off stride.

The thing was to get out quickly. Do it and be done with it. Creep down the hall, sneak past Reception, and hope the elevator came fast.

Maybe it was all a bad dream. Maybe Joanne only meant to frighten her, shock her into the realization that she was taking her responsibilities a little too cavalierly, even for Claridge. She'd fucked up royally, granted, but look what she'd done for them before this bad spell!

Maybe she'd go home and in a day or two there'd be a call. Come back, we need you, we miss you, who else can edit the Roughrider Boys series? Your authors are clamoring for you, they signed a petition.

Her authors. She'd have to write letters to her favorites. She'd have to call Bob Rothman and a few others herself. Bob wouldn't believe it, wouldn't believe they could do it to her. After three and a half years.

Judith looked down at Melinda's playpen. She carefully unscrewed the clamp on the mobile. Melinda loved the mobile. Then, just as carefully, she screwed the clamp back on. Better to leave it. Leave everything. Let them tell Maintenance or the night cleaning woman, or whosever job it was, to clear out Judith Winograd's effects. Let the goddamn playpen stand as a reproach for a few days. They'd forget her soon enough.

She put a few yellow legal pads and a box of Claridge and Palmer pencils into a large interoffice envelope, slung her pouch bag over her shoulder, and closed the door behind her.

Finis. -30- The End.

JUNE 25, 1982, AFTERNOON

Marianna's taxi pulled up in front of the house just as the ditz next door was going up the brownstone steps. "Yoo-hoo," she called. "Hold the door for me, will you?"

The ditz heard her all right, but she pretended not to, so Marianna called out again. "I need help with my bag. Just stay there and hold the door open."

Judith stayed there while Marianna got a receipt from the cab driver and hauled her coffee-colored leather suitcase up the steps.

"Three flights to go. Whew," Marianna said, tossing her blond mane. "No rest for the weary. It was murder on the expressway, let me tell you."

Her neighbor didn't answer, so Marianna kept talking, although she knew she should save her breath for the stairs. "I just came back from the most fantastic assignment. We creamed the other networks, I had all the hostages sewn up. You've been following that bank robbery in Duluth, where the gunmen kept the tellers and two vice-presidents locked in the vault all week? It's been the lead story every night. Well, anyway, I got an exclusive on the hostages when they came out. Don't ask me how, that's little Marianna's secret, but they spoke for our cameras and for nobody else. One of the tellers, you wouldn't believe it. She fell in love with the younger gunman. Wants to attend his trial. A classic case of the Stockholm syndrome. You *did* read about that, didn't you, it was in the *New Yorker* a few years ago. Where the victims identify with their captors, sort of like what happened to Patty Hearst? Of course Patty came to her senses and reversed herself later on. I imagine they all do eventually. Anyway, 'Tell him I'll wait for him,' she says to my reporter while the videocam is rolling. Only a woman!"

They had reached the third-floor landing. While Marianna located her key in her pocketbook, Judith unlocked 3-A across the hall. She hasn't said a word, Marianna thought. And I'm so keyed up I'm speeding.

"Shouldn't you be at Claridge and Palmer?" Marianna asked with what she hoped was an appropriate show of interest. "I'm so dog-tired I forgot it's the middle of the afternoon."

"I'm working at home this week."

156

"What luxury! If I could ever manage to work at home! But then I wouldn't be in television, would I? There's such a different pace in books. Well, I know what I'm going to do right now. Take a steaming hot bath with half a gallon of Badedas. They call it Vitabath in the States, but I pick mine up in Europe. Short of Valium, it's the best thing to calm your nerves. If you haven't tried it, I recommend it without reservation. You might even throw a capful in the tub for Melinda, although now that I think about it, what do babies have to be nervous about? It's all eat, sleep, and elimination, isn't it?"

She waited while Judith struggled to make a response.

My God, Marianna thought, he's always going for the jugular, and she's practically catatonic. They must be a barrel of fun at a dinner party.

JUNE 25, 1982, EVENING

Bob Rothman came over as soon as she called. The three of them—she, Barry, and Bob—had a funereal dinner. Barry gave her some Percodans to see if they'd numb the psychological pain, but nothing could lighten her mood. Even Melinda was very subdued.

"Look at it this way," Bob said. "You've been wanting to get back to your novel."

"Yeah, that's what I told Joanne Owens."

"So?"

"So nothing. I'm not a novelist, Bob." She looked at Barry and made a face. "I'm a forty-year-old unemployed children's book editor who was fired for fucking up on the job. *Goddamn them,* they did it a week before my birthday." She started to sniffle.

"You're also a mother, sweetheart," Barry said, stroking her cheek.

157

"Right. I'm a mother."

"Don't say 'right' that way, Judith. Get your priorities straight. I'll go up there and break their kneecaps for them if you give me the word, but let's discuss this rationally. Big deal, they gave you a lofty title, but how much were you taking home? Rothman, you know the publishing business, it stinks. I wouldn't get out of bed to represent a subway flasher at his arraignment for what she took home at the end of the month. They never appreciated her in that office. Tell him about the astrology series, Jude. She came to them with a brilliant proposal last month—I helped her with the concept—and they shot her down. I'll tell you the real reason they let her go, Rothman. Because she was head and shoulders ahead of them in the brains department, and it bugged them. Listen, it's not such a tragedy. I know someone in this house who's going to be mighty happy that the sun doesn't rise and set anymore on Claridge and Palmer."

The baby was at Barry's feet, sitting quietly. Judith got down on the floor and hugged her hard. Melinda yelped and reared back.

"Oh, shit."

"You scared her for a second, that's all. She's touchy. Go get her some cornflakes." He rubbed the baby's neck.

Judith came back from the kitchen with a single-portion box of dry cereal and put it on the floor. The baby poked her fingers happily into the flakes.

Barry turned to Bob. "She takes everything personally."

"Which one?"

"Both of them. I'm living with two prima donnas, if you didn't notice. One's a blondie, the other's going a little grey."

Judith flinched.

"I like it, hon, I like it. Did you hear me say I didn't like

158

it, Rothman? She thinks she's fooling me with that Clairol junk she slops on her head." He grinned and got up to put in another cassette. "Early Beatles. Boot."

Bob nodded and turned back to Judith. "Listen, Jude," he said. "The thing is not to lose momentum. Promise me you'll call Macmillan first thing Monday morning."

"No." She stood up. "Barry's right. I'm finished with the straight world. I'm finished with their fucking hypocrisy, with the pretense that they're one big happy corporate family of thin, well-exercised superachievers who just adore each other and who *love* their authors and who, who . . . aren't getting a day older. I never fit in there, I could feel they were talking about me behind my back. Why do you think I put on that Clairol slop, as he so charmingly calls it? Because one day out of the blue Harvey Erickson said to me—he's Joanne's lackey, he thinks he's in line for her job—one day he says, *dig this*, 'The grey isn't becoming on you, Judith. It looks good on Joanne, but not with your type of frizz.' Like they had been discussing it at a meeting."

The phone rang, and she went over to answer it. "Oh. Yes. Well, I have company over." She got off as soon as she could. "Sally Milton. She claims she didn't find out until five p.m., after I'd gone. Do you believe that? If you believe that, I can sell you the Brooklyn Bridge."

She burst into tears.

JULY–SEPTEMBER 1982

The summer went by for Judith in a haze. She took Melinda out of the cooperative nursery. Barry and she agreed that the childcare and home responsibilities were now primarily hers because she wasn't bringing in a salary. If he was going to support her like a husband—a relationship both of them had pridefully avoided since the day she moved in, but one he was prepared to accept until she got back on her feet—she had to fulfill her domestic obligations. They both freely acknowledged that housekeeping wasn't her strong suit, but she was actively looking forward to being a full-time mother to Melinda. It would give her invaluable hands-on expertise, she told Bob Rothman, if and when she did try to get another job in children's books. And of course, it wouldn't look bad on her résumé either. Lots of career women were quitting their jobs to stay home with their children during the formative years, she'd just read a long piece about it in the *Times*.

During her first month of unemployment she wrote down lists of all the things she loved about New York but never had time to do because she was working or she was too tired at night. She took Melinda uptown by subway to the Metropolitan Museum, and when that went well, to the Guggenheim and the Whitney. She was surprised by the number of mothers with infants who rode the subway during the day, most of them black or Puerto Rican. The narrow circuit she had grown used to—Greenwich Village to Claridge and Palmer to Greenwich Village—was nearly all white. She and Melinda came home from their excursions on the Fifth Avenue bus, which was a lot more convenient than the Lexington IRT once the right bus came along. When it did, they had door-to-door service.

Barry told her about the TKTS booth on the little island in the middle of the traffic above Times Square. If she got there by three p.m., she could get half-price orchestra seats the same night to practically any show on Broadway. She overdid it the first month. She and Barry saw *Annie, Sugar Babies,* and Lena Horne. When she said she was going to try for the Japanese Kabuki at Lincoln Center and what night did he want to go, he warned her to slow down and save something for August.

She got a rude shock when she went down with Melinda to file for unemployment insurance. The claims investigator told her she wasn't eligible because she had voluntarily resigned, but she could appeal the ruling and demand a hearing if she wished. It happened all the time, he said, and the claimant generally won. The idea of a hearing was so abhorrent to her that she waived her claim. The investigator said that if she took on some free-lance assignments or got a temporary job in her field, she could establish a new base year and make her eligibility that way. She thanked him for his advice. "It's the law," he shrugged.

Barry was furious with her when she told him about waiving her claim. He said he'd represent her at the hearing and shoot those assholes out of the water. She didn't want to upset him further, so she told him she'd go back to the New Claims section and start over again. She never did, and he seemed to forget about it.

One nice thing had happened at the unemployment office. She'd run into her downstairs neighbor Gunther Heald on line. He was "between shows," he told her, that was the actors' euphemism for "out of work." She loved the phrase and said she'd use it whenever she ran into somebody she knew. "I'm between shows," she said with a grin. "Terrific!" Gunther inquired after Barry and admired Melinda in her stroller. He said he'd be happy to do some free babysitting if she gave him enough advance notice. He'd grown up in a houseful of kids back in Minnesota.

Usually when she needed a sitter she called a student service that was semiofficially connected to NYU, but their rates had just gone up, and she was beginning to worry about money. Gunther would be ideal if he really meant what he said. He was much friendlier than Jim, the man he lived with. Melinda could be parked downstairs in their apartment if that wouldn't upset Jim, whom she considered prissy. But when she told Barry about Gunther Heald and the free babysitting offer, his reaction was sour.

"What do you want to involve the neighbors in our lives for?" he scoffed. "The walls are thin enough, let them pick up their gossip that way." That made her blush. She wondered what the neighbors did hear when she and Barry had one of their fights. She hoped they were sound sleepers. Anyway, she wasn't going to dwell on it. He had been altogether sweet to her since April. The bad days were behind them.

Melinda was approaching her first birthday. Whatever they and the cooperative nursery had been doing was obviously right. So much for the mystique of childcare! The baby was eating with a spoon nicely, if messily, and could handle a cup at least some of the time without spilling. Usually they fed her little bits from their dinner, a few pieces of cooked carrot, a bite of chopped meat, a stringbean or two, some slices of apple without the peel. They didn't sweat it. If she didn't want to eat, okay. Mashed potatoes were a big winner with both of them, father and daughter, but it was her job to clean up the gobs that landed on the floor and the wall.

Melinda had also learned to stagger around the apartment clutching at the sofa and chairs in something approximating a walk. Barry was tickled that she was an early walker. "You know she's going to be verbal," he told her, "but the kids who really succeed in life are the golden ones with great physical coordination." He wanted an athletic child, he said. A ballerina in high school and an equestrienne at college. She puzzled over that one. Both of them had gone to city schools. Obviously Melinda was headed straight for out-of-town prep school and the Ivy League.

Since the weather was so glorious and it stayed light for so long, the three of them went to Washington Square

162

Park when Barry came home in the afternoon. Some parts of the park were a little hairy. The great liberal battles against police brutality in the sixties had left a curious legacy twenty years later. Once upon a time the cops arrested folksingers who gathered around the fountain, and charged them with loitering or disturbing the peace. Now a different kind of music prevailed unchecked. Acoustic guitars had given way to bongo drums and blaring transistor radios.

"It's all rather jungly," she said to Barry, adding that she hoped she wasn't becoming a racist just because she had turned forty. The noise was deafening, and whites were definitely a minority. In her day the fountain had been a rendezvous for the A-trainers from Harlem and the bagel babies from Brooklyn. She supposed there was a time in her life when she qualified as a bagel baby, but it seemed so very long ago. Now it was all A-trainers, as far as she could make out, and the beautiful white marble arch, a copy of the Arc de Triomphe, was a mass of graffiti. It made her want to go back and reread Henry James— *Washington Square,* of course, but also *The Bostonians,* with its description of wood paling, grass-plats, and plashing fountains. The fountain in the Washington Square Park that she knew hadn't "plashed" in a long time.

Another great liberal battle had been fought and won against bus traffic going through the arch. In the long run, what had the liberals gained? Now there was drug traffic. Like the music, it was unchecked. Sinister-looking types hissed "sens, sens" at them on every path. It made her laugh. They had better sinsemilla at home than these guys ever smoked.

"We ought to work out a deal with them," she said to Barry one day when she was feeling merry. He wasn't amused. For as long as she'd known him he'd done a little dealing here and there, as a favor to friends. Once he told her it had put him through law school, but then the next

163

day he said he was kidding, hadn't she learned yet when he was pulling her leg? Lately there had been larger quantities of grass and coke in the apartment than ever before. It was something she didn't ask about.

"You're stupid, Judith, you know that?" he said when she made her crack about dealing with the sellers in the park. She winced. Her comment *had* been stupid. But his irritation vanished in a minute or two, so she hadn't spoiled the day.

Usually when they took Melinda to the park they stayed near the swings. By some unwritten law that the druggies respected, that was still the family section. She tried not to be nervous when Barry put the baby in one of the old-fashioned seats with the metal crossbar and gave her a push. "Whee," she'd say with her heart in her mouth, "whee, look at Melinda!" She thought the baby was too young to go sailing through the air like that, but Melinda was a daredevil just like he was; she loved getting pushed and wasn't afraid of heights.

Some evenings Barry didn't come home after work. He went straight from the office to City Island, where he kept his boat. Weekends she packed a lunch, and the three of them drove out to the Whaler. Barry took them for a cruise in the Sound, or went down the East River through Hell Gate, back up the Harlem, and into the Hudson. Then they'd cruise the length of Manhattan Island to the Battery, circle the Statue of Liberty, and go back the way they came.

The Whaler was fast. Barry loved to chase the Circle Liners and leave them behind in his wake, or cut across their stern, drenching the three of them with salt spray. "What's the matter, Judith?" he'd say when she grabbed for a towel. "You're losing your capacity to have fun, you're becoming a stick-in-the-mud."

Her stomach began tightening the minute she got on

the boat, and it wasn't only because she got seasick from the rocking, the noise of the outboard, and the smell of gasoline. She could never do anything right on the Whaler. She couldn't remember when to unsnap the canvas awning, where to sit for ballast, or whether he wanted a beer or a Perrier from the ice chest. Her hands were full with Melinda, and on top of that she had to deal with her nausea. She tried to anticipate his needs, but at least once on every outing he accused her of sabotaging the day.

She developed a morbid fear that Melinda was going to fall over the edge and drown or get cut to ribbons on the outboard's propellers. It was utterly irrational, he told her she was getting phobic, but that was how she felt. To calm her, he rigged Melinda out in an infant's life preserver with an elaborate harness, but it didn't make her feel any safer. She preferred it when Barry and Melinda went off without her. That way her anxiety was less specific, although she didn't have any peace of mind until they returned.

One day he told her he was tired of powerboats and was going to switch to sails. He had a line on a twenty-three-foot Seasprite with a fiberglass hull. She shuddered. From what she'd heard about sailboats, she was terrified that she'd fail miserably if she had to play first mate.

SEPTEMBER 11, 1982

Goldie and Max came into Manhattan for Melinda's first birthday party. Barry and Judith were holding the festivities at six p.m. on Saturday evening, one day after the real date, because the Winograds had gotten the four of them tickets to a matinee performance of *Cats*. News of the spectacular English musical, which had been such a hit in London, had even reached Bayonne. Barry hated ma-

165

tinees, but Judith didn't have the heart to tell her parents.

Just as she expected, Barry was bored to tears by the show, and so was she. Her parents came home with them afterward and waited downstairs while Judith picked Melinda up at Gunther and Jim's apartment—Barry had reconsidered Gunther's offer since, as he put it, the price was right. Then they took the birthday girl for a walk through the Village. Max went ahead with Barry, who let him wheel the stroller.

Goldie said she couldn't believe all the changes in the neighborhood. Judith involuntarily winced. They went through exactly the same conversation every time her parents came for a visit.

"Sutter's has been gone for years, Ma. We use Jon Vie on Sixth Avenue."

"What could be as good as Sutter's? What happened, they lost their lease?"

"I don't know." She showed her mother the community garden on the site of the old Women's House of Detention. Goldie did not look impressed. Her parents had slowed down a lot in the last few years, the pace of the walk was excruciating. Barry must be going out of his mind, she thought.

"You're not touching up your hair anymore, Judith? It doesn't look good, the grey."

She held her tongue. Her mother still went for her weekly shampoo and set at a neighborhood place where every six weeks she had them "put in the blond." It seemed to Judith that her own hair had given up the fight to stay brown the minute she left Claridge and Palmer. She'd let it go for the summer, but even if she wanted to do something about it, it was beyond the covering power of Clairol's Loving Care. She'd have to investigate some serious dyes.

They were back on Waverly Place. Mrs. Laemmerle opened her door when they started to climb the stairs, and Judith introduced her ground-floor neighbor to her parents. Barry glowered when she invited her to come up later for a piece of Melinda's birthday cake.

Bob Rothman, the only nonfamily guest, arrived with a bottle of wine for dinner and a beautifully wrapped present for Melinda. Judith served a casserole from a Claridge and Palmer cookbook. It had chopped meat and macaroni in it, so it made a fine meal for the birthday girl too.

"What do you call this, Judith?" her father asked. "It's got a foreign taste."

"Pastitsio, Daddy, it's Greek."

Her father raised his eyebrows.

"Max is reserving his judgment, Goldie, but you're adventurous," Barry chimed in with a laugh.

Judith noticed that Barry was hitting the wine pretty hard. She was grateful that Bob had brought only one bottle.

Gunther and Jim came up for birthday cake and coffee. It was the first time Jim had been in their apartment. He made a big to-do over the better view one flight up, and sighed that they probably got more sunlight in the morning too. They agreed all around that their apartments were dark, except for the front rooms, which got two hours of sun in the morning.

Judith brought out a pink iced cake with one candle. They all sang "Happy Birthday," and Max put Melinda on his lap and helped her blow out the candle. The baby stuck her finger in the icing, and everyone applauded.

Then they opened the presents. A hooded pink snowsuit one size too large ("She'll grow into it") from Max and Goldie, ABC building blocks from Barry, a pail and shovel from Bob, Play-Doh from Judith, and a wooden pull-train from Gunther and Jim that became Melinda's instant favorite.

167

"Nobody got her a doll," Bob observed. "Do you think that's because of women's liberation?"

Just then there was a knock on the door. It was Mrs. Laemmerle with an antique doll—from her own collection, she said. She didn't understand why they all burst out laughing.

MARCH 1983

Barry's pro forma appeal to the Second Circuit Court in New York on behalf of the Hethingtons had been turned down. He wasn't surprised, he told Paul Scorvey, and put the matter out of his mind.

But he was very surprised a few months later when he learned that Ellie's father had hired a new lawyer in Burlington, a former prosecutor who was making a good name for himself handling court-assigned cases. The Burlington lawyer went back into Federal District Court before the Eisenhower appointee and filed new papers. He requested that the Hethingtons' original conviction be overturned and that the defendants be granted a new trial on the grounds of ineffective assistance of counsel. He had sworn affidavits from the Hethingtons that the chief counsel of record, Barry Kantor, had been high on cocaine during the trial.

Barry learned about the new motions when the assistant U.S. attorney called to ask whether he wanted to appear as a government witness. That was standard procedure in an ineffective-assistance-of-counsel hearing.

"Not particularly," he said to his former adversary.

The prosecuting attorney laughed and said, "I guess we can manage without you."

Marianna went to bed with a cold on Friday evening, intending to stay put all weekend. Sunday was Easter. At least her system had collapsed over a long slow-news weekend when the only filmable story was the Pope blessing the faithful in St. Peter's Square. Of course, since the Agca assassination attempt in '81, you couldn't take anything for granted.

She felt perfectly miserable and alone. Almost everyone she knew had gone out of town. She ordered enough groceries and boxes of Kleenex to last through the siege, and had the liquor store send up a bottle of brandy. After making herself a cup of hot tea with brandy, lemon, and honey, she got under the covers and had turned out the lights by ten p.m.

In her dream she was in a Venetian gondola, gliding down a silent canal. She was looking for the house of Marco Polo. The gondola maneuvered through a narrow passage. It was dark, past midnight, and the only sound besides the *whop, whop* of the oar hitting the water was a boatman's answering cry in the distance. *Oooray. Oooray, oooray.*

The cries were growing more insistent. *Oooray.* Her boatman waved his oar frantically—there had been a collision.

Marianna bolted upright and snapped on the light. The sound was coming from across the hall. A pitiful, wailing, shrieking *oh, oh, oh.* Over and over.

She checked the time. Four a.m. Briefly she considered putting on her bathrobe and going across the hall to knock on their door.

What would she say?

She could say she heard a cry for help and wondered if the baby was ill. Would they like her to call a doctor?

They'd see through that in a minute.

She could say she woke up from a nightmare and heard the noise and—

Goddammit, she could say she heard a bloodcurdling scream that sounded like someone was getting murdered.

Did she have the nerve? No, that was not the issue. The issue was, did she have the *right* to interfere like that?

Marianna went to the door and listened.

Silence.

She stood there for eight minutes, counting to herself, just like that crazy time in the videotape room fifteen years ago when she forgot her stopwatch and was too ashamed, too embarrassed, to tell the engineer. Seven thousand fifty-eight, seven thousand fifty-nine, eight thousand.

Whatever duet in hell they were playing across the hall had stopped.

Marianna padded back to the bedroom, crawled under the covers, and willed herself to fall asleep.

She slept late on Saturday morning, then got up and made herself a cup of tea. English Breakfast. It was quiet across the hall. Too quiet?

This is ridiculous, she told herself crossly. They've got you so discombobulated you've begun to think bizarre is normal and normal is bizarre.

She called the assignment desk just to hear a friendly human voice. Bernie Hopper picked up the phone. He told her all was quiet on the western and eastern fronts, and ditto for the north and south borders. "Bring me a ham on rye and a news story," he kidded. "We may have to lead tonight with the weather."

"Yeah, well, I got a battered-woman case across the hall. Want a live actuality? I can put my Sony under the door and get some wild sound, but I don't know what we'd do for cover shots."

He laughed and told her they hadn't sunk that low. They could always do a feature on the bear cage in Central Park.

"Call again," he said as he hung up. "I'm bored and lonely too."

It started again in the evening. The *whop, whop* that sounded like oars hitting the water, and the muffled scream.

She paced the floor, debating with herself again about whether she had a right to interfere. How did she know if the loonytoon across the hall wanted help or not? She tried calling three friends to discuss the ethical situation with them, but nobody was home. It was just as well, she'd sound like a fool if she tried to explain that she was spending the Easter weekend with her ear to the door listening for sounds of Venetian boatmen.

Off the deep end, Marianna!

She made another hot toddy and got into bed with *Time, House and Garden,* and *Architectural Digest.* An old Carole Lombard movie was on the tube. She turned up the volume, convincing herself that her ears were stuffed up from her cold.

Late Sunday night she finally reached the Laughlins. Bill commiserated about her sniffles and put Maria on the phone.

"You'd think I'd be deaf to it by now," she told Maria, "but it sounds different than it used to. In the good old days they shouted at each other—a lot of name calling and abusive language. I figured she was giving as good as she was getting. This is qualitatively different, I don't know if I can explain."

"There's a child in the house, right? How old?"

"Oh, you know me, I'm so bad about children's ages. Wait a minute, let me figure it out. It was a newborn just before I went to China, when was that? Oh, the little girl must be about a year and a half. Why? You don't think he's beating the kid, do you?"

"I don't know what to think, Marianna, it's not unheard of. But if you're as upset as you sound, I think you have to do something for your own peace of mind."

"You mean move back uptown."

"In this real estate market? I was thinking of something a little more practical and short-range, like calling the child welfare department. Marianna—whatever you do, don't knock on their door. Promise me. He's liable to bop you over the head and drag you in there."

"Oh, pooh, I'm not his type."

"I'm glad to see you've still got your sense of humor. Listen, Bill has to use the phone. You're a resourceful person, scout around for the proper agency to call, and do it first thing Monday morning. I wish I could remember the number I saw in the subway. Some twenty-four-hour abuse hotline."

"I don't ride the subway."

"I didn't think you did."

Marianna got out the White Pages and the Yellow Pages. God, when she was starting out in TV as a talk-show booker, she could locate the private telephone number of any celebrity in fifteen minutes flat. How did you find the number to call for child abuse?

Her fingers were all thumbs. She was shaking. In the front of both directories was a toll-free number for reporting child abuse and maltreatment. She dialed and got a recorded announcement saying all available lines were busy but please stay on, her call would be handled in sequence. Where was she calling? Some central clearinghouse in Arizona?

She hung up, composed herself, and dialed again.

This time she got no answer.

She dialed a third time, and an operator said, "New York State Hotline."

"I want to report a suspected case of neglect." Why had she said neglect? She meant to say abuse, mayhem, horror. "I have reason to believe a child in my building is being ill cared for."

Marianna reeled off the name, address, and apartment number. "I hear terrible sounds of crying," she whispered. "All the time."

The calm female voice at the other end double-checked city and borough, and asked for her name and telephone number. Marianna was unprepared for the question.

"*My* name?" she asked. "What do you need my name for? Where is your switchboard located?"

"You don't have to give us your name," the voice said reassuringly. "You're calling Albany. We telecopy the information to Special Services for Children in New York. Some people like to get a confirmation of the investigation."

"Will there be an investigation?"

"Oh, yes."

"And the child will be removed from the home if the parents are found unfit?"

173

"There are many intermediate steps, but—"

"That will be sufficient," Marianna said, clicking off.

APRIL 7, 1983

The young caseworker who got the assignment was surprised. Waverly Place near Washington Square Park was a beautiful block. She wished she could afford an apartment on a tree-lined Village street.

This was a low-priority complaint, probably nothing to it. An anonymous neighbor had heard a child crying. Maybe people who lived in fancy brownstones weren't used to hearing kids cry.

Eileen Wilmott found a telephone listing for Kantor and placed her call, taking care to identify herself properly. Most people were unfamiliar with "SSC," Special Services for Children; even the police still said "BCW," for their old name, Bureau of Child Welfare. On top of that, the newspapers decided to call them "HRA," for Human Resources Administration, the new umbrella agency under the mayor's reorganization plan. It made her life more difficult.

A low female voice told her to call back after six p.m. That made her a little suspicious, but when she called back, a man said, "Come right over."

That was yesterday, and here she was, by appointment. She rang the bell for Apartment 3-A, announced, "Eileen Wilmott, SSC," and was buzzed in.

A large dark-haired man with a mustache and glasses was waiting at the door with a child in his arms, a radiant, chubby little girl in a polo shirt and denim coveralls.

"Say hello to Miss Wilmott, Melinda. She's here to see that you're not neglected."

" 'El-lo," the child said. " 'El-lo. Daddy see ball?"

"We were looking for her ball before you buzzed." The

174

man smiled the proud smile of a father who knows his child is a charmer. "Melinda, where did you throw your ball?"

"Down, Daddy," the child said. "Down."

"You want to get down and look for your ball?" The father gently put his daughter on her feet and watched her fondly as she toddled into the living room. Eileen Wilmott observed the plant-filled front windows; the long room was immaculate except for some children's toys that were lying about. Building blocks, a gaily painted rocking horse, a wooden pull-train.

"Here ball!" The little girl clutched a red rubber ball in her hands and presented it to the caseworker with a beatific smile.

"What a lovely child," Eileen Wilmott said. "How old is Melinda?"

"One year and seven months."

"Remarkable."

"We think so. I'm sorry my wife isn't here for your visit. Her mother was hospitalized this morning with an ear infection. Judith felt she ought to be there."

"Of course." My kind of man, she thought. Rumpled, bearish, a bit of a potbelly, obviously sensitive, and *physical*—why are men like that always taken? She cleared her throat. "You understand that once a complaint is made, by law we must follow through. I don't write the rules, I just carry them out."

"Certainly. That's the meaning of bureaucracy." He flashed her a warm, sympathetic smile. "Paperwork, tell me about it. I put in a stint at the welfare department before I entered law school."

"You're an attorney?"

He nodded. "My wife is an author of children's books. There's one of them on the table. She uses a professional name."

"Yes, I saw the name on the mailbox."

"She works at home. Melinda is never unattended."

"Of course not!" For a moment Eileen Wilmott forgot the purpose of her visit. The child snuggled into her father's lap.

"Mr. Kantor, do you mind if I take a peek into the kitchen? It's one of those rules."

"Melinda, let's show Miss Wilmott the kitchen."

They let the eager child lead the way.

Feeling altogether foolish, the caseworker opened the refrigerator. Her eyes swept over the half-gallons of milk and orange juice, the carcass of a roasted turkey covered in cling wrap, a large jar of Skippy peanut butter, two kinds of jelly, a loaf of pumpernickel and another of whole wheat, a dozen eggs, a quart of cottage cheese, a head of lettuce, Entenmann's chocolate cupcakes, a bowlful of grapes.

"Miss Wilmott is worried that you're not getting enough to eat, Melinda."

"Oh, no, really I—"

He lit a cigarette. "May we know who made the complaint, Miss Wilmott?"

"I couldn't tell you even if I were allowed to by law. Look, I—I'm sorry to have caused you a disagreeable experience. I don't want to take up any more of your time."

She picked up her briefcase and held out her hand.

"Bye-bye," the little girl cooed without being prompted. "Bye-bye."

As she was leaving the building, a tenant on the ground floor opened her door and peeked out. Collateral interviews, the caseworker suddenly remembered—she was supposed to ring a few bells and talk with some neighbors. But really, this thing had gone far enough. The old crone was probably the person who had placed the anonymous call.

Eileen Wilmott wrote up her report that night. "Child

is extraordinarily precocious and evinces no sign of neglect. Happy home environment. Father unusually cooperative. *Amply* stocked refrigerator." She underlined "amply" three times.

The Kantor neglect case was marked "Unfounded." By law, all details of the investigation were expunged from the records.

MAY 1983

The Federal District Court judge in Burlington heard oral arguments from the Hethingtons' new lawyer. Ellie and Don took the witness stand and described how their previous counsel had sneaked cocaine into the courthouse and gotten high during their trial.

Cross-examination by an amused assistant U.S. attorney was brief. Barry Kantor did not appear as a government witness.

From the tenor of his questioning, it was clear that Judge Haywood could not believe that prior counsel's shenanigans had occurred in his court. He seemed personally affronted by the argument that Ellie and Don were denied their constitutional right to a fair trial in a case over which he had presided.

An enterprising reporter for the *Burlington Free Press* called lawyer Barry Kantor in New York for a comment. His printable comment was that the woods were full of disgruntled clients, they were as common as maple trees. The Hethingtons, he said, were simply trying to get out of serving their time in jail.

The reporter threw him a surprise question. What did he know about the missing bail bond money? Had he absconded with twenty thousand dollars that was intended to serve as Ellie Hethington's bail?

He replied that the bail bond was a figment of someone's imagination. The sister had paid him money due on his retainer, this was the first he'd ever heard about bail.

Shortly afterward Judge Haywood handed down his opinion. Motion for a new trial was denied.

Judith

Melinda was a daddy's girl from the moment she came into the house. There are some things, like her bath, that she never lets me do—it has to be him. I have given up trying. I go after her with a washcloth and keep her face and hands pretty clean, and leave the tub baths to Barry.

He has developed a fail-safe routine. He fills the tub with water, then strips and gets into it himself. Melinda climbs on his knees, and he gives her a good scrub. He found a rubber sponge in the shape of a fish with a slit in its belly for a bar of soap. They play that they are going fishing. She gets so involved in the game that she overcomes her fear of the bath, and soon I hear the sounds of her splashing. He washes her hair that way too. He invites her to come in when he takes a shower, then he lathers her up with shampoo, rinses her off, and calls me to dry her hair with a towel. When I try the same thing myself, she screams that I get soap in her eyes.

We get through meals okay as long as I let her choose her own bib, cup, and spoon, but she will finish everything on her plate only when he is around to applaud her.

But all is not lost! It happened when she was eighteen months. Melinda and I discovered a common meeting ground at last. Oh, how I had waited for the moment, how I had hoped and prayed and laid the groundwork!

I entered the date in my journal: *Melinda asked me today to read her a story.*

"Read me, Mommy." That's what she said.

I'd been reading poetry and short stories to her for months, usually before she went to bed, but I had no idea if it was registering or not. Reading aloud was just something I could do—something that Barry didn't do, maybe that's what I'm saying.

One night she came into the kitchen and watched me closely as I did the dishes. She knew she was supposed to go to bed after dinner, and usually we had a scene. But this night she looked at me gravely and said, "Read me, Mommy." I burst into tears.

A breakthrough. A breakthrough with my daughter. I was so happy I called my mother in Bayonne to give her the news. "I have a little companion now," I told her proudly.

That's when the reading began in earnest. Of course I had the entire line of Claridge and Palmer picture books in the house, the simplified *Mother Goose,* and the Grimm and Andersen classics retold for preschoolers. What else? The Roughrider Boys series that I edited is too mature for her, but it doesn't seem to matter. I even try her on some of Bob Rothman's things—his book on toxic waste, which was the first book I brought in as an acquiring editor. We have no shortage of children's books in the house. I started taking them home as soon as we got Melinda. A bunch of them may still be at the nursery school she went to before I lost my job.

She loves anything with animals, *Bobo the Lion, The Moose and the Mouse, The Duck on the Truck, The Snake in the Lake, Funny Bunny and the Frozen Strawberry Yogurt Machine.* What else? I must say it. I really believe her favorite is *Vegetables That Grow Underground.* Every time I read from it, I tell her that this is the book I wrote for her before she was born.

JUNE 1983

Barry acquired a black-hulled Rhodes-22 with a teakwood cabin and a furling genoa and innermast main from a client on Long Island, who transferred the custom-fitted fiberglass sailboat to him as the final installment on his retainer. He had worked out a deal so the client, a low-level chauffeur for the Mafia, could plead to one count of criminal trespass in a messy case. He had broken into his ex-wife's home in the middle of the night, cracked her jaw, and raped her while his two children cowered in the other bedroom. Then he went on a rampage with a hammer, smashing all the major appliances, the porcelain sink, and the toilet bowl before the police arrived. "Next time you pull something like that," Barry quipped, "try to avoid the property damage."

He named his sloop the *Melinda Maru* and berthed it at Higbee's Marina in Patchogue. The Rhodes-22 was small and classy, you'd never mistake it for an O'Day or a Catalina. Without bothering to tell Jeff Kellerman, he sold their powerboat to somebody on City Island.

JULY 1983

Jeff Kellerman learned in a roundabout fashion that he no longer owned part of a Boston Whaler when the marina on City Island started dunning him for unpaid bills.

He raised the subject during one of Kantor's rare appearances in the office. "What gives?" he said. "First you sell the boat, and then you stick me with two thousand dollars' worth of hauling, landing, and storage charges."

"Gimme that," Barry said. "It's a mistake, I paid them in full." He went into his office and closed the door.

Jeff assumed the boatyard matter had been taken care of, but whenever he asked Barry for his share of the Whaler's proceeds, he got a stall. Finally Barry agreed to pick up the full rental on their office suite for the next two months.

AUGUST 15, 1983

Barry wangled a pair of seats from a promoter who owed him a favor, and took Judith to see *Richard Pryor Live at Midnight* at Radio City Music Hall.

"A great improvement over the Easter Show," she murmured, surveying the hip crowd.

He squeezed her hand, and she whispered, "I love you." They were trying to forget the pain of last week, when she got hysterical and wanted to go to St. Vincent's after her left eye shut tight. He had put round-the-clock ice packs on her and crooned her to sleep. Two days later she was able to joke that Muhammad Ali had survived much worse. It was important that she let him know during the good times that this was the Barry she loved and adored.

Judith scrunched down in her seat when she spotted Sally Milton a few rows ahead. Her former co-worker had called the house a few times to ask if she was ready to take on some freelance assignments. Each call had caught her fast asleep. It wasn't her fault that she sounded groggy. She had taken to napping with Melinda in the afternoons, the only peaceful time in her day. Usually she woke up about four p.m., when Melinda brought her a book and said, "Read me, Mommy." Then she had to rush around and get things together for dinner. Where did the day go?

AUGUST 16, 1983

Sally Milton came into the office around noon and went straight into Joanne Owens' office with her news. Judith Winograd had been sitting a few rows in back of her at *Richard Pryor Live*.

"She was trying to avoid me, so I didn't say hello. Guess what. She's still with Barry."

"I guess I'm not too surprised. Did she seem all right?"

"He had a great tan, and she looked awful. She was all covered up in long sleeves, like she was hiding bruises on her arms the way she used to, and she had on a pair of dark glasses. Pryor was terrific. He did his 'Richard Pryor Burned by Fire' number from the record, the one where he does a riff about what happened when he was freebasing, but I tell you, seeing Judith ruined it for me."

OCTOBER 1983

Barry Kantor and Jeff Kellerman ended their professional association when their lease was up. Jeff joined three friends of his in the same building, and Barry went in with Paul Scorvey. "The piker took all the lawbooks with him," Jeff told Cindy Owens. "Most of them were mine."

Jeff learned a week later that Barry hadn't paid the rent on their suite for the last two months, which wiped out the deposit Jeff had forked over to the management company when they signed the original lease. On top of that, the City Island marina was still dunning him for arrears. "This is one burn too many," Jeff told his new partners. He filed a suit against Kantor in Civil Court. Then, for good measure, when he got back to his office he went across the street to the Bar Association and filed a complaint with the disciplinary committee.

NOVEMBER 24, 1983

Things had been so difficult around the time of Melinda's second birthday that Judith did not invite her parents to come into the city for a party. Instead she took Melinda across the river to Bayonne for Thanksgiving. Barry did not accompany her.

Some of her cousins whom she hadn't seen in years were at the dinner table. Her aunt Ruth had brought a fully cooked bird and her famous prune and apple stuffing. Everyone oohed and aahed over Melinda. It was obvious that she was head and shoulders above her cousin Julie's fat blob of a child, Gerald, who was four months older and not yet toilet-trained.

Julie got on her case and asked her twice why Barry wasn't there.

"He's having dinner with his own mother," Judith snapped.

"I don't think that's right, do you, Mort?" Julie said to her husband. "Children are very sensitive to these things. The least he could do is put in an appearance."

"You don't know what you're talking about," Judith said, fussing over Melinda's bib.

"You're not still working at Claridge and Palmer, are you?" Julie went on. "Oh, no, that's right, you took a leave of absence or something."

Judith got up to clear the dishes and pretended she didn't hear.

After dinner the children were encouraged to perform. Melinda sang "Twinkle, Twinkle, Little Star," with Judith helping her over the rough spots. Max and Goldie led the applause.

The most Julie's Gerald could manage was to bang on a pot with his spoon.

"Isn't the little guy terrific?" Mort exclaimed. "Hit it, Gerry! We've got a professional jazz drummer on our hands."

Judith glowered. She wanted to grab the pot out of Gerald's sticky fingers and bang it over her cousin Julie's head.

Afterward, when she was leaving, Max slipped her fifty dollars to buy something nice for Melinda. She threw her arms around his neck and kissed him on the cheek. Her father was surprised and embarrassed. They were not a demonstrative family.

Judith wondered if he had an inkling that her money situation was tight. Probably not. Why should anyone think she was short of cash? She had no idea what Barry was making these days, but he was always after her for being a profligate spender.

Mort and Julie drove them to the bus station. "Don't be such a stranger. Keep in touch," Mort said kindly.

He said it like he almost meant it, Judith thought. Her eyes filled with tears.

FEBRUARY 1984

Marianna got a dandy assignment to produce feature pieces on the Winter Olympics in Sarajevo. After that she was scheduled to hook up with the Gary Hart campaign. She had asked for Mondale because he was the Democratic front-runner, but one way or another, between the primaries and the general election, she figured she'd be on the road till November.

She sublet her apartment to a researcher in the election unit. In the long list of instructions she typed out for her tenant, she included a paragraph about her neighbors across the hall. "They have periodic brawls, you'll get used to it," she typed. "If things get out of hand, you can try 911, and if you're worried about the child, you can ring up the hotline."

Gunther Heald was out of town for most of that winter and spring. He had gotten the juvenile lead in a dinner-theater road company of *Most Happy Fella*. One of the stops was a two-week engagement in Minneapolis. He was looking forward to a grand reunion with his family, who hadn't seen him perform since high school.

Jim felt bereft. Gunther called him collect three or four times a week, but all Jim had to report was that he'd seen a new movie—alone. One evening he'd gone straight from *Silkwood* to *Terms of Endearment*.

Gunther tried to cheer him up by asking for the building gossip. "So how's the Akita across the hall?"

"Larger."

"Mrs. Laemmerle?"

"Deafer."

"Any new developments with Maggie and Jiggs?"

"The same."

FEBRUARY 12, 1984

In response to an anonymous call, Special Services for Children sent a weekend investigator to the Kantor apartment on Waverly Place. The caseworker found Mr. Kantor at home in his bathrobe on Sunday morning, reading the *New York Times* and watching the Olympics on TV. She interviewed him for fifteen minutes and examined his daughter Melinda, who bore neither bruises nor signs of neglect. The child was alert and animated, and followed the events on the screen, a four-man bobsled competition, snuggled in her father's lap. Mrs. Kantor was not available for an interview.

When the caseworker ran a computer check on Kantor, she found a previous unfounded complaint in April 1983, but the details of the investigation had been expunged from the records. Eileen Wilmott, the investigator, was no longer with SSC. She had gone back to school to study landscape design.

Troubled by the earlier complaint, the caseworker took the matter up with her supervisor when she came in to work on Wednesday. They agreed to schedule a follow-up visit. This one would be unannounced.

FEBRUARY 21, 1984

A second caseworker went to the Kantor residence on a Tuesday evening. He found Mr. and Mrs. Kantor and their daughter Melinda at home having dinner. The wife, who said she was an author of children's books, looked older than her husband and was uncommunicative and withdrawn, in the investigator's opinion. Her husband did all the talking.

Mr. Kantor was outraged by the unannounced visit. In view of his attitude, the investigator was surprised that he had opened the door. "What is this, Nazi Germany?" he had yelled. "Anybody can accuse anybody of anything— I'm a lawyer, I know the difference between an unsubstantiated charge and a prima facie case."

He ranted about Gestapo tactics through the entire visit. The child, who bore no signs of abuse or neglect, clung to her father's legs and did not seem frightened by his loud behavior.

186

When the caseworker attempted to have a private word with Mrs. Kantor in the kitchen, her husband barked, "Leave her alone, she's got an upset stomach from all this aggravation." Mrs. Kantor excused herself and went into the bathroom.

The caseworker found Mrs. Kantor perplexing. Her reticence bordered on unconcern or lack of interest. But he was there to examine the little girl, and he had to concede that the child did not appear underfed, ill-treated, or fearful. On the contrary, she was remarkably self-possessed for two and a half years. When he got up to go, she tried to present him with her red rubber ball. "Good-bye, mister," she articulated quite clearly.

He overcame his slight misgivings and filed a "No Action Recommended" report. His paperwork went into the shredder the following month. Only the dates of the two visits and the final determination of "Unfounded" were logged on the computer.

MAY 4, 1984

Judith put a pan of water on the stove to boil. "This is fun, like heating the baby formula. Now what?" she asked.

Barry consulted the recipe card. "Three parts coke to one part baking soda. By weight. Add enough water. Use your eye."

"Use your eye? What does that mean?"

"It means it's not an exact process, but it works. Where's the jar?"

He wetted down the ingredients and put the jar in the pan. "Swirl it around. Is anything happening?"

"It's fizzing like Alka-Seltzer."

"Lemme look." He whistled. "I'll be goddamned. Add some more water. Okay, now stick it in cold water."

"Stick it in cold water?"

"Yeah, we got the separation already."

She ran the cold water.

"Get me a strainer and a paper towel."

She moved fast.

"There you go, sweetheart. The rock."

They smoked it that night.

JUNE 1984

Barry tried to put together a deal with the Durst Organization to buy out a small welfare hotel on Forty-second Street near the Pussy Peep Arcade. The Times Square Redevelopment Project was planning a major overhaul of the neighborhood, and people on the inside track could make a fortune.

He couldn't get a line of credit, and the deal fell through.

Two owner-occupied apartments he had bought in a co-op building on East Ninety-fifth Street were giving him a headache. His monthly maintenance had gone up, the rents hadn't. He was paying the difference, and the sonofabitch tenants wouldn't move.

JULY 12, 1984

Marianna had her camera crew at the state capitol in St. Paul when Walter Mondale announced his running mate for the presidential campaign. There was a loud spontaneous whoop followed by cheers and applause when the senator from Minnesota said, "I looked for the best vice-president and I found her, Gerry Ferraro."

To her surprise, Marianna found herself hugging the woman next to her, a print journalist for one of the New

York dailies. Both women laughed and introduced themselves. Cindy Owens said, "Who cares if my reaction isn't professional? Hot damn, this is an historic occasion."

The two women shook hands and said no doubt they'd run into each other again, probably the following week at the Democratic convention in San Francisco.

JULY 15, 1984, 1:30 A.M.

The ringing phone woke Max and Goldie. It was Judith, crying hysterically.

"Take me home, Daddy, take me home. He's going to kill me."

Max sat up in bed and put his hand to his heart, listening in the darkness. His daughter was sobbing into the phone. He could make out about one in three words.

"I can't take it anymore, Daddy, I want to die."

Her father shook himself awake and turned on the bed light. "He's there now, Judith? Let me speak to him."

"No, he went out an hour ago—a half-hour, I don't know, I lost track of the time. I'm here alone with Melinda. But he'll come back and he'll kill me. He told me he'd be back to finish me off. Daddy, come get me now. *Now,* while he's gone."

Goldie got on the phone. "Judith? Can you hear me, Judith? You want I should call the police?" She listened to the incoherent sobbing for a few minutes and gave the phone back to her husband. "She wants you."

Max put on his glasses and pawed the floor with his bare feet, trying to locate his slippers. "Snookie," he said. He hadn't called her that in thirty years. "Snookie, I'm getting dressed." He fiddled with the buttons on his blue-striped pajamas.

"Just a minute, Max." Goldie took the phone from him. "Judith, listen to me, Judith. It's one-thirty in the morning, your father is seventy-two years old with a heart condition. Judith, listen to me, if you don't want I should call the police, ring the neighbor downstairs, the nice fellow we met at the birthday party. Tell him you want to sleep down there. Max will take the car in tomorrow morning."

Max got back on the line. He sounded relieved. "Your mother is right, Snookie, it's already Sunday. You stay with the neighbor, and I'll be there bright and early."

Goldie got on again. "Judith, let me give you some good advice. If he comes back, you tell him your father's going to be there in the morning. You hear that, Judith? Make sure he knows your father's coming so he don't try any more monkey business."

She put down the receiver and looked at her husband. "*Ver ken vissen,* you think this time she means it?"

JULY 15, 1984, 9:00 A.M.

Max took the stairs slowly, stopping to catch his breath on the landing. When he got to the third floor, he found Barry waiting at the open door, haggard and unshaven, eyes bloodshot behind his glasses. Max brushed past him without a word.

The living room looked like the aftermath of a tornado. Chairs knocked over, table upended, rug askew. Wrenched from its fixture, the Tiffany shade hung from the ceiling by a single wire, a broken umbrella of colored glass. Judith sat huddled at one end of the green sofa, staring dully. There were large red welts on her neck, burn marks running up her arms from wrist to elbow. For one confused moment he couldn't locate the little girl, and then he saw her. She was playing quietly with her building blocks in the corner.

190

Max stood rooted in place, afraid to approach the terrible apparition that was his daughter. "Your mother had me bring a suitcase, it's down in the car," he said in a choked voice. "Pack what you need for Melinda, you're getting out of here."

"Just a minute, Max," Barry interrupted.

"I have nothing to say to you, buddy. Look what you did to my daughter."

"Max, take it easy, you don't know what happened."

"Judith, get your things, I'm taking you to Bayonne."

"Judith, tell your father to calm down."

She looked from one man to the other without comprehension, as if she were watching a movie in a foreign language.

"Jail isn't good enough for you, buddy. If I were a younger man, I'd horsewhip your hide."

Melinda started to cry in the corner. Judith stared at her vacantly.

"Come over here to Grandpa, Melinda," Max said. "How would you like to go with Grandpa for a ride?" The child toddled over to where he stood and looked back at her father. "We'll go for a ride and see Grandma Goldie. Judith, can you stand up? The car is downstairs."

"Max, she can go if she wants, but Melinda stays here. Do you understand that, Judith? Melinda stays here."

Judith spoke for the first time. "Daddy," she said in a hoarse whisper. "Thank you for coming."

"Go get your things."

"Max, I want to speak to her alone. Give me fifteen minutes."

Max looked at his daughter.

"It's okay, Daddy, I'm not afraid anymore."

Barry picked up the child. "Melinda, how would you like to take your grandfather for a walk? You can show him the library where your mother gets you all the books.

191

Do you know the way? Do you think you can show him?" The child nodded. "If you ask Grandpa nicely, he'll buy you an ice cream cone."

He turned to Max with a beseeching look. "Take her downstairs, she needs some fresh air. Give me fifteen minutes alone with Judith. Max—please, Max, we've been together for fourteen years."

After Max closed the door, Barry got down on his knees and buried his face in her lap. "You hold all the cards," he said.

"I know," she whispered. Her throat hurt when she spoke.

"What are you going to do?"

Do? What could she do?

"I can't take it," she said finally. "It was worse this time. We need help."

He didn't answer.

"I try to be there for you, but you shut me out. I—when you turn on me, I feel so helpless. What am I doing wrong?"

"I hate this rotten fucking city, everything's turning to shit. You're all I've got. I'll fall apart without you, Judith. You and Melinda are all I live for. If you leave me, I'll fight you for her. You'll never get her, she'll go to a foster home, you'll live with that for the rest of your life."

"Barry, I need time to think. Let me go to my father's for a couple of weeks."

"If you walk out on me, don't come back."

"I'm not walking out, I need to be by myself."

"They poisoned you against me. Your old man always hated my guts."

"That's not true."

"He walked in here like he owned the place."

"He's sick, Barry, he's got a heart condition. I'm his only daughter."

"Judith, they've got each other. You belong here with me."

She stared at the ugly hole in the ceiling, the hanging wire, the jagged shards of glass. Last night. They were sitting at the dinner table, talking about what? The coffee. He said the milk was sour. *But the milk wasn't sour, she tasted it, the milk was okay.* She ducked, the shade went crashing into the wall, the next thing she knew he was screaming he'd kill her. Nowhere to hide, she had nowhere to hide. He dragged her out from under the table. Oh! The lamp chain.

The rest of the evening came flooding back. It was part of their terrible curse that every insult, every blow, was etched on her brain, while he remembered nothing, nothing. Next week he'd look at her like a hurt puppy and say in a wounded voice, What are you bringing that up for, Judith? Why *now,* when we're getting along so well?

And of course he'd be right. It was important not to break the spell of the good days, to restring the fragile necklace one bead at a time. How long is the lamp going to stay that way, Judith? he'd say eventually, looking at the broken pieces like he was seeing them for the first time. What's wrong with you, Judith, take the shade to a repair shop and have it fixed.

"Something's wrong with me, Barry," she said. "I'm losing ground. Little things scare me that didn't used to, I get afraid on the street, I can't write anymore. I don't understand what's happening. We're locked into this together. If I don't leave you now, I never will."

"Judith, we'll take the boat out tomorrow. I can think better on the water, we'll work it out, you'll see. We'll draw up a contract, we'll make new rules. You can't throw away fourteen years like this, Judith, it's not fair. Where

193

will you go? What will you do? Take a good look at yourself, sweetheart, when was the last time you held a job?"

The doorbell rang. A cold spike of fear pierced her chest.

Max came in with Melinda.

The child hurtled across the room into Judith's arms. With exaggerated calm, Barry took his place on the green sofa.

Her father blinked at the family picture.

Judith lowered her eyes. "I'm staying, Daddy," she said.

JULY 16, 1984

Barry stayed home on Monday. Some of the burns on Judith's left arm were becoming watery blisters. He got out the tube of Bacitracin, applied it gently, and wrapped her wrist loosely with gauze.

In the afternoon he took Melinda with him on a secret errand. They came bounding into the apartment two hours later with a tricycle from Macy's. Barry wanted them all to go to the park together for Melinda's first ride, but Judith said she couldn't go out the way she looked, everyone would stare.

"Nobody stares at anybody in the park," he said. "It's all in your mind. Put on a long-sleeved shirt."

She told him she'd rather stay home and put the living room in order.

Melinda looked crestfallen.

The tricycle was a great hit, Melinda hadn't wanted to leave the park. But Barry got her home and fed her dinner. He produced his second surprise, two tickets for

Twyla Tharp that evening, fifth row center. They had to hurry, the curtain was at eight. He wanted Judith to call a sitter.

Judith said she couldn't move so fast on such short notice, they'd never get a sitter at this late hour. And besides, she'd already told him she didn't feel ready to face the outside world. Her neck hurt.

Barry looked at Melinda. "Okay, kiddo," he said. "You're going to your first dance concert on Broadway. Best behavior now, scout's honor. No wriggling around in the seat."

After the two of them went out, Judith called Bob Rothman at home. She wouldn't have dared to make the call with Barry in the house, and these days she didn't like to have a personal conversation in front of Melinda. The little girl was all ears. It was hard to know what she took in and what went over her head.

She gave Bob a short account of the hellish weekend, concentrating on the Tiffany lamp, the choking with the iron chain, and her father's abortive rescue mission, which she attempted to tell with a comic twist—how the two men in her life had stood there yelling "Judith, Judith" at her—but she didn't mention her burns. Talking to Bob was a good release. He was the one person she trusted enough to confide in, but she always left out the most painful details. If she told him the whole story, he'd think she was crazy. Who would believe what really went on with her and Barry? She didn't even mention the beatings in her journal. There were great blank spaces in it, weeks when she couldn't bring herself to make an entry. Some things were better left unsaid. When she reread the journal, she knew exactly what the ellipses meant. It was safer all around not to spell it out. She didn't want to give Barry any extra provocation.

Bob Rothman listened. He had heard many similar accounts from Judith over the years. Long ago he had realized that his role in her life was to serve as a sponge when the anxiety grew too great for her, but that was the extent of it, nothing more. He accepted the terms. Judith and he had been pals for ten years, and he suspected that at this point he was probably the only friend she had. Judith had been a wonderful, supportive editor when she worked at Claridge and Palmer, the first one to give him a book contract—he believed he owed her his attention and sympathy during these difficult conversations.

Judith was going downhill. He could tell by the spiritless tone of her voice, the way her excuses for Barry got lamer and lamer. Bob's heart went out to her, but what could he do? It wasn't as if Judith were some poor woman on welfare with five children; she had marketable skills and plenty of resources, she could get out from under anytime she wanted. He had concluded years ago that Judith's destructive dependence on Barry defied rational understanding. A couple of times he'd suggested the Horney clinic to her, and once he'd made an appointment in her name at the Alfred Adler consultation center, but she wouldn't go. Judith didn't want any advice from him, and she wouldn't tolerate any criticism of Barry. "It's nobody's business but mine," she said.

Bob had stopped thinking that she would ever have the guts to leave the fucker. So he listened when Judith called, and made the appropriate noises when she wound down. Usually she ran on for close to an hour, even longer if he let her. Just by listening, he felt, he was providing a therapeutic service.

But this time she said something that frightened him. After he hung up, he tried to remember the exact words.

She had said, "I hope the next time he really hurts me. Then maybe he'll see what he's doing."

AUGUST 1984

Bob Rothman put together a tape for Judith. He'd been listening to a Billie Holiday record when he realized he had the same song in the house by Bessie Smith.

> *If I should take a notion . . . to jump in . . . to the ocean, ain't nobody's business if I do.*

Judith's theme song. He wondered if she knew it.

He played Bessie, then Billie, over and over. Uncanny the way the two great blues singers had glommed on to the same anthem. Bessie's version was purer, just a piano accompaniment, but Billie's cover, with piano, bass, and drums, had been recorded live in some smoky cabaret, and on the last verse you could hear a laugh of self-recognition from a woman at one of the tables. Eerie.

> *I'd rather my man would hit me . . . than to jump a ride and quit me, ain't nobody's business if I do.*
> *I swear I won't call no copper . . . if I'm beat up by my poppa, ain't nobody's business if I do.*

He dubbed the two sides back to back on a fresh cassette, put it in a brown envelope, and mailed the small package to Waverly Place.

SEPTEMBER 10, 1984

Judith put Melinda on the phone to speak to her grandparents on her third birthday. She hadn't been out to

Bayonne since last Thanksgiving, and Barry had made Judith promise that there would be no more visits from Max and Goldie to Waverly Place.

She didn't have the heart to tell her parents they were both persona non grata. It was easier to stall them, make a tentative date and then break it. "I'll come for Rosh Hashanah, Ma," she said before she hung up, "and I'll bring Melinda. That's only two weeks away." She'd have to find a good excuse in two weeks. Maybe not. Maybe she would actually go out there.

Her parents had sent a beautiful gift anyway, a child's tea service with table and chairs. Five minutes after the big carton was unwrapped, Melinda was conducting an imaginary tea party, but Barry threatened to give the set away. He said it was just something else to trip over in the living room.

OCTOBER 1984

He had changed the rules again and enrolled Melinda in nursery school, not the cooperative one she used to go to, but a big expensive one, the best in the Village. They worked out an arrangement. He walked Melinda to school in the morning, and she picked her up at three o'clock. The school was costing him a fortune, he complained, he wanted her to start looking for a part-time job or take in some freelance work. He got a copy of the *Voice* and showed her the ads in the back from people who needed manuscript typists. She'd actually drummed up the nerve to call a couple of numbers, but they weren't interested when they found out she didn't use a word processor. Things were changing in the publishing world. She wondered if Claridge and Palmer had converted to computers.

Judith

With Melinda out of the house during the day, I am free. I thought I'd catch up on my reading, or maybe try to write a short story, but it is so hard to concentrate. I can barely get myself to make a notation in my journal. Instead I make lists of projects. Scrub tops of kitchen cabinets. Scrape old paint off chest of drawers and refinish. Recaulk loose tiles under bathroom sink.

No more Balducci's, the highlight of my afternoons. Just walking in the door used to give me a lift. The electricity of the place! So much energy and excitement. Every shopper on a serious mission, hunting and gathering for an important dinner. I'd pretend I was one of them, how would they know I wasn't? I'd go over after lunch with Melinda and start cruising the aisles. I could lose all sense of time as I circled the trays of homemade chicken and pasta, the marinated mushrooms, the cucumber, avocado, and endive salads. I'd finger the crusty breads, compare labels on giant bottles of tarragon vinegar, extra virgin olive oil, goose leg confit. I'd inch along the crowded cheese counter until I arrived at one particular, pungent round of goat cheese nestled among the equally delectable logs and triangles and squares.

I'd make my selections, tuck the grocery bag into Melinda's stroller, and go home.

I was being so thoughtless! "Look, Judith," Barry said to me, "if you can't pull your oar, cut down on the food bills. No more Balducci's. Walk the extra block and a half and go to Sloan's, what else do you have to do all day? And use the shopper coupons for Chrissake, it's good money."

Stupid, stupid. I was so wrapped up in my own problems, it never occurred to me that I was spending money we didn't have. Now I clip the twenty-five-cent coupons from the Sunday papers and take the grocery cart to Sloan's, where I load up on house brands and weekly specials. I hate the supermarket's unfamiliar aisles and dreary produce, but I want to show him I am trying. I *can* manage the household. I can. All it takes is planning. He is right—lack of organization was my downfall at Claridge and Palmer. If I get things running smoothly at home, the skills will translate to my next job or book, whatever I choose to do. Why am I so resistant?

Yesterday I left the cashier's receipts on the kitchen counter so he could see how much we were saving, but then at dinner he announced that supermarket meat made him gag. When he shoved his plate away, Melinda followed suit. "Mommy made poo-poo," she squealed, holding her nose and looking to him for approval. She must have picked up "poo-poo" at the nursery school. It is her all-around term for anything disgusting. Barry hates it when Melinda uses baby talk, but "Mommy made poo-poo" cracked him up.

NOVEMBER 1984

Jeff Kellerman won a default judgment against Barry Kantor after Barry failed to show up twice in Civil Court. "Let him try to collect," Barry muttered to Paul Scorvey when he got the notice in the mail.

"I hate that sonofabitch so hard it hurts," Jeff told one of his new partners. "He knows he has to pay up, but he'll do anything to cause a little more aggravation." Jeff waited another month and then put a freeze on Barry's account at Manufacturers Hanover with a *duces tecum* subpoena and restraining order.

A check for the full amount arrived two days later.

When Jeff signed it for deposit, he saw that Barry had scrawled "Fuck you" across the back.

JANUARY–FEBRUARY 1985

Barry brought home a dog that winter, a frisky black-and-tan German shepherd pup about seven months old. He walked in the door with it one cold January afternoon.

"Finally, finally," he said, rubbing his hands. "A suitable replacement for Thor. You remember my Great Dane, don't you, Judith?"

Judith watched in trepidation as the shivering, uncertain puppy nosed around the apartment. "Is it housebroken?" she asked.

"Yeah, it's housebroken. I got to hand it to you, Judith, your mind is always on shit. His father was best-in-show at Westminster, the guy showed me the ribbons."

She kept her mouth shut. One of the shepherd's ears stood out at an angle, but if she called it to his attention, it would only lead to a fight. He'd accuse her of deliberately finding fault with anything he brought home. When he discovered on his own that the dog's ears didn't match, he'd turn on the poor animal for being less than he expected, and deep down he'd crucify himself for getting snookered. She knew him so well.

"I'm going to train it right," he announced, grabbing its muzzle. "We need a watchdog around here." He waved toward the bedroom, where he kept the shoeboxes and scales. She nodded. His other business, the private deals for his clients. Brokering, he called it. There were always large sums of money around the house, money she wasn't supposed to touch. Once, in an unguarded moment, he had let on that he kept safe-deposit boxes at three different banks.

When Melinda saw the puppy, she threw her arms around its neck. Barry told her the dog's name was Champion Great Thunder of Schleswig-Holstein, but they would call him Shep. The next day he went out and bought Shep a studded leather collar and a chain leash.

The dog was not housebroken, nor did it show any inclination to catch on. They took it to the park twice a day, but as soon as they came back, Shep would make a pile on the living room rug. Judith got down on her hands and knees with the Bissell rug cleaner, but it was hopeless. Barry threw out the soiled rug and put newspapers down on the bare floor.

Barry became obsessed with teaching the dog to obey him. When the weather was good, he practiced in the park with the shepherd for hours on end while Judith kept watch over Melinda. When he thought the dog had a new lesson down pat, he gave Judith and Melinda a demonstration.

"Stay, Shep," he commanded, and then told Judith to call the dog, to show that Shep had learned to answer only to him. But when Judith said, "Here, boy," Shep came trotting toward her.

Melinda giggled.

"Maybe he comes because I'm the one who feeds him," Judith said mildly. Barry had put a forty-pound bag of kibble in the kitchen, but she thought the dog was meat-starved and was buying it hamburger on the sly.

They were in one of their good periods—their honeymoons, she called them. Her journal was filled with positive entries.

MARCH 1985

Orville Rodgers, who owned the Akita in 2-B, knocked on Gunther and Jim's door with a petition and an outrageous story. The people in 3-A were exercising their dog by letting it run up and down the stairs. Yesterday when he had opened his door to take down the garbage, the shepherd bounded inside the apartment and was at Kojo's jugular before he could stop him. He had just come back from the vet with Kojo, he and the dog were still shaking. When he knocked on Kantor's door to show him the bills, the man laughed in his face.

"Out," Orville Rodgers said, "I want them out of this building. That dog is a menace, absolutely wild and un-trained. It's criminal the way some people abuse their pets in the city. In all the years you've known me, have you ever seen Kojo off the leash?"

Gunther and Jim agreed that they hadn't. Jim was only too happy to sign the petition. "Hallelujah, we should have thought of something like this years ago," he cheered.

The tenants on the fourth floor signed gladly and kept Mr. Rodgers for over an hour while they told him their own horror stories about Kantor. He left a note under the door for the woman in 3-B, the television producer who was seldom home. Mrs. Laemmerle was the only holdout. She said she loved the pretty little child in 3-A and she didn't feel right about signing petitions against neighbors.

APRIL 12, 1985

Tax time made him edgy. He hadn't filed quarterly estimates since '81 or '82, when he quit taking the as-signed-counsel cases. This year his reportable income was in the basement.

He came home in the afternoon after a stop at the bank to get a packet of hundreds from the vault. Judith was asleep in the bedroom. He grabbed Shep's leash and took the dog for a walk, arriving fifteen minutes early to pick

Melinda up from nursery school. She ran to Shep and kissed him and then let her father scoop her up for a hug.

"Mommy's not feeling well again," he said. A flicker of pain crossed Melinda's face.

"We're glad to see you, Mr. Kantor," her teacher said with a reproving look. "Yesterday I had to call your house. The child was sitting here crying her eyes out when no one was here at three to pick her up."

"My wife and I got our schedules crossed," he said with a lopsided smile, holding Melinda in his arms. He had half a mind to tell her that for the prices they were charging, it wouldn't kill them to keep the kid an extra half-hour, but he held his tongue. Melinda liked this teacher, he didn't want any scenes.

They went to the park and let Shep off the leash while Melinda told him about her day in school. "Tomorrow we'll take the boat out," he told her. "Just the two of us." She nodded happily as he stroked her hair. Three and a half years old, and already she could pull up the centerboard on command.

APRIL 17, 1985

They sat at the table while Judith brought out the spaghetti.

"Did you get to feed the bunny rabbit today, Melinda?" he asked.

"Uh-huh."

"What does the bunny rabbit eat?"

"Carrot."

"What else?"

"Lettuce."

"Show me how the bunny rabbit eats his lettuce."

Melinda crinkled her nose and made chomping noises.

"What does Shep eat for dinner?"

"Hamburger!" the child said triumphantly, jumping up and down in her chair.

The spaghetti platter in Judith's hands crashed to the floor.

"*Judith!*" he roared.

She froze. Melinda started to whimper.

Barry threw back his chair. The pulse in his neck was pounding. His eyes blinked rapidly behind his glasses.

"*Sneaking bitch!*" He lunged.

Judith darted sideways with a guttural moan as his fist hit the wall. He pivoted wildly and lunged again, tripping over the dog. His glasses went hurtling. The yelping shepherd scrambled under the table.

"*I'll teach you to play games!*" His punch caught her under the ear. She fled screaming to the far end of the living room, the dog at her heels.

He staggered after her blindly. The shepherd growled, barring his path. Barry kicked the dog out of the way and went at Judith with both fists.

The shepherd bared its teeth. Its ears lay flat against its head.

Melinda sat forgotten at the table. "No, Shep, no!" she cried.

APRIL 20, 1985

Orville Rodgers waved to Gunther on the street. "Action," he said. "I knew we'd get action."

Gunther wasn't sure what his neighbor was talking about.

"Our petition worked. The dog is gone. He got rid of it. Of course I was hoping there'd be an eviction proceeding,

205

but he's too clever for that. He knew we had him dead to rights."

Gunther raised his eyebrows and said congratulations. When Jim came home, he told him the news.

JUNE 21, 1985

Carol sat on the park bench on the first glorious day of summer and watched with maternal pride as her younger boy crawled through the jungle gym. An agile little girl with strawberry blond hair dominated the upper rungs. Her self-assurance was a bit galling—Carol had a moment of profound irritation—but Seth seemed oblivious to being bested by a girl. The two children were getting on nicely. A grey-haired woman who sat slumped at the end of Carol's bench obviously was minding the girl. A nurse-maid by the looks of her, Carol decided.

"Mommy," the little girl called, shimmying down the bar, "I'm going to the swings."

"Not now, Melinda."

Carol turned sharply. There was something about the voice, but the hair and the nose were all wrong. "Judith?" she said. "Judith Winograd? It's Carol Altman. I'm Carol Marks Altman. Oh, my God, it's been ten years!"

Judith's eyes filled with tears as the two women embraced.

"Is that yours?" Carol asked. "The little redhead? Oh, Judith, how wonderful. The monkey in blue is my younger one, Seth. His older brother is away at camp. Judith, it's so good to see you. I've wanted to call you so often, you have no idea."

They collected their children and walked to the swings. Judith was moving so slowly, Carol noticed. What happened to all that wonderful animation?

She started chattering to fill up the silence. "Well, I

206

married Jonathan, in case you didn't hear. I was so angry at you I guess I didn't send you an invitation. We just bought a loft in Soho after nine years uptown, so I thought I'd try out Washington Square Park. Whew, it's grungy. But I'm so glad I ran into you!"

Judith nodded. "I come here every day."

"Mothers on parade. Remember when we used to hit the singles bars together? And oh, remember how we went to one of those first meetings of women's lib? Judith, what ever happened to—uh, don't you just love creeping middle-age senility? I used to call him El Mysterioso."

"Barry?" Judith asked. "We're still together."

There was a long, uncomfortable silence. Carol stole a look at Judith's flattened nose.

"Melinda is our adopted child," Judith finally said.

"Bully for you."

Judith gave her a funny look.

"I used to search for your name in the *Times Book Review,* isn't that silly?"

"I wrote a children's book that did very well, I guess I meant to send you a copy. Then I went into publishing. I haven't been well lately. Stomach spasms, something to do with my gastrointestinal tract. I may have to have an operation."

"Rotten when the body starts to let you down. We're both over forty."

"You look wonderful, Carol."

"Three hours a week at Alex and Walter. If I miss a session, my tummy pooches out to here."

Judith giggled, a low rusty sound of unaccustomed mirth.

"Well, I finally got a rise out of you. I was beginning to worry." As soon as the words escaped her mouth, Carol knew she had said the wrong thing. Her old friend looked as if she wanted to crawl into a hole.

"Yipes," Carol exclaimed. "The time! I'm late for the

hairdressers. Seth! Seth, honey—*andiamo*! Judith, give me your number."

A look of panic crossed Judith's face.

"It's under Kantor on Waverly Place. We're still in the same apartment. Carol, I'd—I'm very glad to have seen you," she finished softly.

That night Carol told Jonathan about running into her old friend Judith Winograd in Washington Square Park. "You met her, remember? Ten years ago when we were courting? I had a Valentine's dinner, and she came two hours late. She was going to be a novelist. Anyway, the thing is, she's still with the same guy, and they have this adorable adopted daughter named Melinda, but Judith looked dreadful—it was very unsettling. Jonathan, her nose was squashed in. Squashed in. Judith used to have a beautiful nose. If a plastic surgeon did that to her, he ought to be shot."

"Are you going to see her again?"

"I don't know."

Jonathan switched on the news. He wanted to get the latest on the hijacked TWA jet that was still sitting at the Beirut airport. The Shiites had released another two hostages. He wondered what they'd have to say.

Judith's Journal, Fall 1985

September 10.   Melinda is four years old. B. took her with him to Patchogue for a sailing lesson. Afterward to the Bronx. I wasn't included, and probably wasn't missed. I used the free time to work on the windows. Ammonia better than Windex, but still smeary.

September 15. Call from Bayonne—am I coming for Rosh Hashanah? B. told them I couldn't come to the phone.

September 20. Woke up at five, felt disoriented. Nobody home. Didn't know if it was night or day. Turned on the TV, pictures of an earthquake in Mexico. Collapsed buildings, people buried alive—screaming, crying—they are finding parts of bodies in the rubble. I wish I was under the ground with them, an end to this misery.

October 4. Took Melinda to nursery school this morning and picked her up at three. Haven't done that in a long time. Feeling a lot better.

October 22. Good discussion with B. tonight. Got stoned like the old days and curled up in bed with the door closed. M. asleep on the living room sofa. Everything B. said made sense. The main problem is that I go off into my own world and he can't reach me.

1. My general refusal to go sailing, and my poor attitude and lack of cooperation on the days when he does succeed in dragging me out to Patchogue.

2. The dinners. Check with him in the a.m.

3. Kitchen and bathroom scrubbed twice a week on alternating days. He will make up a schedule.

4. Not true that Melinda doesn't want me to read to her. I am better at this than he is (!)—a lot of her vocabulary comes from the reading. Nature versus nurture. If B.'s theories are correct, the cultural input of two superior people should overcome genetics. Resume reading!!!

5. I must try harder to be there for him when he comes home after a difficult time with court or a client. He is out there battling the world—I have forgotten what the jungle is like. *My insensitivity to the pressures in his life is endangering this relationship.*

6. When I tune out in the presence of one of his clients/friends (from boredom or from feeling unwanted—usually a combination of the two), it damages his position in their eyes. His clients and business associates must be made to realize that B. is a superior person. They are not in his league, B. knows I understand this, but the weak and the inferior always seek to diminish the light that emanates from those who exist on a higher plane. *They cannot stand the radiant glow.* B.'s great talent is that he can create the illusion of camaraderie with people who are not his equals. This allows him to function in the ordinary world—but then his inferiors take the illusion for reality and fail to give him the respect he deserves. I have no gift for easy communication with others, but my role can be crucial. Body language, full attention when he speaks, anticipation of his needs. If I show B. the respect he deserves, others will pick up the cue.

7. Money.

November 4. B. in a funk all weekend—finally I figured out why. The snapshots the woman in the park took of him and Melinda at the swings were awful. He was squinting into the sun, with his round glasses he looked like a tired raccoon. Today—Monday—we went to Cohen's Optical on Greenwich Avenue and picked out new frames. Rimless aviators, imported from Italy. $540 for two pairs. Instant transformation—B. looks like an Italian movie star. *Why didn't I think of this sooner?* It made him so happy.

210

B. is so vulnerable when it comes to his appearance, especially his eyes. His eyes are devastating, everyone comments on his penetrating gaze—*but I am the only one who understands how he suffers. Astigmatism!* What a cruel trick of fate that someone who sees through the sham in all people should be cursed with astigmatic vision.

I have the power within me to heal his wounds, the secret power. We have a mystical bond between us that nothing can break. Oh, how they try—mother, father, old lady K. Nobody understands how much he needs me. B. Rothman *doesn't get it.* The poor dumb fools at Claridge and Palmer. Carol. So strange running into her that day in the park. Nobody gets it. Nobody understands why we adopted Melinda. They think it was me—that I was the one who couldn't have children. They will never learn the truth because I will never betray his secret. I hold his tragic secrets in the palm of my hand and blow them away.

JANUARY 1986

Melinda could walk down the stairs like a grownup. Foot on the step, other foot *down,* foot on the step, other foot *down.* Only babies put both feet on the step. She wasn't a baby anymore, she was almost four and a half. She could get dressed by herself when she woke up in the morning and almost tie her shoes.

The bottom drawer in the bedroom belonged to her. She could go in there anytime and get out her things, but she wasn't allowed to open the other drawers. Those belonged to Mommy and Daddy. Daddy had lots of shirts and sweaters. Mommy didn't have much stuff, she wore the same old dress every day.

211

Daddy was home a lot now because Mommy was sick in bed. He got on the phone and talked to lots of different people all day long. Sometimes he put Melinda on the phone to say hello. She liked that.

Mommy cried a lot. Daddy got mad and yelled at her, and then he hit her on the head. Then Mommy cried some more. Daddy hit Mommy because she was bad. He didn't want to, but she had to learn her lesson.

Melinda was a good girl, Daddy never got mad at Melinda. Daddy said Melinda was making progress. Daddy loved her a lot. Daddy knew everything, he was the best Daddy in the world, and he loved Melinda because she tried to be good and make progress. She wished Mommy would try to be good, then Daddy wouldn't have to hit her.

When Mommy was sick, Daddy let Melinda play downstairs at Mrs. Laemmerle's. Just sometimes. Other times Daddy said no.

Mrs. Laemmerle gave her a glass of juice and cookies and let her bang on the piano. That was fun. But she didn't like it when Mrs. Laemmerle asked her questions. Daddy told her not to answer. Mrs. Laemmerle was a nosybody.

Sometimes Mrs. Laemmerle didn't open her door. Then Melinda had to go upstairs early and knock on Jim and Gunther's.

Gunther was home a lot, he was very nice, but he didn't have any cookies. He showed her funny pictures of from when he was a baby, and he played nice games. He read to her from grownup books, just like Mommy used to do. Gunther read in a big loud voice that made her laugh, he read better than the teachers in school. She wished Gunther could come to school and read to all the children.

MAY 6, 1986

Barry hoisted Melinda onto his shoulders and carried her piggyback down the street. It was a beautiful spring day. The red tulips the Waverly Place Block Association had planted last fall made a brave show under the newly leafed-out street trees, diligent homeowners spaded the earth in their postage-stamp front gardens, a flat or two of mixed impatiens at their side. Even Washington Square Park looked inviting if you didn't get too close. This was the season of glory for Greenwich Village.

Father and daughter made their way around the corner to P.S. 55. The neighborhood public school was one of the best in the city, with a traditional curriculum that warmed the hearts of the lifers down at the Board of Ed.

Some parents who were easily taken with new ideas were inclined to grumble that P.S. 55 was a mite old-fashioned. If they ventured to voice that opinion out loud —say, at a meeting of the PTA—Franklin Chandler, the school's guiding force, would shrug them off with an imperious wave, directing them to P.S. 3, or to P.S. 41 a few blocks away. The old principal held no brief for what he called "that open-classroom-with-gerbils nonsense." Not that the children of P.S. 55 were deprived of gerbils— they had their full complement of the popular rodents, plus rabbits and chicks—but Chandler ran a tight ship through the narrow channel of the traditional Three R's, and most of P.S. 55's grateful parents, who would have been hard pressed to foot the bill for a private school education on their middle-class professional salaries, adored him for that.

It was, therefore, with considerable anguish, delicacy, and politicking that the district school board began its

213

search for a replacement when the beloved principal keeled over and died on the last day of school in June. P.S. 55 was a plummy appointment, and word of the unexpected opening quickly spread through the city. Applications poured in, résumés were scrutinized, interviews narrowed the field. There was a long list and then a short list; favorite-son candidates from warring factions emerged. The assistant principal, who by a regrettable oversight had not been consulted by the screening committee, tendered her resignation. New candidates were proposed, positions hardened, favorite sons were scratched. The search dragged on all summer, unavoidably taking on aspects of a small-town beauty contest, before a compromise candidate, an assistant principal from Queens named Arthur Blattstein, won by acclamation at a stormy district school board meeting that lasted till two a.m.

Bright crayoned drawings festooned the big glass windows of P.S. 55's sprawling facade. *Behold and humble yourselves,* the drawings beckoned, *within these portals lies a children's paradise.* Barry took Melinda by the hand and walked in the front door.

The new principal wasn't in his office. A chirpy assistant in a green plaid dress and pearl earrings informed Mr. Kantor between telephone calls that he and his daughter could have a seat and wait. Mr. Blattstein was touring the classrooms. He might pop back any minute, but there was really no telling, Mr. Blattstein was always on the go.

Barry cooled his heels for ten minutes before he told the assistant he had a pressing engagement uptown. That was a pity, she chirped. Mr. Blattstein was eager to meet with all the parents and prospective students, the door to his office was always open, but if Mr. Kantor only wanted to register his daughter for kindergarten this fall, he could take the forms right now and fill them out at home.

214

The first day of kindergarten was Monday, September 15. Mark it in red on your calendar, she told him. Melinda could be in the hot lunch program for $3.75 a week, the brochure was right in the envelope. Just be sure to sign and return the forms.

JUNE 3, 1986

Barry walked his daughter to Dr. Michael Rochette on West Twelfth. Melinda's pediatrician was always glad to see him.

After the examination, the doctor closed the door to his private office while his nurse helped the child get dressed in the other room.

With Melinda out of the way, the two men got down to business. Over the years he and Rochette had developed a true understanding. A quid pro quo. He fed the doctor's nose habit on a regular basis, an equitable exchange for the medical advice the doctor dispensed with no questions asked when things got a little out of hand with Judith.

The miraculous ice pack treatment was Rochette's suggestion. If he got the ice on her fast enough, it kept the swelling down. It also calmed her—usually all she needed was to calm down. Last month was a lulu. Judith had a bad fit of hysterics and screamed for him to take her to the emergency room at St. Vincent's. But it was only a broken finger, and the pediatrician was able to patch her up just fine in his office.

Barry placed the packet on the desk. Rochette emptied a physician's sample of orange-flavored aspirin into the wastebasket and transferred the coke to the empty bottle.

"Something fell into my lap," the doctor said as he screwed on the cap. "You might be interested. Is Melinda still pining for a baby brother?"

Sally Milton wheeled through her Rolodex for another likely prospect. She promised the guy at Harper and Row she'd have twenty more names by this afternoon. Writers and Editors for Peace in Central America was collecting signatures for a full-page ad in the *Times;* it was so typical of them to forget the people in children's books until they were down to the wire.

Her pencil paused at the R's. Robert Rothman, Sag Harbor. She dialed the 516 area code and tapped her pencil. Another fugitive from the city, he had moved out there permanently last year. The question was, would he be at the beach or at his computer?

Bob Rothman was at the computer. He said he'd be happy to sign the ad and send the committee a check for ten bucks. And he'd get on the horn and make a few calls himself.

"How's Judith?" Sally asked. "Do you still keep in touch?"

"We speak on the phone every few months. Do you?"

"No. We've lost contact. Melinda must be what, about five years old?"

"They adopted another baby, I guess you haven't heard."

Sally nearly dropped the receiver. "It can't be."

"But it is, I kid you not. They named him Ricky Ricardo. Judith's all wrapped up in motherhood, and this time she feels like she knows what she's doing. That's what I hear from Kantor. Usually she's too busy to come to the phone."

"Bob, does he still—let me rephrase that. What shape is she in?"

"Not wonderful."

216

"She never came around asking for freelance assignments. The door was wide open, I want you to know that."

"Don't worry about it, Sally, she doesn't hold any grudges. At this point I don't think editorial work is what's on her mind. When she talks about Claridge and Palmer, it's like once upon a time she lived in a foreign country."

"We used to play tennis together, I bet you didn't know that. What do you think would happen if I called?"

"And asked for a singles match? Or to sign the Central America thing?"

"I hadn't thought about Writers and Editors, but it might be an opening gambit."

"Barry would get on the phone and chew your ear off about Ortega. Then he'd launch into a thrilling tale of his last jaunt to Panama, where he's in thick with the ruling junta."

"General Noriega?"

"Is that the jerk's name? Some big cheese who oversees the dope traffic. I tune out when Kantor gets speedy. It's all in his head anyway, like his rap about Donald Trump flying him to Atlantic City in his personal helicopter to discuss how to improve his casinos."

"What you're saying is, I wouldn't get through to Judith at all."

"Give it a try, who knows? It might be one of her good days. You want the number?"

"Thank you, I've got it. She's still in my Rolodex."

"Sloppy housekeeping," he said.

"Whose?"

"Yours."

Sally took a few deep swallows at the water cooler. What could possibly happen if she made the call? He couldn't bite her head off on the phone.

217

A man picked up on the first ring. "Petroleum Industries."

It had to be the wrong number. "Judith Winograd, please. I'm calling for Writers and Editors—"

"She can't come to the phone. What do you want?"

Sally pressed down the disconnect in a fluster.

AUGUST 15, 1986

Melinda reached into the basket and hugged little Ricky. "Can I give him his bottle?" she asked.

"Go to the refrigerator, Melinda," Judith said in a soft voice. "Bring me a bottle from the lower shelf. Don't slam the door, close it gently."

Her little boy. A dream come true. Hold on, hold on, sweetheart. Trust me, he said. I'll arrange something, be patient. Have I ever let you down?

She hummed to herself. A boy for you and a girl for me, and oh, how happy . . .

"Peee-yooo." Melinda drawled out the syllables. "Ricky smells bad again."

"He's a baby," Judith crooned. "A sweet little innocent baby boy." She took the cold bottle from her daughter's hands and gently eased the nipple into the baby's mouth. He began to suck. Glorious miracle. So natural. Everything was so natural. She glanced at the earnest, watchful child at her side. "You don't remember, Melinda," she said, swelling with pride. "When you arrived, you were just as little."

Melinda looked at her mother with questioning blue eyes. She couldn't ever have been that small, she'd have to ask Daddy when the plane brought him back home.

Judith turned away, absorbed with the babe in her arms. "Nobody in this world will ever hurt you, Ricky," she crooned. "Nobody. I'll always be here to protect you. I'm your mommy, little Ricky, and I love you very, very much."

"Why can't he use the potty?"

SEPTEMBER 4, 1986

Cindy Owens went straight from the paper to her sister's Gramercy Park apartment for dinner. Poor Joanne was emerging from a terrible career crisis, and Cindy was giving her all the support she could. In the last management reshuffle at Claridge and Palmer, the new publisher had reorganized her department and put Harvey Erickson in her job. Everyone expected Joanne to leave, but she had hung in there for three wretched months. Now they were going to give her an imprint of her own. She'd still have to check with Harvey on the decent-sized advances, but it was better than nothing.

Joanne's silver pot of fresh-brewed amaretto decaf sat on its trivet. Cindy breathed in the pleasant aroma. Joanne ground the beans herself, so the denatured coffee was almost as good as the real thing.

"Jo, I want to ask your advice about something," Cindy began. "It's for my series on battered women. I've got great stuff on the shelters, and I'm getting a woman who killed her husband, her lawyer said no problem after the trial, but my editor threw me a curve the other day. He said what about the women who don't kill and don't leave? Of course he's right. They're sort of the silent majority." She broke off.

"It would be ghoulish and in poor taste, wouldn't it, if I called Judith Winograd? I mean, what would I say?"

Joanne looked at her sister as if she had never seen her before. "You can't. You just can't. *Cindy!*"

"That's what Jeff said. I called him. Okay, okay, it was just an idea. You see why they give me the soft features? I don't have the tough hide to be a real investigative reporter." She reached for the Sweet'n Low in Joanne's silver bowl from Georg Jensen. "You want to know something weird? Until I started this series, I never thought of Judith as a syndrome. Did you?"

SEPTEMBER 23, 1986

The afternoon sun picked up the silver highlights in Arthur Blattstein's trim beard as the dynamic young principal made his way through the Little Yard.

"Good afternoon, children."

"G'afternoon, Mr. Blattstein," they chorused back.

Wonderful. An alert bunch of kids. He knew half their names already. Horace, Kwame, Melissa, Melinda, Tyrone, Jennifer, Jessica, Gabrielle, Margot, Cheryl, Jeremy, David, Danny, Ari, Robert, LuBelle. Just the right ethnic balance. He liked to see the poor unfortunates from the welfare hotels distributed evenly through the kindergarten classes.

Seven or eight girls were playing Duck, Duck, Goose in a circle. A striking red-haired child named Melinda was It. Small for her age, pretty, she was usually brought to school by her father. Little Melinda looked as though she wouldn't tire of Duck, Duck, Goose until she got to the third grade. He gave the circle of girls a benevolent smile and wandered toward a boisterous group at the far end of the yard.

"Miss Cavetti," he said to the teacher, "what in God's name is that?"

She winced. "I'm afraid that's television tag, Mr. Blatt-

220

stein. It's a variation on freeze tag, but instead of freezing they shout out the name of a TV show. You'd be surprised how many shout *Miami Vice.*"

"Where do they come up with these things?"

"Beats me." They both laughed.

"Miss Cavetti, tomorrow a photographer from *Scholastic* is coming around. A timely topic—the swell in enrollment caused by the Baby Boomers spawning their own little broods. I'm going to send him to the yard when Kindergarten Two is having recess." He scrutinized the teacher's baggy sweater and pants. "I'll be wearing a suit. The last time a *Scholastic* photographer showed up, your colleague Miss Ely was mortified that she didn't get advance notice."

"I'll get my nails done."

"Ah, we needn't go that far, Miss Cavetti."

And off he went.

OCTOBER 17, 1986

Marianna adored the Laughlins' dinner parties. The food was magnificent, and the conversation never flagged. This time she kept the table entranced with her account of the Reykjavik summit. They ate up her Gorbachev stories and begged for more. Of course all her tidbits were secondhand—she hadn't laid eyes on the man all week, but who was to know? The truth was, she hadn't gotten out of the studio control room the whole time she was in the confounded place.

When Maria brought in the chocolate torte from Sarabeth, Bill turned to the woman on his right. "Well, Cindy," he said with an encouraging smile, "we all read your series with interest. A real eye-opener. It ran while you were away, Marianna."

Marianna was miffed, but that was the Laughlins' hard-and-fast rule. Every guest at their table got a chance to shine.

"I'm in the dark," she said with a forced laugh. "Somebody fill me in." She directed her gaze across the chrysanthemums to a modest-looking woman with a good haircut. A print reporter—she should have known by the short fingernails and plain face. "I'm afraid I didn't catch your by-line when we were introduced."

"Cynthia Owens," Bill said loudly.

"Actually, we've met before," Cindy said. "The first Mondale-Ferraro press conference. In Saint Paul."

"A lot of water under that bridge," Bob Aschenhoover joked.

"Cindy just completed a six-part feature on battered women," Bill explained to the table. "Part Six was about the women who wind up killing their mates. Powerful stuff. What she found was that the women's self-esteem was pitifully low. They were victims of the learned helplessness syndrome—am I quoting you accurately, Ms. O.?" he said with a smile.

"Well, not me, but the psychologist I interviewed. Dr. Lenore Walker."

Marianna glanced at Bill. It was so obvious that Cynthia Owens was not going to shine. "Did you tell Cindy I live next door to a battered woman?"

"No," Maria answered for her husband. "We thought we'd just introduce the topic and let you two take it from there." She served Bob Aschenhoover a second piece of cake. "Do you think of the lady across the hall from you as a victim?"

"I think of her as a moral zombie," Marianna exploded. Cindy looked startled.

Marianna reached for the Pouilly Fuissé. "I've watched the deterioration over the years. My God, they have two children in there now. Two! Don't tell *me* about learned helplessness and lack of options—that's the easy part. This is not one of life's unfortunate creatures from the lower end of the socioeconomic scale whose welfare payments are threatened by Reaganomics. I'm talking sick-in-the-head irresponsibility. She could take the children and leave anytime she wants, but she won't, that's my point, she's utterly in his thrall. And it isn't because she doesn't have anyplace to go. She had a good job in publishing until she gave it up for that creep."

Cindy looked down at her plate. Bill Laughlin changed the subject. He got Peter Feldman and Bob Aschenhoover going on the West Bank.

When they moved to the living room, Cindy skirted Bob Aschenhoover and sat next to Marianna on the sofa.

"You don't happen to live on Waverly Place, do you?" she asked in a quiet voice.

"Why?" Marianna laughed. "Does it show?"

OCTOBER 20, 1986

Jennifer Westerhof raised her hand and went to the front of the classroom. She had brought in a beaded evening bag for Show and Tell.

"It's got a comb and a mirror inside," she recited in a singsong voice as she opened the clasp. "It's my mommy's, but she said I could have it 'cause she and Daddy never go out anymore and it just sits in the drawer."

Miss Cavetti suppressed a giggle.

"Thank you, Jennifer. Anyone else? Daniel."

Daniel Sidell stepped forward, pulling a chunk of pink quartz from a chamois bag. "I got a crystal. My mom and dad bought it off a guy on the street who said it was magic."

"Do we believe in magic, Daniel?"

"I dunno."

Melinda Kantor raised her hand. The sassy little girl bounced to the front of the room. Her hands were empty.

"My daddy has a big sailboat, it's bigger than this whole room. We got a deck and a cabin, and we can sleep on it whenever we want, 'cause it's got lots of beds and an itty-bitty toilet."

"Where do you sail on your father's boat, Melinda? Do you know where you sail?"

The child looked puzzled. "On the water. We sail round and round. Sometimes we stop and eat lunch, and then we sail some more. When we go back, Daddy makes a good knot."

"Thank you, Melinda. Anyone else? No?"

Miss Cavetti clapped her hands. "Boys and girls—those who brought lunch, get your lunchboxes, please. Let's have two orderly lines."

The student teacher brought up the rear as Kindergarten Two marched, straggled, and skipped to the lunchroom.

NOVEMBER 14, 1986

Barry ducked his head into the Carousel Lounge at eleven-thirty p.m., just in time to hear a thumping three-piece jug band wind up a set. The cabaret on Eighth Street was three-quarters empty on a Friday night.

Jerry the bartender gave him a warm greeting. "Leon's in back, Mr. Kantor, I'll tell him you're here. We just closed the kitchen."

Leon, the two-hundred-forty-pound owner, came out wearing a white apron. "Barry, where the hell you been? I left four messages on your machine."

"Out of the country. How's business?"

"Look around, the new law is killing me. You want some chili? Maggie just closed the grill. Barry, they slapped me with a summons. Intolerable noise levels. What do they expect when you have live music?"

Barry glanced at the summons and shoved it in his pocket. "Don't worry about it, it's nothing."

"Nothing, he says. I could murder that Koch."

"That's what you have a lawyer for."

"They're gonna drive us all out of business, that City Council. Hey, you hear about Boesky? It just came over the radio. A fucking slap on the wrist."

The two men sat at one of the back tables while Barry devoured his bowl of chili with extra sour cream.

"The city's changing, Barry, I don't like it. The yuppies come in here like they own the place. Credit cards up the kazoo. Your building go co-op yet? We just got our red herring. A fucking tenement on the Lower East Side and they're pitching it like luxury housing."

"Send me the book," Barry said between mouthfuls. "It might be a good investment."

"A good investment for who?"

"Where are you putting your spare change these days, Leon?"

"What spare change, are you kidding?" Leon mopped his brow. "You got a good deal?"

"Yeah, I got a couple of ventures going—nothing for the faint of heart." He wiped his mouth. "Whaddya know about oil concessions? You follow the futures market, the international situation? Price per barrel in '79 went from thirty-six dollars to fifty to a hundred, remember? What happened this January? It falls below ten, knocks the

Saudis on their fat behinds, Texas is crying uncle. Everything's cyclical, Leon. What goes around comes around.
Nowhere for oil to go but up." He leaned in close. "I'm in
with a guy in Houston who's asshole to asshole with the
former governor. Fifty thousand cuts you in, no guarantee
that you'll see a penny."

Leon turned white.

"Hey, sweetheart, how do you think Boesky did it?"

"Not with cash register receipts."

Barry got up to go. "Okay, Leon, keep booking the jug
bands."

Leon trailed him to the door. "I got a client for you,"
he whispered. "One of my dishwashers. Gun possession.
The guy is a collector—no kidding, a buff. I thought as a
favor—"

Barry's face was wreathed in a big smile. "You springing
for the retainer?"

"Maggie's gonna take up a collection."

"Tell him to call."

DECEMBER 27, 1986

Saturday night in the Bronx. He had finally persuaded
his mother to move from Morris Avenue to the relative
safety of Kingsbridge Road. All the furniture he remembered from his childhood had been crammed into the
new apartment, which was a clone of the old one. His
room was intact, down to the maple dresser and the college pennants over his bed.

The familiar odor of chicken boiling in the pot with
carrots assailed his nostrils as he got off the elevator. She
opened the door, a shapeless figure in black. He dutifully
bent down and kissed her creased forehead. Melinda
trailed after him into the dark apartment.

226

"Come kiss Grandma," she commanded. The child looked at her father and quickly obeyed.

A *yahrzeit* candle flickered dimly on the counter, he didn't ask for whom. His mother had a long list of the dead.

Old lady Kantor shuffled to the table three times with cracked china plates of stringy, dry chicken. Melinda toyed with her dinner. "Wonderful, Ma," he said.

Mother and son sat in the kitchen talking in low voices while the bored little girl rolled walnuts on the linoleum floor.

Finally it was time to go. He hadn't had a cigarette in nearly three hours, his mother didn't know he smoked.

The old lady reached into her pocketbook and took out a quarter. "Chanukah *gelt*," she said to the child.

Melinda took the coin and looked at her father. He motioned for her to reach up and kiss the withered old cheek.

Too late. His mother's gimlet eyes fastened on his.

"A grandchild of mine doesn't know about Chanukah? Barry, Barry, what is the world coming to? How many times did you sit on my knee while I told you the beautiful story? You knew it by heart. You'd put your hand on my lips and finish it for me. Remember? Abe was so proud, may he rest in peace. Barry! Judah Maccabee and his glorious brothers! The oil burned for eight days, and they wouldn't surrender."

"We learned it in school," Melinda piped up. "It's the Jewish Christmas."

Old lady Kantor clutched her breast.

"Ma—"

"A heart attack I'll get—you want to kill me? The *meshuganah* bride is so busy clucking on the telephone she can't give her daughter a Chanukah lesson?"

Within him the uncontrollable rage started to grow.

Barry told her that morning to wash and iron a dress for Melinda and find something clean for the baby. He was taking them all to a New Year's Eve party in Queens, at one of his clients'.

"Nice family people," he said with a wink. "Uncles and cousins and brothers. The women have been cooking all day. Empanadas, music, and dancing. Maybe you'll learn the merengue."

At his prodding, Judith went out in the afternoon and got her hair done. She hadn't been inside a beauty parlor in years. On the way home she bought Melinda an inexpensive pair of patent leather shoes on Eighth Street.

Barry warned her they had to be ready to leave the house at six p.m. She laid out Melinda's clothes on the bed for her—the new shoes, white tights, and the pink party dress with the white ruffled bib that Goldie had sent for her birthday. She brushed Melinda's shoulder-length hair till it shone, and clipped the side with a pink barrette. Melinda pranced around the apartment while Judith zipped Ricky into a green jersey romper, another of Goldie's offerings. Her mother was still hoping for a rapprochement.

Judith went into the bathroom and did her eyes—a little black mascara and a trace of blue shadow, just like the old days. She hadn't forgotten, her hand was steady.

She was applying her eyeliner when she heard a smack and a cry. Her hand shook hard, smearing the line. Melinda, Melinda, what was wrong with her lately? This wasn't the first time it had happened. Why did she do things that got him upset? Judith gripped the sink. The child had to learn. *She* had learned. Melinda had to learn

228

too. Please, let it go well tonight, please, dear God, she said into the mirror.

When she emerged from the bathroom, Barry was pulling his black sweater over a fresh white shirt. Melinda sat quietly crayoning in her coloring book. Judith gave her a quick look. The child's cheek was red. Nothing serious, the mark would be gone by tomorrow. The knot in Judith's stomach began to ease.

Barry had finished dressing, and now he was pacing back and forth. Warning, warning. Judith flew to the drawer and pulled out her own black sweater. Matching outfits. She looked at him for approval.

"That's what you're wearing for New Year's Eve?" he said. "You look like a simp from Claridge and Palmer. Okay, let's go."

Jaime Gutierrez Calderon was honored that his American lawyer had come with his family for New Year's Eve. But he knew already that Barry Kantor was not a typical American lawyer. He had told him last week that he was more like a *paisano.* Barry Kantor liked that a lot.

Jaime showed his guests the fine house from top to bottom and introduced them to all the Gutierrez and Calderon relatives, some of whom had their own little ones in tow. Melinda didn't need any encouragement, she was off in a flash with the other children. Jaime's mother hovered in the big Hollywood kitchen with his sisters, overseeing the food. There was plenty to eat, drink, and smoke. Barry dived in.

In contrast to the men of the house, who wore casual sport shirts tucked into their pants, the women were decked out in satin and high heels. Judith sat close to Barry in the kitchen, red with humiliation—such an obvious misfit in her sweater and skirt. He poked her to get up and socialize with the other women. She smiled and

229

tried to look interested, but most of the conversation around her was in Spanish. She took a little coke to make Barry happy, but she knew what she needed to get through the night. Get bombed on heavy Colombian grass. Wait for Eva Tanguay to sing in her head. *I don't care, oh I don't care.*

After they ate, the babies were put upstairs for their naps. Jaime, his brothers, and Barry went into another bedroom for a private talk. The rest of the party filtered down to the pine-paneled recreation room in the basement, where they kept the Christmas tree. Balloons and crepe paper streamers hung from the ceiling. Someone put on the salsa music, and the women cajoled the men off the sofas. After a couple of numbers the men begged off, so the women danced with each other in their satin dresses.

Judith took a deep drag on her joint. Kind, these people were very kind. Eva Tanguay was singing in her head. *I don't care, oh I don't care.* A ribbon of thought curled through her mellow haze, she tried to catch it before it slipped by. The living room. Absurd. The Gutierrez family did not use their formal living room for parties, that was it. The womenfolk didn't want any spills and stains. She wanted to tell them about Brooklyn, about all the big untouched living rooms in Brooklyn and Queens and Long Island.

She went looking for Barry to tell him her universal insight, but he wasn't around. Ricky was sleeping on someone's bed. She sat with him for a while before going back down to the basement.

Melinda hopped among the dancers, imitating their steps. The music was different from the dances at school, and she couldn't get it at first. A look of passionate determination crossed the child's face. Step, step, wriggle, wriggle. Step, step, wave, wave. The Gutierrez women laughed and applauded. Some *muchacha.* Their own children were fast asleep. Jaime's nephew Roberto put another cassette in his Panasonic camcorder. Melinda kicked off her new shoes and pranced for the camera, mugging into the lens, a twirling pink tornado with strawberry hair and a loose barrette.

Barry checked in on the party downstairs. Judith sat in a corner, lost to the world. He turned away.

"Hey, Barry," Jaime's nephew called out. "I take many pictures of your kid. She's a good little dancer."

Their *abogado* lit a cigarette and grinned. He was feeling the effects of the very good flake. Barry had a word with Jaime's brother, touching his arm familiarly as he watched his daughter pirouette and strut to the Latin beat.

The exhausted little girl wouldn't quit. *Daddy's watching.* She tugged at a helium balloon on the ceiling. One of the Gutierrez women threw a paper garland around her neck. *Daddy's watching.* Melinda twisted and whirled in her stocking feet, a feral smile on her tired face.

The Kantors said their goodbyes shortly after midnight. They had a long trek back to Manhattan. Ricky was fast asleep in Judith's arms.

JANUARY 21, 1987

"Okay, children, the day of the week is . . . *what*?"

Miss Cavetti flashed a printed card at the fidgety toddlers who sat in a ragged semicircle on a mat near the blackboard.

"*Wednesday,* that's right." Miss Cavetti beamed at her tiny charges.

Unmindful of the morning's calendar lesson, a couple of boys played with their building blocks at a corner table. At another desk, a solitary girl dipped her brush into a paint jar and filled in a tiny square on a large empty sheet of white paper; a student teacher stood at her side. Kindergarten Two's overfed grey rabbit blinked placidly in its wire cage.

"Bobby, don't push. Peter, come sit over here." Miss Cavetti flashed another card. "And the month is . . . *January*. Good. And the date is . . . the *twenty-first*."

The teacher deftly turned the morning attendance check into a simple arithmetic lesson. Today there were three absences, the same as yesterday. The names Melinda, Joia, and Carlos were chalked on the blackboard.

"Okay, children," she said. "We have sixteen girls in our class. Melinda and Joia are absent. So, how many girls are in class today?" She pointed to the numbers chart. "*Fourteen*. Very good."

Melinda Kantor darted through the open door. Miss Cavetti looked up. The child's father was framed in the doorway, a winning, apologetic smile on his face.

Miss Cavetti nodded curtly as Melinda nimbly hung her coat on her peg and squeezed herself into the semicircle.

"Now, class," Miss Cavetti said at the blackboard, erasing Melinda's name. "Melinda is *present*. So, how many girls are absent today? *One*. And how many girls are present? *Fifteen*. Very good."

Miss Cavetti sighed. Since the New Year's break, Melinda Kantor had been absent or late a half-dozen times. The darling child was so popular with her classmates and so eager to learn, the teacher didn't know what to make of it.

FEBRUARY 1987

Ricky was now a perpetual motion machine that rolled, crawled, and lurched around the apartment. The minute

Judith's back was turned he'd wriggle out of his carrier, topple off the sofa, or bang his head on the coffee table. Ricky didn't just howl when he took a fall, he bellowed nonstop.

"Inadequate mother, I am an inadequate mother," she scribbled into her journal in her downward slant.

"Leave him alone, he just wants attention," Barry instructed the first time the baby went into a rage. That was the first time. Now, after ten minutes' exposure to Ricky's phenomenal lungs, Barry would storm out of the house, and she would go to the medicine chest for a Valium or roll herself a huge joint.

Ricky wasn't bringing them closer together, he was driving them apart. Her ficus tree was chucked onto the street when Barry caught the baby eating dirt. Ricky's newest trick was to pull open their chest of drawers and dump out the clothes. "Do something, Judith, restrain him," Barry would yell as he kicked at the clothes.

Judith got slammed in the face and felt she deserved it when Ricky tore the pocket parts out of Barry's lawbooks. The updates to McKinney's *Consolidated Laws of New York Annotated* lay in shreds on the floor.

"Where were you? In a goddamn stupor?" he shouted when he saw the torn pages. "Are you trying to sabotage my practice?" She must have been woolgathering in the bedroom when Ricky got into the lawbooks—she wanted to die.

He stormed out of the house and came back with a secondhand wooden playpen. "The best solutions are always the simplest," he announced, rubbing his hands. "A Skinnerian box. Leave it to the experts."

Judith watched with excitement and dread. He had always been firmly against playpens! Barry collected the baby's toys and threw them in a pile near the window where the ficus used to stand. Then he plunked Ricky down on top of the pile. Before the surprised baby knew what was happening, the upside-down playpen went over his head. Ricky peered through the bars and howled.

"Give him time, he'll love it," Barry told her. "His own private space."

There was no way Ricky could climb out. It was fool-proof.

Melinda cried when she came home from kindergarten and saw Ricky in the cage. "I can't hug and pet him," she blubbered.

"He's not going to live in there, Melinda," her father explained. "It's for nighttime and time out during the day when your mother can't cope. Watch. Your mother can tip the playpen and take Ricky out anytime she wants. Show her, Judith."

Judith gave her daughter a demonstration. "He's not going to stay in there all day, Melinda," she soothed.

"Promise?"

"Cross my heart and hope to die."

"Oh, Mommy, that's what the kids say at school when they're telling a lie."

"Leave him alone," Barry ordered. "See? He's settled in nicely already."

MARCH 7, 1987

Judith ran barefoot into Sixth Avenue's speeding traffic. A taxi ground to a halt. "Please," she said. "Please. Take me to the hospital." The cabby punched the meter and sped up Sixth.

"No, not Saint Vincent's," she pleaded. "Bellevue. Take me to Bellevue. I have money. Please." She thrust a ten-dollar bill through the opening in the plastic partition.

234

The cabby went north and east, dropping his fare at the emergency entrance. She didn't wait for her change.

The receptionist at the Intake desk looked up at the disheveled woman.

"Hide me," Judith croaked in a hoarse voice. "Put me away. I don't want him to find me. I can't take it anymore, I'm losing my mind."

"Calm down, will you calm down for me?" the receptionist said as she looked her over. "Have you been here before?"

Judith shook her head no.

"What is it, honey, a bad trip?"

She wanted to run.

"Give me your name and address, dear. Do you have some identification? All right, I'm going to call the psychiatric resident. Come on, we'll put you in an interview room, you can sit there and wait for the doctor."

Judith shook violently as she followed the woman down the hall.

Two hours later Barry Kantor, Esq., presented his card at Intake and requested to see the night resident on duty. He stated his business in crisp, economical terms. He was looking for a Judith Winograd. He had good reason to believe she had come to Bellevue.

A first-year intern came out to see Mr. Kantor. Barry put his arm around the intern's shoulders and walked with him through the door.

They found Judith sitting alone in an interview room.

"Hello, Judith, you know who I am, don't you?" Barry said in a quiet voice.

She stared at the floor, defeated.

He unsnapped his briefcase. "Are you ready to come back with me now?"

She nodded.

"Put your shoes on, Judith," he said softly. "I brought you your shoes. You don't want to waste any more of these people's valuable time."

"What was that all about?" the receptionist asked the intern.

"Pretty interesting. He's a lawyer who works as a professional deprogrammer. He deprograms people after they leave the cults. Reverses the mindbend, intensive stuff. She got away from him in the middle of a session. Couldn't take it, I guess. Her folks told him try Bellevue, they know her patterns. Got to hand it to him, the work can't be easy."

"One less for us," the receptionist said.

MARCH 10, 1987

Judith sat on the park bench in the stiff March breeze, her hand resting warily on Ricky's stroller. She gazed at the dealers with unseeing eyes. The dealers returned her gaze with hooded disinterest.

Radios blasted, parkies loitered, a patrol car circled, dealers chanted their wares: *sens, crack, indica, nickel and dime.* Something larger than a squirrel, with a hairless tail, scurried across the path.

She had to stay in the park for at least two hours, that was her promise to Barry. The baby needed fresh air.

MARCH 11, 1987

A large brown rat emerged from the bushes and darted behind Ricky's stroller.

236

Judith screamed. She grabbed the handlebar and wheeled the stroller out of the park with a shriek.

For a split second two crack dealers broke off their confab to stare at the crazy mother.

"Wha' happen?"

Both shrugged.

MARCH 12, 1987

Bleecker and Hudson converge with Eighth Avenue at Abingdon Square, which is not a square but two facing triangles intersected by speeding traffic. The enclosed spit of pavement that forms the northern triangle is named Abingdon Square Park, and it contains a fine set of swings. Abingdon Square Park, alas, is not for children. It belongs to the homeless men and alcoholic transvestites who panhandle on the street for small change.

To avoid confusion with the panhandlers' park, the southern triangle is named Bleecker Street Playground. This playground does not have swings, a sore point with the mothers of Greenwich Village, who zealously defend their sandbox, slide, and jungle gym against the derelicts across the way. The demarcation line between park and playground is strictly drawn and maintained.

Judith wheeled Ricky all the way over from Waverly Place to Abingdon Square. The playground was teeming with youngsters in the late afternoon sun. She lifted the baby into the sandbox, grunting from the exertion, and took her position on one of the benches.

An extra twelve blocks each way. The air was cleaner here, it was peaceful and quiet. If she had the strength, she'd take Ricky to Abingdon Square every afternoon.

If she had the strength.

MARCH 19, 1987

He liked the routine. On Tuesdays and Thursdays he picked Melinda up after school and took her to Deena Ribelow's dance class for children in a third-floor loft on Sheridan Square. Usually he watched the little girl do her bends and stretches on the hardwood floor for five or ten minutes before he went to the restaurant-bar downstairs to make some phone calls. When the class was over, he took her to the restaurant for a hamburger while he made more calls.

Half the kindergarteners at P.S. 55, or half the girls, at least, supplemented their school day with aerobics and ballet at Ribelow's. Melinda was always the first one into her leotard, ready to prance.

On this particular Thursday, Deena Ribelow thanked him for the check and crossed off the unpaid balance in her notebook. She said she was glad not to be losing Melinda—she'd been teaching children for twenty years, and his little girl had amazing coordination for five and a half.

Next fall Ribelow was starting a more advanced class, on Mondays and Wednesdays, adding beginner's tap to the program. Parents could buy the shoes through the studio at a discount, and she hoped he'd enroll his lovely daughter.

MARCH 20, 1987

Judith sat on her bench and stared straight ahead. They were whispering about her again. Cruelty—why was the world so cruel? Don't let them get to you, don't give them the satisfaction, pretend you don't notice, they mustn't see.

Cackling hens in their fancy jackets and boots, who did they think they were fooling? She wasn't deaf and blind. They didn't want her and Ricky in their precious park.

Humming tonelessly, she took Ricky from the sandbox and lifted him into his stroller. She straightened up too quickly, and the terrible pain shot through her shoulder. Slowly, very slowly, so the bitches wouldn't see how she favored her right ankle, she wheeled the stroller out of the playground.

Across the street, the transvestites stopped what they were doing to watch the slow procession coming their way.

"Hey, lady, this is our turf."

A young derelict in an army jacket weaved unsteadily in her path. With a fixed smile, she detoured around him and made for the empty swings.

The baby was getting so heavy, she could barely lift him into the metal seat. Her shoulder was aching.

"La la-la," she crooned as she pushed the creaking swing.

Ricky beamed up at her, gurgling with joy.

"La la-la."

APRIL 4, 1987

He took Melinda with him to Patchogue. Time to put the boat in the water. The season of renewal—he could live again.

APRIL 14, 1987

Max telephoned on Passover. Barry complained for a while about the new tax law and finally put Judith on the phone.

Her voice was faint. "They slew all the firstborn sons, Daddy. There was blood on the door."

Goldie got on the line. "Judith, are you all right? Your father can't understand what you're saying."

"I'm fine, Ma. I'm fine. I'm very happy."

Barry picked up the extension. "Judith's in terrific shape, Goldie. You should see her. What? Oh, she's reading to the kids from the Haggadah. Yeah, listen, Goldie— you reminded me, I gotta hang up and call my mother."

MAY 22, 1987

Gwen Faber, a fashion consultant who lived on Morton Street, had begun to sell some of her own designs and needed a lawyer to incorporate her fledgling business. Leon and Maggie of the Carousel Lounge recommended a Village attorney named Barry Kantor.

Her new attorney suggested they meet for an early bite at Florent. She warmed to the choice. The obscure diner in the heart of the city's wholesale meat market on Gansevoort Street was a popular rendezvous for Village types and the limo crowd since a couple of Frenchmen, inspired by the old Les Halles, had transformed it into an all-night bistro.

Kantor brought along his little daughter, who seemed quite at home in the bustling diner. Gwen was instantly charmed. The lawyer put the graceful little girl through her paces. She was in kindergarten at P.S. 55. As part of the school's enrichment program, she had gone with her class to the Museum of Modern Art.

"Tell Gwen about Miró, Melinda."

The little girl animatedly described the blotches and squiggles.

"Show Gwen a Picasso, honey."

It was uncanny. The little girl pantomimed a sad clown, and Gwen could almost see the Blue Period painting before her eyes.

Kantor had brusquely told the waiter not to pour him any wine, but he kept taking sips from Gwen's glass. She was mildly perplexed when he ordered a bottle of Kahlua with dessert and polished off most of the sweet liqueur himself.

When Melinda went to the john, the lawyer abruptly stubbed out his cigarette and said he was having problems at home. Melinda was adopted, he told her, so was their boy Ricky. Years ago, on a hopeless quest, he had taken his wife to the best fertility clinics on the Eastern Seaboard—well, that was before the surrogacy business. The joke was on him. In his wild youth he had paid for abortions for three of his girlfriends, but it had never occurred to him during those carefree years that he'd end up with a barren woman.

He gazed at her intently with his mournful black eyes. Gwen was getting the impression that Barry Kantor was laying the groundwork for something. A proposition, a quickie, an affair? What did he want? She wasn't sure. His intimate revelations embarrassed her. The entire evening had been more like a date than a business discussion between attorney and client. She thought he was awfully attractive, and obviously he was a doting father, but she had a firm rule about married men.

Melinda came back to the table just as Gwen reached over to pick up the check.

"Can we take home the sugar cubes for Ricky?" the child asked.

"Melinda, Miss Faber is going to think we don't have any food in the house."

The child drew back, as if her wrist had been slapped. Her new lawyer, Gwen decided, was a strict disciplinarian. Well, his technique had certainly worked with his daughter. She was an angel.

Gwen made a mental note to draw up some sketches for children's dresses. The Kate Greenaway look in soft pastel cotton, with a straw bonnet and ribbons to complete the effect. A Victorian party frock in black velvet, cut on the bias, with a touch of white lace at the collar and cuffs. Her model would look just like Melinda—long straight hair, demure, yet somehow worldly for her years.

Adding an upscale children's line to her portfolio was an inspired idea. She couldn't wait to get back to her sketch pad.

JUNE 10, 1987

Miss Cavetti noticed a change in Melinda Kantor. The girl was a bundle of energy in the yard, it was a pleasure to watch her on the jungle gym, but for three days now, she had had trouble waking up from the afternoon nap. Perhaps she wasn't getting enough sleep at home?

The teacher had a brief chat with Clara Zaretsky, the school's guidance counselor, who suggested that she have a word with the child's father when he picked her up that afternoon.

At first Mr. Kantor ridiculed Miss Cavetti's gently offered suggestion that his daughter was tired. Then he laughed and said none of them were getting enough sleep, Melinda's younger brother Ricky was quite a handful.

Miss Cavetti was on the verge of asking what the sleeping arrangements were in the house—perhaps Melinda could be moved to another room—but something told her she had gone far enough.

She was right. Mr. Blattstein called her into his office the next day.

"Nice chap, that Kantor fellow." The principal stroked his short beard. "Successful attorney, keeps a boat on Long Island."

The father had gone straight to the principal's office to complain about her!

Mr. Blattstein spent ten minutes smoothing Miss Cavetti's ruffled feathers. He assured her he always stood up for his teachers when touchy parents felt their authority at home was being usurped.

To end the disagreeable discussion, Miss Cavetti said that perhaps she had been too hasty.

"No action can be too hasty when a child's welfare is involved, Miss Cavetti," the principal admonished with raised brows.

JUNE 26, 1987

On the last day of school, Miss Cavetti had her restless kindergarteners tell how they were going to spend their summer vacation.

Half the class was headed out of the city—the Vineyard, the Hamptons, Fire Island, and Woodstock tripped familiarly off their confident tongues. Four little tykes were going to Europe, several were looking forward to sleep-away camp, and one boy was flying to California to visit his father.

Melinda Kantor brought in some blurry pictures of a black-hulled sloop. She told the class she was going to sail all summer on her father's big boat.

JULY 9, 1987

Barry switched dentists.

While Lieutenant Colonel Oliver North redefined the

meaning of patriotism for the American people on a small black-and-white screen above his head, Dr. Ethan Zimmer fitted his jumpy new patient with a full upper plate.

Mr. Kantor told the receptionist to send the bill to his office at 104 Waverly Place. His secretary was in charge of his checkbook.

JULY 12, 1987

Dylan and the Dead, billed as "alone and together," gave a one-night performance at the Meadowlands arena.

At the last minute, Barry scrounged a pair of comps from a record promoter and went with Melinda on the funky trip down memory lane. In the parking lot of the mammoth New Jersey stadium he spotted a familiar face, a guy he had seen around the Village for years. Randy Carter, a black jazz musician who filled in behind the bar at the Carousel Lounge, was a fan of Jerry Garcia, the Dead's lead guitarist. Carter was at the concert with his daughter Tyra, a cute little girl about Melinda's age.

The two fathers and their daughters hit it off. Carter made no bones about his recent, angry divorce. Kantor volunteered nothing about his home situation but left the impression that he and his wife led separate lives. They found good seats together in an empty section after hundreds of teenagers in machine-made, fake-tie-dyed T-shirts—the new generation—jumped the police barriers to get near the stage.

Tyra and Melinda ate themselves silly on hotdogs, peanuts, and ice cream. Their fathers commiserated with each other about middle age as computerized psychedelic images of Jerry and the band beamed on two giant screens. The men joked that they felt like a couple of old fogies, surrounded by Deadheads who all seemed to be nineteen.

244

Barry invited Randy and Tyra to join him and Melinda some weekend when they went sailing. The little girls hugged each other and jumped up and down.

JULY 25, 1987

"Hey, Mindy, come here."

The red-haired little girl in the faded T-shirt and shorts glanced up at her father before she scampered across the wood dock.

"I want to show you a picture," the marina's office manager said. He opened a copy of *Cruising World* and flattened the magazine on his desk.

"See this, young lady? This pretty gal is twenty-one years old. Her name is Tania Aebi, and she's sailing around the world solo, in a boat that's not much larger than yours."

Melinda stared at the picture. "*Va-ru-na*," she read aloud slowly. "That old tub is her boat?"

The manager laughed.

"Daddy and I could sail around the world," she said with her hand on her hip.

"I bet you could, Mindy, I bet you could. You're gonna be the next Tania Aebi."

Her father was calling.

She remembered to thank the man for showing her the picture before she skipped down the dock.

Shiny and black-hulled, the *Melinda Maru* slapped against the rubber tires buffering its narrow slip. Her father scowled as he adjusted the rigging.

"Goddammit, Melinda, I'm not spending all day in the fucking marina."

The agile child hopped aboard.

245

Certain obvious economic facts relating to the law of supply and demand could not escape his attention. Simply expressed, a flooded market drives down the price, which translates into shrinking retainers for counsel. The wild-men of Colombia had become so megaproductive that a key of sixty to seventy-five percent pure that went for forty thousand dollars a couple of years ago was selling for ten thousand today. *His assets were depreciating on the shelf.*

But, whereas, and however you cut it *(no pun intended, we aims to please, Inositol for weight, Lidocaine for freeze),* while the cocaine market spiraled downward, the stock market was soaring. He had never trusted Wall Street. Over the years he had built a cautious portfolio of treasury bonds and triple-exempt municipals, and then watched with a sick heart as it dwindled, shrank. He was not a poor man, to use the phrase he'd learned from his father. Judith would keel over in a dead faint if she knew he had a cool million socked away in bonds, plus the tidy packets of sweet hundreds he kept in the vault. Piddling. Collier Brothers habits. Hetty Green. Under the mattress. Guys on Wall Street with one-tenth his brains—cocksuck-ers, assholes—scarfed a million bucks as their annual bonus. There was only one way to keep up with inflation, what every yuppie seemed to know at birth: invest in the bullish market. It was time to get over his queasiness, chuck the T-notes, liquidate the bonds, and take the plunge.

He called a discount broker and placed his order, reel-ing off the names of the blue chips and leading performers he'd held in contempt for so long. IBM at 162½, CBS at

185, Digital Equipment at 163½, Eastman Kodak at 88⅜, General Electric at 57⅛, Du Pont at 124, Procter and Gamble at 91⅛, Minnesota Mining at 72⅛, Disney at 71½.

When he hung up, he kicked himself for having waited so long.

AUGUST 1, 1987

Gunther had persuaded Jim to table with him for two hours on Sheridan Square. They had a stack of literature on the current status of AIDS research, a petition, and a jar for contributions.

Barry Kantor walked by with Melinda. Jim was not prepared to meet a Waverly Place neighbor, and particularly not *this* Waverly Place neighbor, on his first time out as a gay activist. His initial impulse was to crawl under the table, but he collected himself and managed a "Hi."

While Melinda talked up a storm with Gunther, her father picked up a flyer and scanned it. He put it back, murmuring, "Good cause." Jim was flabbergasted when his neighbor reached into his wallet. He stuffed a bill into the jar and sauntered off down the street with the little girl.

"Quick, I'm dying, what did he put in?"

Jim fished out the bill. "Jesus and Mary, you won't believe this! One hundred dollars!"

AUGUST 3, 1987

He came home with a pair of gravity boots and a metal exercise bar, and spent the afternoon on the stepladder, bolting the bar to the ceiling in the narrow hallway that led to the bedroom.

"Got to do something about the gut," he muttered.

Melinda sat on the floor and watched her father hang upside down, suspended on metal hooks attached to the foam-padded braces on his ankles.

"Daddy, can I try?"

"Boots are too big for you," he puffed. "Go away, read a book. I'm exercising."

AUGUST 25, 1987

Tuesday from one to three was Stevie Cutler's birthday party. His mother went down the kindergarten class list, rounding up all of Stevie's friends who weren't away for the summer.

On the day of the party, Barry picked up a small Lego set for Melinda's present and walked her over to Jane Street, quizzing her along the way.

"So, what kind of questions do your little friends ask you?"

"Mostly they want to know if I have my own room, stuff like that," she answered.

"What do you say?"

The child was silent.

"Melinda, when a child or his parent asks you something that's none of their business, like 'Do you have your own room?' you know what you tell them? You say, 'Doesn't everybody?' That shuts 'em up fast."

"Daddy, can Stevie come play at our house sometime?"

"Maybe. Melinda, do you hear what I'm saying? This is very important. Grownups ask nosy questions because their lives are empty and boring and it gives them a cheap

248

thrill to make trouble for other people who live by rules they don't understand. Children are very impressionable, they pick up the grownups' bad habits. I'm giving you the best-case scenario. The worst-case scenario is that sometimes the children are put up to perform dirty tricks by their parents. Let's suppose Stevie asks you a personal question. It might sound innocent to you, and it could very well be innocent. But suppose Stevie's father, or his mother, or your teacher at school, gave him orders to get as much information on you as he can, because they're evil people who want to destroy us. They're looking for dirt they can use against us. Understand? Okay, let me give you an example. Suppose Stevie's mother calls the state adoption bureau and says, 'I happen to have information that Melinda Kantor doesn't have her own bedroom, I happen to know that Melinda Kantor sleeps on the living room couch.' And suppose the adoption bureau sends an investigator who knocks on the door and says, 'We hear you've got a child in there named Melinda who doesn't have her own room, oh, my, I guess we'll have to take her away.'"

"*Daddy.*" The child looked stricken. "Daddy, you wouldn't let anyone take me away?"

"Of course not, sweetheart, I can fool all of them. We were just playing Let's Suppose."

"Daddy, will they take Ricky away?"

"Nobody's taking anyone away, I'm describing a hypothetical situation. Now, what else do your little friends ask when you're playing together?"

"Nothing."

"Nothing?"

"Daddy, can I have an allowance? All the other kids get an allowance."

"Do they ask you about your mother?"

"Sometimes."

"What do they ask?"

"Cara's mother asked if Mommy was in an accident."

"An accident?" Her father chortled. "What did you say?"

"I said she should ask Mommy."

"Good girl." He gave her a hug.

The children were playing Pin the Tail on the Donkey when the bell rang at two-thirty. Barbara Cutler was surprised to see Melinda's mother climbing the stairs. Mrs. Cutler invited her in for some cake and coffee.

"Melinda has to get home," Judith murmured at the door.

Mrs. Cutler had trouble getting Melinda to leave, but she couldn't get her mother inside the door either, so she filled a shopping bag with birthday cake and party favors for the child to take home. Melinda's mother didn't want to take the package, but the little girl grabbed it.

"What a cold fish," Barbara whispered to her friend Gretchen Mehling when she closed the door.

"I feel sorry for her."

"I feel sorry for her husband."

"Who, Ma?" her son asked.

Gretchen giggled.

"Little pitchers have big ears," Stevie's mother replied.

SEPTEMBER 7, 1987

Randy Carter was in a sour mood when he delivered Tyra back to his ex-wife at the end of the Labor Day weekend. Regina Carter supposed that spending three days with full responsibility for an active six-year-old had wiped him out, but Randy said no—the weekend had been a drag for another reason. A Village neighbor named Barry Kantor had called on Friday to ask if he had any holiday plans. They worked out a trade. Randy would take the girls to the Bronx Zoo on Saturday, and Barry would give them all a full day of sailing on Sunday.

Randy had enjoyed his part of the bargain. He and Tyra picked Melinda up in front of the Waverly Place brownstone on Saturday morning and drove to the zoo. The kids had a great time at the gibbon island, and they loved the African rail safari. He bought them balloons and whistles and treated them to franks and ice cream. Melinda ate up everything in sight. Randy got the idea that she hadn't had any breakfast. She was an appealing child, but demanding. Not at all shy. Tyra wanted to know what had happened to her beautiful red hair—a big chunk was cut out of the back. "Bubble gum," the child said. She shrugged. "Mommy had to cut it out with the scissors." When Tyra asked her father to carry her for a while, Melinda set up a clamor. "I'm your little girl too, aren't I?" she asked. Randy spent a lot of the day carrying first one six-year-old, then the other, on his shoulders.

Sunday was less successful. Kantor called at eight a.m. to say he'd prefer that Randy not bring along his new lady friend. He gave the lame excuse that his boat was for serious sailing, not for partying with chatty broads. Randy thought that was out of line, especially since they were using his car to drive out to Patchogue, but he didn't push it. The sailing experience turned out to be a big drag. Kantor was playing Captain Queeg or something, barking orders at Randy and the children nonstop. They crossed Great South Bay, had lunch and a swim at Cherry Grove, and then sailed back to the marina. "How do you feel, how do you feel? Isn't this the life?" Kantor kept asking. Randy wanted to say that he felt used and bored, but he held his tongue.

Randy spent all day Monday trying to make up with his new lady friend for leaving her in the lurch over most of the holiday weekend. He omitted that part of the story when he dropped Tyra off at Regina's apartment.

SEPTEMBER 14, 1987

They came from all directions, an exuberant procession of nervous, relieved moms and grateful, proud dads leading their fresh-scrubbed, poking and pulling and dawdling charges. Timid newcomers, eager adventurers, nonchalant old hands. Solemn bookworms and sniveling crybabies. Cocky whiz kids and saucer-eyed slow learners. Angel-faced brats and insufferable goody-goodies. Chronic bed-wetters and finicky eaters. In short, the future professional class of Greenwich Village—doctors, lawyers, artists, writers, teachers, clinical psychologists, molecular biologists, space-age technologists, perhaps a few presidents of multinational corporations—streamed toward the center of their universe on that particular morning.

The first day of school! Melinda skipped down the street in her brand-new sneakers, her blue cloth bookbag flying behind her.

Her first-grade classroom was up one flight of stairs. She pulled her father by the hand, leading the way. He deposited her at the door and introduced himself to Lila Rumson, her new teacher.

SEPTEMBER 15, 1987

Lila Rumson punched her card in the timeclock before checking her pigeonhole. There it was. Another lengthy, rambling missive from Arthur Blattstein on bile-green paper. Frank Chandler had used buff-colored paper for his infrequent memos, which were always concise and to the point. She found the change in color exceedingly irritating.

SEPTEMBER 16, 1987

Judith tried to focus on the green sheet of paper.

Dear Parents,

Your child will require the following supplies this week.
1. One hardcover composition notebook, 7½" × 10"
2. One box of crayons
3. One bottle of Elmer's Glue, 1½-oz. size, to keep at home for homework assignments
4. One old, large shirt for art activities
5. One box of Kleenex
6. $2.00 for a one-year subscription to *Scholastic News*
7. $2.00 for music program
8. One folder with two pockets for homework assignments

Please label the above items with your child's first and last name. Please label your child's personal belongings, such as coat, mittens, scarf, and bookbag, with your address and phone number.

Note: Children may eat breakfast at 8:30 a.m. in the cafeteria ($1.75 per week). They are expected to be *in the classroom* at *8:40.*

Note: Dismissal is at 2:55 p.m. Please be prompt!

Note: Your child may participate in Show and Tell daily. Items for Show and Tell may include things from nature, crafts, photographs, etc. Stories may be told aloud.

Note: Personal toys, especially war toys, baseball bats, candy, and gum, are not allowed in the classroom, and are not permissible items for Show and Tell. Responsibility begins at home. Your cooperation is crucial.

Note: At the beginning of each month, you are expected to provide a box of munchies that your child can share with the class at snack time. Sugary junk-food is to be avoided. Suggestions for storable, nutritious snacks include granola bars, whole wheat crackers, little boxes of raisins, etc. *Do not* send carrot sticks, cheese, or other perishable items.

Please note that the school will be closed on Sept. 24 and 25 for Rosh Hashanah, and on Oct. 12 for Columbus Day.

> Arthur Blattstein, Principal
> Lila Rumson, First Grade

Judith wearily put the sheet of paper aside.

"Mommy, I have to have all these things by tomorrow."

"Melinda, don't *nudge.*"

"Mommy, I need the money *now.* The stores will be closed."

"*Melinda!*" She was taken aback by a raspy croak that wasn't her natural voice.

Yesterday, the night before, last week? The last time his fingers gripped, she had to claw—when did it happen?

So hard to remember.

She shuffled into the kitchen. "Don't bother me now. I'm making Ricky his supper."

When her father came home, Melinda ran to him with the school letter.

"Fucking fascists," he exploded, crumpling the paper. It sailed across the room.

When he wasn't looking, the child retrieved the crumpled wad and carefully smoothed it out. She'd show it to him again later. Daddy never stayed mad at her for long.

SEPTEMBER 21, 1987

Leon had a problem: his lawyer never opened his mail. When he called the house, he got either the answering machine or Barry's airhead, who said things like "Just a minute, I'll see if he's here" and left the phone hanging.

Maggie didn't think that was funny. They had just gotten their second eviction notice; apparently Kantor had done nothing about the first one. "Change lawyers or communicate through a messenger service," she told her husband.

Leon called a messenger service.

SEPTEMBER 22, 1987

Melinda loved Bobby DeLessio, who sat at her table. She told Jennifer Westerhof, who crossed her heart and swore not to tell anyone in the whole wide world.

The romance was hardly a secret to Mrs. Rumson's first-graders. During recess when they played Duck, Duck, Goose in the Little Yard, Melinda chose Bobby every time she was It.

SEPTEMBER 23, 1987

Judith put Ricky in the stroller and wheeled him toward the Hudson River. She had to decipher the message.

When the light changed at West Street, she grabbed the stroller and pushed fast.

The abandoned pier at Morton Street had been closed off. A sign on the chain link fence read, WARNING. DANGER. NO TRESPASS. She pressed herself against the metal links and breathed in the salt air. The message was still there—she hadn't imagined it. It was scrawled in red paint on a concrete barrier that ran the length of the rotting pier.

SAVE THE PIERS. DUMP KOCH. SILENCE = DEATH. FREE SHARON KOWALSKI.

What did it mean?

SEPTEMBER 24, 1987

The candy store owner was red with anger. "I told you last week, I told you the week before, I told you in July," he shouted. "I don't sell parts of the Sunday paper on Thursday. It's against the law, they'll take away my delivery. Nine-thirty Saturday night you can buy the whole paper like everyone else."

"Mr. Hummel, how many years have we been doing business? You got fifty real estate sections sitting in the back room. Why can't I buy one copy? Here, take the dollar."

"Mr. Kantor, don't aggravate me, life is too short. Do me a favor, take your business elsewhere."

SEPTEMBER 28, 1987

After Show and Tell, Mrs. Rumson read *The Story of Babar* to her rapt first-graders. Then she asked the children to go back to their tables and make up their own stories of Babar's adventures.

Amy Campbell, the student teacher, handed out big sheets of drawing paper and found a perch for herself in the rear of the classroom. It was exciting to observe the Writing Process in action after absorbing the theory in lectures. The children were learning to express themselves phonetically with the alphabet before they could read. Letters were game play, the idea was to sidestep the fear of writing.

At the window table, Bobby DeLessio threw a crayon at Melinda Kantor. Melinda looked up and punched Bobby's arm. Grinning, she hunched over her drawing and carefully lettered BA BA GTTB WDADA N ME FO MY at the bottom of the page. She was the first one finished.

"That's a very good elephant, Melinda," Amy Campbell said, looking over her shoulder. "Now read me your story."

The eager child turned up her face. "Babar goes to the bank with Daddy and me for money."

Backlit by the strong sun coming in from the window, Melinda's shoulder-length red hair took on hues of burnished gold. The student teacher barely noticed. She was transfixed by the purple bruise under the child's left eye.

THURSDAY, OCTOBER 1, 1987

"Could I have the Sunday *Times* real estate section, please," the little girl piped up.

Mr. Hummel jerked around. The child's father was standing outside the shop, smoking a cigarette near the curb.

"Get out of here, you want me to call the cops?" the store owner shouted. "I told your father, we don't sell the paper on Thursday night."

He complained to his other customers for the rest of the evening.

TUESDAY, OCTOBER 6, 1987

At 8:25 a.m. Officers Pennetto and Haney from the Sixth Precinct went to 104 Waverly Place in response to an anonymous complaint from a female neighbor.

At first they heard nothing inside Apartment 3-A. After a few more hard bangs with the door's fancy eagle-crest knocker, an irate male voice shouted, "Go away."

Officers Pennetto and Haney were not so easily dissuaded. Identifying themselves, they insisted the man open up or they'd be back with a warrant.

There was a rattle of locks and chains. A male subject approximately forty-five years old opened the door.

The place was a pigsty. A little girl was running around half naked, whimpering, "Daddy, Daddy, I'm late for school."

"You hit this kid?" Officer Haney asked.

"Take a look at her," the man barked. "You see any bruises? Melinda, get dressed."

"Who's in the other room?" Officer Pennetto asked.

"Stay out of there," the man shouted. "She doesn't want to see you."

The officers exchanged wary looks.

Haney took the man's name and jotted down the number on the telephone while Pennetto walked down the hallway and rapped on the French doors. The glass panes were painted over.

"Judith, you don't have to see them," the man shouted. He grabbed for a pencil and paper. "Give me your shield number, I'm a lawyer, I know my rights."

"You're a lawyer? What kind of lawyer?"

"My kid's late for school. I gotta get out of here, you're holding me up."

Pennetto was getting nowhere at the French doors. He tried the handle. Locked from the inside.

"Lady," he said, "we're here to protect you. Don't be afraid, just step out for a minute, lady, so we can see you're okay."

The panicky man changed key. "Listen, officer," he said in a smooth, conciliatory voice. "My wife and I had a little argument this morning. You know how it is. Are you family men? Then you know, you know about these little spats between a man and his wife. Confidentially, we got a crazy menopausal neighbor across the hall, she listens with her pussy at the keyhole."

Haney laughed.

"Here's my card, I'm a criminal lawyer. You know Harry Kovitz, Sergeant Harry Kovitz? He used to work out of the Sixth Precinct, he's a friend of mine for twenty years. Call him up right now. Here, use my phone."

Pennetto rapped on the French doors.

"I'm fine," said a wavering voice. "Leave us alone."

"See?" the man said.

"See what?" said Pennetto. "Lady," he called, "don't make our job any harder. We can stand here all day if we have to. Just open up."

"Judith, they're not going away," the man whined. "They won't go away, Judith. Judith, put on your robe and come out."

Minutes ticked by, and then the door slowly opened.

Judith stood there in a terrycloth bathrobe. Her nose was flattened, her swollen eyes blazed with defiance. With as much dignity as she could muster, she leveled her gaze at the two alien intruders who represented the law.

"Is this what you wanted to see?" she said in a cold, stony voice. "Are you satisfied? Now leave us alone."

Officer Pennetto blinked several times at the human wreckage. "Judith," he said. "You look like you've had a rough time. There's nothing to be afraid of, Judith. We'd like to help you, but you have to help us. We want you to come to the stationhouse and sign a complaint."

"Leave us alone. Go away." She drew the bathrobe tighter around her body.

Pennetto retreated. "Lady, it's your business what you do with your life, you're a grown woman. If you don't want to press charges, it's no skin off my nose. I'm not the one with the double shiner. But let me tell you something—"

"Look what you've done! *You frightened my daughter.*"

The officers had forgotten the little girl. She stood solemn-faced next to her father, clutching his hand.

From the back room came the lusty sound of an infant wailing.

"You got another kid in there?"

"Melinda," the man said, "give Ricky his bottle." The child obediently went into the kitchen.

Officer Pennetto checked out the crying infant. When he returned, his partner gave him the sign to go.

"Weird, weird, weird," Pennetto said as he copied the names on the mailbox into his memo book.

Officer Haney was thinking of the container of coffee he'd left on the dashboard. He hadn't become a cop to make house calls on nut cases.

WEDNESDAY, OCTOBER 14, 1987

The man behind the counter at the Korean grocery store on Sixth Avenue watched the poorly dressed woman with the baby stroller as she fingered the pears. She picked up an Anjou, examined it closely, and gravely put it back in its place. His eyes followed her movements as she pushed the stroller down the aisle and stopped at the shiny green Granny Smith apples. Hurriedly, as if she'd forgotten something, she wheeled the stroller out of the store.

He turned to his wife at the cash register and made a circular gesture near his head.

"*Michin nyon!*" she said with a laugh.

FRIDAY, OCTOBER 16, 1987

"Off for the weekend?" Mrs. Laemmerle smiled brightly.

"Please, Mrs. Laemmerle." Marianna put her suitcase down on the curb. "I'm flying to Midland, Texas, wherever that is. The child in the well."

Mrs. Laemmerle clutched her bosom. "That poor little girl, I have such a fateful feeling. You're much too young to remember, dear, it must have been, oh, don't hold me to it, but I'd say 1949. Some things never leave you. Kathy Fiscus, I'll carry that name to the grave. They drilled for three days, the whole nation was praying for little Kathy Fiscus."

"Very interesting, Mrs. Laemmerle. This child is Jessica McClure."

"When the rescuers found her—"

"There's my taxi."

"Will I see you on the television?"

Marianna slammed the cab door.

261

Black Monday. A wave of institutional selling. The lines were jammed, he couldn't get through to his broker.

That evening he checked the closing prices against his July purchase orders. IBM at 103¼, down 59¼. CBS at 152½, down 32½. Digital Equipment at 130, down 33½. Eastman Kodak at 62⅞, down 25½. General Electric at 41⅞, down 15¼. Du Pont at 80½, down 43½. Procter and Gamble at 61⅜, down 29¾. Minnesota Mining at 52, down 20⅛. Disney at 46, down 25½.

Down the tubes. A loss of three hundred thousand dollars.

Judith

She watches him now, all the time. I see the look in her eye. We are like wolves in a lair, alert to every movement and gesture. When he walks in the door, I see her hesitate for just a fraction of a second, with a look on her face that I know so well, before she runs to his arms.

He stands at the open door and sniffs. What is different? What has changed? He waits. And then she runs to him. *"Daddy."*

The tension is killing me—it has to break soon. When I hear the key in the lock, I make myself as small as possible and hide in the back room or busy myself in the kitchen. I wait for the cry. *"Daddy."* Then it is all right and I can come out.

I hear the murmur of voices, the two of them talking. Her childish chatter rises above the buzz in my ears. His voice rises and falls. He is telling her the things he used to tell me. It is almost as if I weren't in the same apartment.

Do they know that I am watching them too?

TUESDAY, OCTOBER 20, 1987

Lila Rumson did not know she was clenching her jaw, although she'd pay for it later. Another bile-green memo was stuffed in her pigeonhole.

"A gentle reminder that Friday, October 30, is the day before Halloween."

Her jaw clenched tighter as she continued to read from force of habit: "Teachers might consider appropriate play activities for this day, such as ducking for apples, carving or painting pumpkin heads, etc. Please bear in mind that children in the primary grades are easily scared. Apples and pumpkins are preferable to witches, goblins, and ghosts."

Oh, really, she muttered. Where does he think I've been for the last twenty-three years?

Her lovely Halloween routine hadn't varied since 1964, and Arthur Blattstein could go jump in a bile-green lake. As for carving pumpkin heads, she knew a good place to start.

Another migraine was coming on.

WEDNESDAY, OCTOBER 21, 1987

In Syracuse, Assistant U.S. Attorney Chip Maguire of the Northern District got a call from defense counsel Barry Kantor. His client Vincent R. Snell would not be surrendering today on the federal warrant. No problem, no problem at all. Mr. Snell was in Miami, he was due back tomorrow, the lawyer would deliver him in person on Friday morning.

Maguire called the DEA and passed on the news.

THURSDAY, OCTOBER 22, 1987

Len Cohen was enjoying the shoot. He liked photographing kids, he had two of his own. This was a one-day assignment, catalogue work for an educational publisher. His client was a peach about lugging his camera bags, that was a help. She was also doing heroic work keeping the principal, a bearded type in a three-piece suit, out of his hair. So far things were going smoothly; every classroom on the checklist seemed to know they were coming.

The photographer reloaded and checked the other Nikon around his neck. Too bad the client only wanted black-and-white. He would have liked to shoot some color.

He saw the little heartbreaker as soon as he walked in the door. Maybe it was the way she bounced around, begging for attention, or maybe it was just his practiced eye, but how could you miss her? This was a squeaky-clean school where every second kid could pass for a professional model.

She had a bruise under her right eye and another one on her left cheek. Her limp, uncombed hair hadn't connected with a bottle of shampoo in a long time, and somebody had chopped off a clump in the back. There was dirt under her fingernails, and the long-sleeved white sweatshirt under her beige corduroy jumper needed a wash.

Cohen glanced at his client. An hour ago she had surprised him by saying she didn't relate much to kids on a personal level. Now the look on her face said this kid had gotten to her.

"What do you think?" he whispered. "I'll shoot around the, uh, grimy moppet."

The grimy moppet would not be ignored. "Hey," she shouted. "Over here, over here."

"I'll get to you, sweetheart, be patient."

Cohen spotted an overstuffed easy chair at the back of the classroom. He moved it a half-foot forward to set up his shot: three kids reading from a large picture book.

"Don't look at the camera, honey, look at the book. No, don't look at me, look down at the book."

"*Jessica!* He wants you to pretend you're reading!"

The photographer turned around. It was the grimy moppet. She had pushed up the long sleeves of her sweatshirt. Another bruise mark was visible below her elbow.

"Ah, I've got a little assistant! Here, sweetheart, hold the cap for me while I change lenses."

"I'm not an assistant, I want to be *in* the pictures. Hey, how come you got *two* cameras?"

He couldn't get over her *chutzpah*. To make her happy, he picked up his other Nikon. "This one makes little girls look pretty. Now give me a big smile."

She raced to her chair near the window. "Take us together," she commanded, pointing to her table mate. "He's my boyfriend."

The student teacher quietly spelled out the names for the client while the photographer clicked the shutter. "Robert D-e capital L-e-s-s-i-o and Melinda Kantor, with a K."

"How'd you get that mouse under your eye, Melinda?"

"My name isn't Melinda, it's Mindy."

"Okay, Mindy. Who gave you the shiner?"

"My baby brother hit me. Hey, is my picture gonna be in a book?"

"Maybe. If I get a release back from your mother."

Cohen's client wanted to say something to the teacher before they left the classroom, but the moment passed.

"It's so obvious," she whispered. "They don't need me to point it out."

THURSDAY EVENING, OCTOBER 22, 1987

Karen Handelsman had been horrified by the appearance of one of Jessica's classmates when she dropped off her box of cookies for the afternoon snack. The little girl looked like a battered child.

Mrs. Rumson disliked interruptions, so the mother pulled the student teacher aside. Amy Campbell knew instantly which child she meant. Amy whispered that she was in agony over Melinda Kantor but didn't know what to do. Melinda always told the same story—her baby brother had hit her.

"What is Mrs. Rumson doing about it?" Mrs. Handelsman whispered back. "Has she spoken with the parents?"

"I don't know," the unhappy student teacher replied.

The only information Mrs. Handelsman got out of her daughter that evening was that Melinda was absent a lot. Other than that, she learned that Melinda was very popular with her classmates and did chin-ups like a boy in the Little Yard.

After Jessica went to bed, Mrs. Handelsman called her family doctor and described at length the bruise she had seen under the child's eye. He suggested that she have a word with the teacher, if only for her own peace of mind.

FRIDAY MORNING, OCTOBER 23, 1987, 8:00 A.M.

Judith hunted everywhere in the apartment for the photographer's release form Melinda was crying about. It had vanished into thin air.

"Melinda. Please, honey," she said wearily. "It's no big deal. I'll write one out for you, it'll be just as good, I promise. I used to handle releases all the time when I worked at Claridge and Palmer. Here."

She found a pad of yellow lined paper and chicken-scratched in her downward slant, "I hereby release all photographs of Melinda Kantor," added the date, and signed her name. She paused, and then wrote "Kantor" after "Winograd."

Melinda grabbed the sheet of paper with a disbelieving look.

"It's true," Judith said softly. "I used to publish lovely books. I did."

FRIDAY MORNING, OCTOBER 23, 1987, 11:00 A.M.

Chip Maguire got a frantic call from Barry Kantor. His client Vincent R. Snell had missed his flight from Miami, he wouldn't get into New York before late afternoon. Could the Northern District hold off the surrender till after the weekend, and could Vinnie be processed in New York City instead of in Syracuse?

"You pull that," Maguire told him, "and I'll ask the Southern District for detention and a three-day continuance so I can get down there."

Saturday. In Syracuse. Ten a.m. The DEA people would be waiting, and Magistrate Hawkins would open his court for the initial appearance.

"How do I bail him upstate on a Saturday?" the lawyer whined.

"That's your problem."

The assistant U.S. attorney had never met Mr. Kantor but already disliked him intensely.

FRIDAY AFTERNOON, OCTOBER 23, 1987

Karen Handelsman had every intention of cornering Mrs. Rumson, but first she wanted to take a good, close look at the person who picked Melinda up after school. If the child seemed afraid to go home, Mrs. Handelsman knew what to do—she'd march straight into the principal's office.

The first-graders were let out at 2:55. Mrs. Handelsman stood back and watched Melinda race toward a tall man in a sweater who was lounging near the flagpole. He swooped her into his arms.

"Daddy, Daddy!" the little girl burbled. "Look what I drew!"

"How's my best girl?" Tenderly the father touched the child's cheek.

It was a picture-perfect reunion with hugs and kisses and family chatter. Karen Handelsman pulled Jessica along rather sharply on the way home.

FRIDAY EVENING—SATURDAY MORNING, OCTOBER 23–24, 1987

The rental car was parked in front of the house, a white Chevrolet Corsica. He had promised her a big adventure, an overnight trip and a chance to see Daddy in court. She filled him in on her day in first grade as he drove seventy

268

miles an hour to Fulton, New York, to hand-hold Vinnie Snell. Father and daughter arrived at Vinnie's palatial house in time for dinner.

On Saturday morning, Vinnie took them for breakfast at his mother's diner. His sister Kitty brought around her Mercedes so Barry wouldn't rack up additional mileage on the rental car. The atmosphere during the short ride to Syracuse was hyper and festive. Melinda snuggled in her father's lap as he went over the surrender and arraignment procedures for the fourth or fifth time.

"The Drug Enforcement people do what they do, then we go into court and ask for ROR. We got a good shot," he said to the brother and sister in his gravelly voice. "Release on his own recognizance," he explained to Melinda, chucking her under the chin. "The twenty-five thou is for backup." Kitty nodded, patting her purse. The lawyer put his hand on Vinnie's shoulder. "I wouldn't want to face your mother if I come home without you."

After a couple of wrong turns, the three adults and the child arrived at the federal building on South Clinton. Trim and earnest, Chip Maguire was waiting at the side entrance. He led them to the DEA office, where Vinnie was taken away to be photographed, fingerprinted, and placed under arrest. Barry excused himself for a minute and left Melinda with Kitty while he found the men's room and did a toot. Their next stop was the United States District Court in the same building. Maguire escorted them to Magistrate Hawkins' third-floor courtroom for Vinnie's arraignment.

Magistrate's bench, witness box, counsel tables, three rows of pews—every blond oak surface in William S. Hawkins' blue-carpeted domain was polished and shining. In lieu of a court stenographer, four microphones and a tape machine, the latest models, would record the proceedings.

The six-year-old's bare legs dangled in the front row as she took in the modern equipment, the spotless carpet, the matching blue vinyl chairs. "I thought it would be bigger," she whispered to Kitty.

Her father entered Vinnie's plea of not guilty to the charge of conspiracy to possess with intent to distribute cocaine. The haggling over bail began.

Chip Maguire asked the court to detain the thirty-four-year-old defendant until trial. For the last five years Mr. Snell had made monthly purchases of a pound of cocaine, eighty percent pure, from a downstate distributor named Fernandez, currently under indictment, whereabouts unknown. When the federal search warrant was executed, coded records of Mr. Snell's cash sales were found in a locked safe in his home. Mr. Snell himself had a cocaine dependency. His last income tax return had been filed in 1982 with the notation "deceased." He was unmarried, had a passport, a gun permit, and two vicious guard dogs, and was likely to flee.

Barry stood up and consulted his notes. His tongue was thick, his speech slurred, as he began a rambling attempt to put a reasonable face on Vinnie's employment. A prize-winning used-car salesman who bred Doberman pinschers on the side, Vinnie had fallen into the clutches of a cocaine habit through overwork and exhaustion, damaging his health, his income, his family's heart. A seller of cocaine? Never. A purchaser? We concede that, your honor, but for a personal dependency, not for profit. Vinnie had entered a voluntary rehabilitation program this summer; for the last—how many days, Vinnie? eighty?— eighty days he had been drug-free. "In all my years of practice, your honor"—*honest Injun, cross my heart and hope to die*—"in all my years of practice, if ever a defendant was a candidate for ROR, this defendant is it."

Magistrate Hawkins spoke from the bench. "There are

some sharp issues of fact here, Mr. Kantor. The picture I'm getting of this defendant is totally unclear."

The lawyer scratched his head and grinned like a little boy. This was the part he liked best. Absolute believability, his stock-in-trade, his triumph, honed since childhood on the Morris Avenue hills. *No, Daddy, I didn't steal the skates, I won 'em in a game. Judith you're such a klutz, I didn't shove you, you walked into the door. This is our adopted daughter Melinda. Aw, Ma, come on, we got married ten years ago in Hawaii, remember, I sent you a postcard.*

"Your honor, the gun permit, let me dispose of that quickly. I had the opportunity to speak with this defendant's mother and sister this morning. They saw no guns in the house on any occasion. As for the allegation on the income tax matter, we deny that, your honor. I myself witnessed a copy of the defendant's 1985 return, and he assures me that all his other returns are in order. Let me summarize. Yes, he has a legal permit to possess a gun. No, he has no weapons. Yes, he purchased cocaine for his personal consumption. No, he did not sell it to others. With all due respect to the government attorney"—he bestowed a brotherly smile in Maguire's direction—"when the facts come out, my client will not be as culpable as he thinks."

The magistrate jotted down some notes. "If I do set bail, Mr. Kantor, I hope you understand that there's no possibility your client can be released this weekend."

Barry focused on his words, befuddled. "I don't get that, your honor."

The justice looked up. "The clerk's office isn't open on Saturday. There's nobody here to process the papers."

"You're going to detain him?" The lawyer braced himself against the table. "Just a minute, your honor, I don't understand. You're going to detain him?"

The room was spinning. He slammed his fist down, the microphone teetered. Magistrate Hawkins froze.

"Fundamental fairness, your honor. A man's freedom is involved. I asked for a bill of particulars. The government produced absolutely no evidence"—*bang*—"not one iota of contraband"—*bang*—"paraphernalia, scales, any of the things we see with somebody who's dealing, selling, packaging. Not even one bag. This client voluntarily surrendered"—*bang*—"to this courtroom."

"He had the opportunity to surrender all week, your honor," Chip Maguire cut in. "We were prepared to handle it Friday when the clerk's office was open."

"Come on, judge, be reasonable," Barry wheedled. "Sixteen ounces a month? I'm a New York counsel. Coming from New York City, that's *minute.*"

A look of horror crossed the magistrate's face.

"Not that quantity makes it morally correct or incorrect," he stumbled on in a rush. "Your honor, this is a fundamental due process issue."

He sat down, shaking. He had walked Vinnie into their trap, the yawning jaws were about to snap shut.

Magistrate Hawkins set bail at one hundred thousand dollars cash and ordered the prisoner confined until bail was met. The eyes of the little girl in the front row popped when the federal marshals took Vinnie away in handcuffs.

The hearing was over.

"New York lawyers," Magistrate Hawkins said to the government attorney in his chambers. "They barrel up here with their subway manners and think we're pushovers." He walked to the window and gazed at the peaceful view. "But every once in a while they stumble over one of us. And fall."

The white Chevrolet Corsica was holding up the line. Angela Bonelli watched with annoyance while the agitated driver searched for his wallet.

It was only when the driver got out of the car to shake his jacket that the toll collector noticed the little girl in the front seat. Her body was convulsed with sobs, and there was a red welt on her forehead.

"What happened to your little girl?"

"Nothing. She hit her head on the windshield. Sharp turn getting on at Interchange 39, you ought to do something about the grade." He reached across to the glove compartment and took out a bag of hard candy. "This'll fix her up."

His wallet was lying behind the bag. He fished out a twenty and received his change.

Angela Bonelli noted the rental license plate as the car sped off. Milk cartons with pictures of missing children danced in her head. She picked up the phone.

"White Chevrolet," she reported. "New-model Corsica. Four-door. License plate ZBB956. I think we may have a kidnapping."

Twenty-five miles south of the Woodbury toll area, the state troopers spotted the white Chevy Corsica, ZBB956, approaching the Tappan Zee Bridge. They pulled the car over and asked the driver for identification.

"Hey, what's going on here?" he said, all smiles. "I was under sixty."

"This your little girl?"

Melinda sat in the front seat, dry-eyed and scared.

"We had a report that a little girl was sobbing."

"Yeah, well, look at her. She's fine. I'm an attorney, I

had a court case in Syracuse this morning. We're on our way home. She's tired. She gets cranky when she's tired —wants to try out every rest stop on the road. Do you find something suspicious about a father and daughter riding in a car?"

"On a Saturday? What kind of case? Custody hearing?"

"Unbelievable! I represented a client of mine at an arraignment. Here, look at my briefcase. Call the judge. I got to reach a bail bondsman tonight. You're detaining an officer of the court, I ought to report you for obstruction of justice."

"Would you come with us, please."

The troopers took them into the Tarrytown Plaza toll building. They sat Melinda on a desk and took her picture.

"What's your name, little girl? Do you know your telephone number?"

She recited the number by heart. On the eighth ring, Judith answered.

Barry pulled into the Howard Johnson's before he got back on the thruway. He treated Melinda to a chocolate ice cream soda, and he had a hot fudge sundae with extra whipped cream.

MONDAY, OCTOBER 26, 1987

Lila Rumson gritted her teeth and walked into the principal's office.

"One of my first-graders," she said without a preamble. "Something's wrong at home. She doesn't look—"

"From the welfare hotel."

The teacher felt her gorge rising. He had spoken with absolute certainty, cutting her off before she finished her sentence. The arrogance of him, the unmitigated arrogance, the way he airily waved his hand, dismissing her before she had finished her sentence!

"*Not* from the welfare hotel." Her voice was shrill. "*Not* from the welfare hotel," she repeated.

TUESDAY, OCTOBER 27, 1987

Barry's neck muscles twitched as he paced the length of the principal's office.

"I'll pull her out, I'll pull her out right now. I've got friends down at Livingston Street, the Board of Education will hear about this. I'll file a suit for defamation of character. What kind of fascistic operation are you running here, Blattstein? Some repressed old maid leaps to a fantastic conclusion—did you speak to Melinda? What did my daughter tell you?"

"Essentially what you did," the principal soothed. "And of course we believe her, but—"

"*What* but? *What, what?*"

"Mr. Kantor, don't shout, there are classrooms down the hall. No one is suggesting that the facts are other than have been presented. Mrs. Rumson has been with us a long time, we respect her judgment." Involuntarily the principal shuddered. "Her feeling is that Melinda may be suffering from pressures at home, something that it might help us to know about."

Barry abruptly sat down. "Pressures at home?"

The principal gave him a hopeful, encouraging nod.

Barry stared out the window. Two young lovers were walking arm in arm. He took off his glasses and rubbed his eyes.

"Blattstein," he said in a doleful voice, "the minute I

laid eyes on you, I figured you for an unusually perceptive fellow. Melinda *has* been under pressures at home."

The principal allowed himself a self-congratulatory shrug.

"Blattstein—" The lawyer dropped to an intimate register. "It's not my habit to unburden myself to strangers, but at this moment I think I need a good friend. I guess I owe you an apology and an explanation." He rubbed the bridge of his nose. "Judith is a wonderful mother to Melinda, I want you to know that in my presence she's never raised a hand to our daughter. There are times— sometimes weeks at a stretch—when my wife is the happy, vibrant woman I fell in love with seventeen years ago. That's what gives me the courage to go on."

The principal's eyes were bulging. Barry paused to let the full effect sink in.

"When I think how we used to walk arm in arm through the Village! Life seemed so simple then, so full of promise. Blattstein, do you know what it's like to live with a clinically diagnosed depressive schizophrenic? To get up every morning and wonder if this is the day she's going to throw herself off the roof? Last winter she went on a month-long crying jag. I took her to Bellevue. They shot her up with Thorazine, turned her into a bump on a log. It broke me up to see her so lifeless, I signed her out the following week. Look, I won't bend your ear with the tragic details or show you the bills from the fancy Park Avenue specialists who took my money and ran. I'm not asking for sympathy. What's money for if not to spend it on our loved ones? Maybe I've been deluding myself that we could stay together as a family unit. It was suggested to me a long time ago that she ought to be institutionalized—for everybody's health and welfare, not just for her own. But what do I do? Kiss her goodbye and throw away the key?"

The principal stroked his beard in the electric silence.

276

"Mr. Kantor," he said humbly. "May I call you Barry? I'd be honored if you called me Art."

"Art," Barry echoed. "Art, I've been so wrapped up in my personal troubles that I guess I failed in my responsibilities toward my little girl and boy."

"Coming to terms with mental illness is never easy, Barry. In our family we had an Aunt Ida, my mother's sister who lived with us in the Bronx, a situation not very different from the one you describe. But there's something I learned from Aunt Ida that I'd like to share with you now. Guilt-tripping yourself doesn't accomplish a thing. I sense that in the short time we've spent here together, you've gone through a welcome catharsis. I believe you know in your heart you've been reluctant to face something that has to be done."

"Listen, Art, I need a couple more months. I want her to go voluntarily, with the understanding that it's for her own good. The other day after she blew up at Melinda, she said something that made me think for the first time that she's ready for intensive treatment."

The principal nodded. "You understand that our obligation here at P.S. 55 is to Melinda. If we have reason to believe the child is in physical danger, we'll have to step in."

"I hear you loud and clear, Art, I hear you. You're right, talking to you so openly like this has been a catharsis. I guess it takes an objective observer to put things into their proper perspective."

The lawyer rose to go. "What part of the Bronx?"

"Pardon? Oh. Mosholu Parkway. We moved to Forest Hills when I was ten."

"Son of a gun! My mother still lives on Kingsbridge and Jerome. I went to DeWitt Clinton, did my undergraduate work at Fordham. Yankees or Giants?"

"Yankees."

"*Yeah*, stick with the winners! You were gonna be the

next Mickey Mantle, right? So how do you figure the season? They started out okay until they came up against Detroit."

"No pitching."

"On the noggin. And we'll never forgive them for trading Reggie, right? I tell that to George every time I see him. Steinbrenner's an old friend, I had him on the boat this summer with Billy Martin. Hey, when was the last time you took in a game? Gee, I wish I'd known about this sooner, Art, anytime you want I can come up with a pair of box seats." He turned at the door. "Melinda's teacher, Old Rumpot—"

Despite himself, Arthur Blattstein laughed.

"Art, I don't have to tell you how it works, you've been ahead of me every step of the way. One busybody gets the lowdown and blah-blah-blah, it's all over the school. It's not my feelings I'm worried about, it's my daughter's. What do I tell her when she comes to me in tears after some classmate blurts out, 'Hey, my mommy says your mommy's a psycho'?"

The principal shook his hand. "Count on me, Barry. Everything we discussed will remain confidential, you have my assurance."

WEDNESDAY, OCTOBER 28, 1987

Kitty Snell came into the city with the property deeds to Vinnie's house, her Florida condo, and the lot and trailer Vinnie had bought last year for their mother. Barry took her to see Alberto Cruz, his favorite bail bondsman.

She laid it on the line to him afterward, when they went for coffee.

"Barry, you and Vinnie go way back, so I want you to know this is my decision." She stubbed out her cigarette and immediately fished another one out of her pack. "I've been speaking to some friends. I'm getting Vinnie a Syracuse lawyer."

"Yeah. So?"

"No hard feelings?"

"I think it's a good idea," he said evenly, toying with his lighter.

THURSDAY EVENING, OCTOBER 29, 1987

They were asleep when he came home.

He belched. Sour stomach from too much eating and drinking and smoking. He decided to work it off with fifteen minutes in the gravity boots.

Cursing, he strapped on the boots, grabbed the guide rope, and jackknifed, hooking one ankle over the bar. There was an ominous crack. He crashed to the floor.

"*Judith!*" he bellowed.

In the downstairs apartment, Gunther and Jim woke up to a familiar thud-thudding.

"Put on the Mahler," Jim groaned.

FRIDAY AFTERNOON, OCTOBER 30, 1987

Carrie Westerhof had knocked herself out putting Jennifer's costume together. After slaving for two days over a pair of gauzy white wings, late last night she had finally figured out how to pin the contraption to Jennifer's shoulders. *Voila!* A white leotard and tutu from dance class, a wand and tiara from Lamston's, and her daughter was transformed into a fairy princess. The proud mother rummaged among her art supplies for a box of gold paper stars. She pasted a few at random on the short, stiff tutu for a finishing touch.

The first-grade Halloween party was scheduled from one to two-thirty, and Carrie wasn't going to miss it for anything. She had arranged with Mrs. Rumson to photograph the entire event.

Batmen and Supermen dueled with Darth Vaders in the First Graders' Halloween. Carrie made a quick count of one pirate, two clowns, three dinosaurs, two spiders. A couple of girls were doing She-Ra from *Masters of the Universe*. They strode around the classroom giggling, in boots, capes, and tights. Fairy princesses, alas, were a glut on the market, although to her mother's credit, Jennifer was the only fairy princess with wings.

Carrie took out her makeup kit and put some blusher on Jennifer's cheeks.

"Paint my face, paint my face!"

It was Jennifer's little friend Melinda Kantor. She wasn't in costume; she had on a purple-and-white jersey that was two sizes too large.

"Paint my face, *please*."

"Do it for her, Mommy. As soon as you finish me."

Carrie appraised the child's peaches-and-cream complexion.

"Melinda, honey, how do I know your mother would approve? Go ask the teacher if it's okay."

Too late. Attired in a sweater and pants for the strenuous activities ahead, Mrs. Rumson was marshaling her charges for the Grand Parade. Carrie picked up her Olympus and started shooting.

Apple Ducking followed Pass the Apple according to the precise schedule the teacher had chalked on the blackboard. As Carrie clicked away, she noticed that Jennifer's right wing was dragging. All around her, costumes were coming undone.

"Take my picture!"

Melinda. The child bobbed in front of her, grinning and posing.

Carrie felt a twinge of guilt. "Melinda, I promise I'll take your picture, but not when you're posing. I'm going to sneak up on you and catch you when you're not looking."

A cheeky kid, Carrie thought. Mile-a-minute energy. More confidence than Jennifer. But always posing. How could her mother forget to make her a costume? The child must feel mortified. They lived at a good address—why did her parents dress her so poorly in castoff clothes?

Melinda's mother limped and looked like she had a harelip. On the few occasions she'd seen her in the park, Carrie couldn't bring herself to walk over and say, "Hi, I'm Jennifer's mother, our daughters are friends." Once Carrie had overheard two of the other mothers talking. One called Mrs. Kantor handicapped, and the other said, "My dear, that's an outré word, the correct term is 'disabled.'" Well, there was disabled and disabled. Melinda's father always had a wink and a nod, but her mother gave off vibes that said Don't Tread On Me.

Ducking for Apples was over. Mrs. Rumson put on some music to calm the children down while the student teacher emptied the water bucket and mopped up the spills.

It was time for the story. The obedient children went to their tables clutching their paper cups of candy corn. Mrs. Rumson benevolently patrolled the aisles. She paused when she got to Melinda Kantor. Carrie watched the teacher put her hand on the child's shoulder and give it a warm squeeze.

A hush fell over the classroom as Mrs. Rumson started to read from *Bedtime for Frances,* the popular tale of a little girl who is afraid of the dark. Jennifer sat erect in her

281

chair. Across the room at the window table, Melinda hunched forward. Her blue eyes had turned solemn, she stared straight ahead.

Carrie quietly picked up her camera and focused. Now! She snapped the shutter.

Hallelujah, I finally got her when she wasn't posing, Carrie Westerhof said to herself.

FRIDAY EVENING, OCTOBER 30, 1987

Gunther backed out of his apartment and managed to lock the door. His arms laden with two garment bags and an overnight case, he nearly collided with his upstairs neighbor. Marianna was struggling with her suitcase on the landing.

"Coming or going?" he asked.

"After last Halloween, what do you think? I'm camping out for the weekend with a couple of nice, normal friends uptown."

"Sorry I don't have a free hand, or I'd help you with that. We're headed for Amagansett."

"That should be far enough," she muttered. "Why does the city encourage this thing? Don't they have any idea this is a residential community?"

Gunther's garment bags bumped and scraped along the walls as he followed his neighbor down the narrow stairs. "Three years ago, eight of us went as slices of birthday cake. With candles. The costume gal and set designer from the show I was in worked out the concept. It was fabulous when we danced in a circle. I used to love that parade," he said wistfully, "in the simpler days before AIDS."

"So did I," Marianna called over her shoulder. "Really,

it was most imaginative. Now, wake me up when it's over."

"Jim's bringing the car around," he said when they reached the street. "If you want, we can give you a lift."

"*Would* you?" she said, flashing a radiant smile. "The poor blokes always look so dashed when they find out you're not going to the airport."

SATURDAY, OCTOBER 31, 1987

The pagan custom still flourishes in countries where Celtic traditions are strong. On All Hallows' Eve the hoi polloi are permitted to leave behind their repressed libidos and humdrum lives and take to the streets in an unbridled masquerade of dark fantasy and passion. Jack-o'-lanterns in the window and trick-or-treating for penny candy are a sanitized American version of these holiday revels.

In the far western reaches of Greenwich Village, circa 1975, a few creative types rebelled against the five-and-dime-store Halloween of their childhood and fashioned an eerie parade of papier-mâché creatures that were authentically demonic. Hissing witches and reptilian monsters set the tone and spirit for the neighborhood folk, who happily joined in. The macabre procession was a great success and became an annual Village tradition.

The local news media found the outpouring of ghouls and spooks irresistible. With each passing Halloween, a hundred more drag queens on roller skates joined sixty new Satans on stilts. Eighty more Ronald Reagans shoved past forty additional Richard Nixons. Dancing domino sets and shuffling packs of cards from Tribeca vied with walking cadavers from Soho. Waving Ayatollahs flooded in from New Jersey. Eventually the entire Eastern

Seaboard, or so it seemed, turned out in costume for the Village parade.

The inevitable happened. Gawking tourists clogged the narrow residential streets. Vendors appeared. Pickpockets prospered. Roaming youths practiced their own pagan rites on innocent bystanders lining the route. The Village community board passed angry resolutions demanding a beefed-up police escort, the parade was rerouted, its guiding creative spirit resigned in a huff. The city took over.

By 1987 only one aspect remained of the old parade. A demonic force, a murderous tension, descended on Greenwich Village on Halloween night.

Barry hoisted Melinda onto his shoulders and made his way past the jostling crowds to the corner of Sixth Avenue and Tenth Street near the Jefferson Market Courthouse Library. They were too late. The crowd stood six deep behind the curbside barriers. He could barely see the tops of the floats going by.

"Hey, buddy, don't push."

"Who's pushing? I'm trying to give my little girl a view."

"Yeah, we all want a view. We been standing here since six o'clock. Go back uptown where you came from."

"I happen to live here."

"Big deal."

He gripped the child's knees and worked his way farther down the block.

"Outta my way, I staked out this lamppost."

"Hey, schmuck! Climb down off that traffic light."

"Don't shove."

"You tryin' to start something, asshole? You shoved me first."

"Fuck you."

He gave up in disgust and took Melinda home.

Two hours later he left the apartment alone and went out into the night.

Melinda sat cross-legged on the cold tiles and silently recited her ABCs. She counted up to five hundred. Then she counted backward from two hundred fifty till she got to zero. Except for Ricky, the house was quiet.

Holding her breath, the child unlocked the bathroom door. Nothing happened. She took off her shoes so she wouldn't make any noise and tiptoed across the living room floor, following the magic cracks until she reached her brother's playpen. "Stop it, Ricky, shut up," she said in her bossiest whisper. "If you don't shut up, I won't give you your bottle."

The baby gasped for air and continued sobbing. Melinda reached through the wooden bars and patted the top of his head. "Don't be scared, Ricky, please don't be scared. It's over." She got down on the floor beside him. "Come here, let me kiss you." She tugged at his arm. "Ricky, please don't cry anymore. Do you want to come out? I'll go ask Mommy."

Melinda followed the magic cracks down the hallway until she got to her parents' bedroom. She listened gravely outside the door before retracing her steps to the playpen. "You'll have to stay in there for a while, Ricky. Mommy's sleeping. Don't be upset, you'll get to come out later."

She leaned her head against the bars. "Ricky? If you stop crying, I'll tell you a story."

Judith pushed open the French doors and staggered to the bathroom. She missed the toilet bowl and threw up on the floor. *Clean it up, clean it up,* the voices commanded.

"Melinda," she called weakly.

The child ran to her mother. "Mommy, Mommy, I'm here."

Judith covered her face. "Melinda, I can't walk. I need you to help me. Go get the ice from the freezer. Use the stepladder, be careful. Bring me the whole tray and a bowl."

Melinda did as she was told. Shifting from one foot to the other, the child watched her mother wrap the ice in a towel and hold the compress against her nose.

Inside the mirror the subhuman creature was wearing a yellow-and-purple mask. It sneered *Livergut, livergut* at the woman clutching the bathroom sink.

"Mommy, I can't sleep. I'm frightened."

Judith tried to hide the white powder.

"Oh, Mommy, *don't.*"

"I have to, honey. Just a little. The pain." She put a taste on her pinky and touched her tongue. Bitter. Good. A quarter-teaspoon. Now, fast. She scooped a few grains on the end of a matchbook cover and inhaled through her left nostril. For balance, she took a hit on the right. *Oh Cocaine Bill and Morphine Sue were strolling down the avenooo. Honey have a (sniff) have a (sniff) on me, Oh honey have a (sniff) on me.*

"Mommy, I'm scared. Can I sleep in here with you till Daddy comes home?"

"Melinda, *no.* Go back to the sofa." *They walked up Broadway, turned down Main, looking for a place to buy cocaine. Honey have a (sniff) have a (sniff) on me, Oh honey have a (sniff) on me.* Once he had dropped a gummy brown ball into her lap, the size of a jawbreaker. Try this, he said. The poppy. You smoke it like hash. Oh the dreams were so sweet. Only once and never again. Don't bug me, Judith. Nobody imports opium, too much bulk. If you want a good down, you gotta go with the refined stuff. The Big H. Think of Domino Light instead

286

of brown. Not as good for baking a cake, she said. He laughed and labeled the vials. Yin and yang, hers and his, H and C. The eternal difference affecting the destiny of all creatures. Yang was strong, bright, and masculine. Up. Yin was loose, dreamy, feminine. Down. Two white powders. She learned to tell them apart. Heroin was plaster dust gouged from a wall, dry putty, builder's sand running to beige. In coke straight up, she saw milky crystals, fish scales, mica. Barry, two white powders—how do you tell yin from yang? On your tongue, he said. Yang gives you the freeze. Yin tastes bitter. That's yours.

"Mommy, when Daddy comes home, he won't be mad anymore, will he?"

"I don't know," her mother said in a faraway voice. "I don't know."

SUNDAY, NOVEMBER 1, 1987

He was dressed and shaved by ten a.m.

"Take me with you, Daddy. Take me with you." Melinda threw her arms around her father's waist and buried her face in his stomach.

His temples throbbed. "Melinda, don't whine."

"Daddy, I want to go with you."

"Stay in the house, take care of your mother," he roared.

"Daddy, I don't want to stay in the house." She looked up at him, imploring. Always, always he took her with him on Sunday. "There's nothing to eat in the house, I'm hungry."

Cursing, he sent her flying against the sofa. "You'll eat when I get back. Make your bed, put your clothes in the drawer. Give Ricky his bottle. I want this place *clean* when I get home."

She tried one more time when he was at the door, grabbing his jacket with her strong little fists.

He gave her a crack on the side of the head. Sobbing, she released her hold.

At noon on Sunday, Debbie Potter was walking home with a friend when she saw the little girl she used to babysit for wandering on the street.

"Melinda Kantor," the babysitter called. "What are you doing out alone? Are you lost?"

The little girl looked confused. Her eyes were smudged. She had been crying.

"Melinda, do your parents know you're out by yourself?"

The child didn't answer.

"Do you want me to walk you home? I know where you live."

"My mother sent me to get milk."

"Oh. You're not going to cross Sixth Avenue, are you? I hope not."

"No."

"Melinda, is something wrong? You didn't lose your money, did you? I can lend you a dollar."

The child shook her head.

"How is your mother? Is she feeling better? The last time I saw her—"

"She's okay."

"Your baby brother must be real big by now. Melinda, this is my friend Cissie. Look what we got at Lamston's! It's that fabulous mousse they've been showing on TV. Do you want to come watch while we do our hair? You can call your mother from my house."

"Mommy's waiting for me."

The little girl ran off.

"That was odd," Debbie said to her friend. "She's usually so talkative and friendly."

Alberto Cruz picked up the check. He owed Barry the dinner for sending Kitty Snell to his office. Neither man was in the mood to go home, so they hit a couple of bars on Bleecker Street. Barry was pushing one of his deals, he wanted Alberto to invest in some retirement-home franchise scheme in the Midwest. "No kidding, it's on the level," he kept saying. Alberto pretended he was interested to make him happy.

At eleven p.m. he walked the lawyer to Waverly Place. In the three years they'd been doing business, the bail bondsman had never seen the inside of Kantor's apartment. He waited downstairs while Barry went up to bring him a color brochure on the franchise operation. Who knew? Maybe the lawyer was on to something, he sure talked a big game.

Lights suddenly blazed in the third-floor front windows. Alberto bided his time at the curb. When Kantor came down, his eyes were hard and glinty behind his glasses.

"Snot-nosed brat—" The lawyer cut loose with a string of expletives.

"Take it easy, Barry," the bail bondsman saluted. He put the brochure in his pocket and headed for the Sixth Avenue subway.

The rage grew blacker with every step he climbed. Inside the apartment, Melinda was huddled on the sofa precisely as he left her, her eyes wide, the dirty blue blanket hugged to her chest.

"Get out of bed," he screamed. "I gave you all fucking day to clean up this shithole." He went to the hall closet and started pulling out coats. "You slept for twelve hours, now do some work."

He cracked her across the forehead. The little girl whimpered.

"Judith!" he bellowed. "Come out here. Get your slut daughter off her fat behind. Judith!"

No answer.

The child shrieked as he went in after her mother. Ricky began to wail.

Judith lay in a stupor, a vacant smile on her battered face.

Now in the graveyard by the hill, lies the remains of Cocaine Bill.

"You're zonked," he shouted at her. "Zonked. The minute my back was turned."

She stared up at him weakly. Her flattened nose made him want to retch.

And in the graveyard by his side, lies the remains of his morphine bride.

"I'm not your bride, Barry, I'm not your bride. They made a mistake. Why are they burying us together?"

"How much stuff did you gobble? Answer me before I tear the hair out of your fucking head."

She howled. A sustained, piercing bray. Tufts of grey wool from her scalp were in his hands.

"You're killing me."

"Shut up, you're raving."

Livergut, livergut, the voices sneered.

Disgusted, he kicked her into the living room.

"A couple of prima donnas, I'm living in a shithole with a couple of prima donnas. One's a smackhead, the other's a runty bastard I dragged in from the gutter." He picked up a chair and aimed. It caught Judith across the chest, the force threw her backward.

He pulled her to her feet and punched her mouth. With a soft squoosh the blood from her split lip spurted onto the wall. He stared at his knuckles.

"Get a move on, Melinda, before I smack your ass."

"I hate you," the little girl shrieked from the sofa. "I hate you. You're not my real father."

With a terrible cry, he caught the child's legs and whirled like a shotputter. "Slut," he shouted. "Slut, go back where you came from."

"*Daddeeee.*"

The forty-pound child hurtled through space till she hit the wall. Her head bounced on impact before she slid to the floor with a small sigh.

He let out a whoop and fell on the woman who was not his bride, flailing his legs and fists until he passed out.

Motionless under his weight, Judith waited for the rhythmic whistle and snore. With a rocking motion, she eased herself sideways until his neck was cradled in the crook of her arm. The fingers of her free hand sought out his damp, sweaty hair and came to rest in one of the tangles. Her right leg lay across his thighs. Her swollen eyes were shut tight. She dreamed.

Melinda lay where she fell, her head propped against the wall. A dribble of vomit oozed down her chin.

MONDAY, NOVEMBER 2, 1987

Four hours later, Barry shook himself awake. His bones ached in protest against the hardwood floor. Carefully he disengaged from Judith's sprawled arms and legs. She was breathing heavily in welcome, exhausted sleep. He groped for his glasses and staggered into the bathroom.

The hot shower felt great. His nasal, off-key baritone rose above the hissing water. *Monday, Monday, dah-dah dah, can't trust that day. Monday, Monday, sometimes it just turns out that w-a-a-a-ay.*

Invigorated, he grabbed a towel and stepped to the mirror to rub his hair. Fuck it, his foot slid into something slimy. He decided not to let it spoil his mood. *Oh Monday mornin', Monday mornin' couldn't guarantee . . . that Monday evenin' you would still be here with me.* But she would always be here. God bless her, his poor sweet suffering lady. He racked his brains, figuring how he was going to make it up to her this time. *Oh Monday mornin', you gave me no warnin' of what was to be. Oh Monday, Monday, how could you leave and not take me?* Take a trip, just the two of them. Wait till the Christmas holidays, take Melinda and Ricky. All four of them together, the nuclear family, starting over. Jesus, the nose and the lip. Before they went anywhere, he'd find her the best plastic surgeon in the city. Should have done it before. Should have done it after the first time. Bad vibes! Look forward, not back. He'd asked, he'd asked plenty, but she'd stare him down and say she wanted to bear his marks as a living reminder. No more of that shit, no more living reminders. His brain was scorched with living reminders. Leave the fucking apartment and the whole fucking city. Find a house upstate, enroll Melinda in a country school. He laughed. Yeah, Vinnie Snell's house, he wouldn't be needing it for a while. Get a house in the country like Vinnie's, on the water. Private dock for the boat. Separate room for Princess Melinda, with a chintz-covered dressing table and matching canopied bed. Nursery down the hall for Ricky. Become a country lawyer. A squire. Barry Kantor, a squire. Rambling three-story white clapboard with an upstairs room—no, a complete floor!—for his mother. Why not? Why not make it real? Get the goddamn marriage license for real instead of holding it in front of her (squashed) nose for seventeen years like a carrot on a stick. Say goodbye to the C-stuff, the H-stuff, no more fooling around.

Buoyant, he stepped out of the bathroom to survey the damage. The living room reeked of shit, piss, and vomit. Bad boy, Barry. Bad boy.

He turned on the water for instant coffee in the kitchen and checked the clock. Six a.m. Ricky was dead to the world in his playpen. Melinda was . . . where? The sofa was empty. He scratched his head. Light of my life, red-haired angel of sunshine, Princess Melinda, today is school day, where did you spend the night?

Must be curled up in the back room with her blanket, Jesus the poor kid.

His eyes followed the blue blanket to the puddle of child near the wall.

He knelt beside Judith and shook her shoulder. She strained like a sensor to pick up the signals before she forced open her swollen lids. Last night—oh last night, it had to be over, she couldn't be certain until she looked into his face.

His face.

"Help me," he said in a broken voice.

She followed behind as he carried the limp bundle to the back room and laid it on the bed.

Oh Monday mornin' you gave me no warnin'. He took out the vials. Mechanically he mixed the two white powders, cutting a short hit of heroin into the coke. Speedball.

293

Her tongue worked the cleft in her split upper lip. Following his cue, she bent forward and vacuumed the dust up her battered nose, waiting for the terrible fog to lift. It didn't.

"Blood on your shirt. Soak it in cold water."

They mustn't see! Obediently she changed into her black pullover and limped to the bathroom to soak her shirt. When she came out, he handed her the phone.

"Nine-one-one," he said. "Dial it. Give them the address. Tell them you have a child who stopped breathing."

She did as she was told.

Outside the front windows it was still pitch-black. Dawn would not come for another half-hour, if it came at all. He had taken Ricky from the playpen and tied him securely to one of the bars. Moving swiftly now, certainly, he walked through the apartment, pausing at each light fixture to unscrew the bulb. Her scrambled brain worked feverishly to understand, to comprehend. *Yes, that was it —they mustn't see!*

He reached up to unscrew the last remaining bulb in the hallway. She gazed after him in wonder, barely able to discern his shape in the final darkness as he walked to the back room, to wait.

Her man. He always knew what to do.

A Selected List of Fiction Available from Mandarin

While every effort is made to keep prices low, it is sometimes necessary to increase prices at short notice. Mandarin Paperbacks reserves the right to show new retail prices on covers which may differ from those previously advertised in the text or elsewhere.

The prices shown below were correct at the time of going to press.

☐ 7493 1352 8	**The Queen and I**	Sue Townsend	£4.99
☐ 7493 0540 1	**The Liar**	Stephen Fry	£4.99
☐ 7493 1132 0	**Arrivals and Departures**	Lesley Thomas	£4.99
☐ 7493 0381 6	**Loves and Journeys of Revolving Jones**	Leslie Thomas	£4.99
☐ 7493 0942 3	**Silence of the Lambs**	Thomas Harris	£4.99
☐ 7493 0946 6	**The Godfather**	Mario Puzo	£4.99
☐ 7493 1561 X	**Fear of Flying**	Erica Jong	£4.99
☐ 7493 1221 1	**The Power of One**	Bryce Courtney	£4.99
☐ 7493 0576 2	**Tandia**	Bryce Courtney	£5.99
☐ 7493 0563 0	**Kill the Lights**	Simon Williams	£4.99
☐ 7493 1319 6	**Air and Angels**	Susan Hill	£4.99
☐ 7493 1477 X	**The Name of the Rose**	Umberto Eco	£4.99
☐ 7493 0896 6	**The Stand-in**	Deborah Moggach	£4.99
☐ 7493 0581 9	**Daddy's Girls**	Zoe Fairbairns	£4.99

All these books are available at your bookshop or newsagent, or can be ordered direct from the address below. Just tick the titles you want and fill in the form below.

Cash Sales Department, PO Box 5, Rushden, Northants NN10 6YX.
Fax: 0933 410321 : Phone 0933 410511.

Please send cheque, payable to 'Reed Book Services Ltd.', or postal order for purchase price quoted and allow the following for postage and packing:

£1.00 for the first book, 50p for the second; **FREE POSTAGE AND PACKING FOR THREE BOOKS OR MORE PER ORDER.**

NAME (Block letters) ....

ADDRESS ....

....

☐ I enclose my remittance for ....

☐ I wish to pay by Access/Visa Card Number ☐☐☐☐☐☐☐☐☐☐☐☐☐☐☐☐

Expiry Date ☐☐☐☐

Signature ....

Please quote our reference: MAND